WEDDING PRESENCE

HAUNTED EVERLY AFTER MYSTERIES
BOOK TWELVE

REGINA WELLING
ERIN LYNN

Willow Hill
BOOKS

CONTENTS

WEDDING PRESENCE

CHAPTER ONE

At seven minutes past nine, the power went out in Mooselick River and wouldn't come back on for nearly a week. The house went dark and so silent we could hear the shush of wet snow slapping against the window panes. Next to me, Molly let out a quiet woof, then wiggled her butt into my side to get a bit closer.

"You don't realize how many appliances have lights on them until they all go out," Drew's voice came out of the darkness to my left. Unnerving when even though his body touched mine, I couldn't see him at all.

"Light pollution. It's a thing."

The two minutes before the generator kicked on seemed like they might stretch on forever. Maybe it wouldn't come on, that little annoying pessimist in my head insisted. Then it did. Lights flared, appliances beeped. Once again, I blessed Catherine Willowby, my ersatz benefactress, for sparing no expense when making her home something of a fortress. My parents had installed a similar system in the fall, and it cost, if not an arm and a leg, at least a finger and a toe.

Rising, Drew made the rounds to reset all the clocks that flashed the wrong time while I grabbed my phone and checked the Mooselick River community Facebook group. "At least my phone can get online. There are trees and lines down on just about every road in and out of town," I reported when he returned. "They've recalled the road crews because it's too dangerous to plow. I need to check in with all of the tenants."

My job as property manager for Leo Hansen paid better than it should, but then, Leo took good care of his properties, and so long as I kept the tenants off his back, considered the money well-spent. I'd had worse jobs, I decided, as the blanket text went out to those who used cell phones. Only two current tenants still had landlines, but both were in multi-units, so their neighbors could confirm that the generators were on.

One by one, the responses came back. Each taking a bit more worry off my mind.

"David's good," Drew reported. "He's making jokes about living in the Overlook."

"So long as no creepy twins show up, I guess he's safe." My phone dinged with another text notification. "Patrea just checked in. All's well at the farm. My parents are good, too. Just waiting for Jacy and Neena to give the all-clear." I got up and went to the front windows, hoping to see Neena's lights flicker on across the street—if I could even see that far with the amount of snow coming down.

Drew's phone signaled again.

"Brian," he announced. "They're fine. Jacy's checking in with her folks. Anything from Neena?"

"Not yet. Hush, girl. It's okay," I soothed as a muffled thump from outside set Molly barking and sent my heart rate speeding. "Was that a tree?"

"Could be. I'll check." Drew headed toward the coat closet.

"No," I grabbed his arm. "It might not be safe."

Chuckling, he grabbed what he'd gone in there for. His high-powered flashlight. "I was planning to stay on the porch."

Even so, I watched out the window and when the light popped on, got a glimpse at the changes wrought since a wall of unrelenting gray clouds sent the first snowflakes drifting over town. The power wires coming in from the pole bowed under the weight of the snow-formed tubes coating them. It would be a wonder if they didn't break.

Unable to help myself, I stepped outside with Drew to listen to the creak and pop of branches sagging under the growing blanket of white. One of the birches on that side of the house stooped until its lower branches caught in the wrought iron of the backyard gate. It was silly, but the urge rose in me to shake off the snow so the tree could find the sky again before it toppled.

"It'll hold, I think." Drew must have known something of my thoughts because his tone reassured me almost as much as the arm he slung around my shoulders. Turning, he aimed the light across the lawn and driveway to play it over the garage roof where a large fir bough lay half-buried in a furrow of snow. "That must have been the noise we heard. If we're lucky, that branch will be the only thing that falls." He angled the light higher. The pine towered over the garage, its top higher than the light could shine.

"There's nothing we can do about it now except maybe stay away from that side of the house in case it falls."

Shrugging, he followed me back inside. "It'll hit the garage first."

Somehow, with both our vehicles parked inside, that

thought failed to offer a basic level of comfort. I'd hardly had my new car long enough to break it in. Still, better to lose a vehicle than part of the house.

Since Neena hadn't answered my text and even from the porch, I couldn't make out whether or not her generator was running, I called. When it rang until her voicemail picked up, worry crawled up and wrapped its icy hands around my throat.

"That's it." I headed back toward the coat closet. "I'm going over there. She's probably hanging off the dining room light again."

Drew stepped in front of me to block my way while he looked at me with puzzlement. "Why would she do a thing like that?"

"Never mind. I can't just sit here if she needs help."

"Why don't you call Dolly? Ask her to go over and check on Neena. Snow shouldn't bother a ghost."

"If I do that, she'll stay. For hours. Or at least as long as it takes to give me a rundown of the top ten snowstorms in Mooselick River history. Do you want that? Do you? Because I certainly don't."

"I'll go." He shoved past me to grab his boots and coat.

"And leave me here alone to imagine both of you in trouble. Nope. Not happening." I darted around him and snatched up my own boots. "Besides, the visibility sucks. You could get lost and end up wandering around until you freeze to death. I've read Little House on the Prairie. I know things like that happen."

That earned me a quirked grin. "This isn't the prairie. I think I'll be fine."

"If you're going, I'm going with you. We'll tie a rope around the post on the front steps so we can find our way back."

Later, I'd have to give him credit for not laughing in my face as he indulged my latest flight of fancy. "If that makes you feel better. I'll grab a coil of climbing line, and we'll go see if Neena's okay."

Ten minutes later, regret weighing nearly as heavy as the wet coat on my back, we wallowed through sixteen inches of ever-deepening snow on our way to Neena's front door.

"See, I wouldn't have lost my way. It's a straight shot." Her house loomed before us while the rope I'd insisted on using trailed behind.

"Fine. Be right about that if you want, but I don't hear her generator, and I don't see any lights, do you?"

Maybe some of my worry translated to him because his negative response came in a subdued tone. Once we'd fought our way up the front steps, he banged on the door and called her name loudly. I should have brought her key.

After a minute passed with no response, he didn't bother hiding his concern. "I'll go around and check the other door."

"Not by yourself, you won't. Where you go, I go."

Why we hadn't strapped on snowshoes was one question I barely had the breath to ask myself as I tried to follow his footprints down Neena's driveway. When I slammed into Drew's back, even that one went right out of my head.

"What's wrong?"

"I heard noises in the garage." He changed direction abruptly, and I followed. When we got closer, ours weren't the only footprints through the snow. A set led from the direction of Neena's back door. Relief replaced worry.

"Stupid contraption." Neena's voice, raised in anger, sounded like angels singing to me just before Drew yelled to announce our presence.

"Need some help?"

It wasn't any warmer in the garage, but at least snow wasn't blowing in my face.

Neena stood in the pool of light created by a battery-operated camping lantern, her face a mask of fury tinged with despair.

"I'm glad you're here," she said to Drew. "And annoyed that I need you."

"Thanks," he said. "I think. What's the problem?"

"How should I know? Hudson and his dad set this thing up. They bragged for weeks about routing the exhaust, adding a smart panel to the system, and how it's just the right size for the house and uses far less fuel than one of those on-demand types. You'd think it was a contest or something, the way he went on about it. I followed the instructions, which he painted on the door, even. Switch the power from house to generator, make sure it's full of gas, set the choke, and push the button to start."

So saying, she jabbed the start button. Nothing happened. "So why doesn't it start? Hm? Why? And don't you dare say it's a man thing. I shouldn't have to have a penis to push a button." Turning, Neena kicked the door that gave her access to the lean-to enclosure.

"No. Of course not." Drew held back any comment that might put him in danger. Couldn't say I blamed him. "When was the last time you started it?"

She looked at him like he'd asked the most obvious question in the world. "The last time the power went out."

"That would be last winter? More than a year ago."

"Yes. That's right. Why?"

"Well, I hate to say it, but I suspect your battery is dead. Want me to pull-start it for you? I promise not to use my penis."

His attempt at humor was ill-timed, but after glaring at him for a moment, Neena stepped back and let him do what needed to be done. The engine roared to life, and the lights came on in the house. After a moment, he set the choke and closed the door. "All set."

"Thanks." Calmer now, Neena pushed a dark curl off her forehead. "Sorry. I didn't mean to cause offense to your manhood."

"None taken," Drew smiled. "Once the storm is over, we'll see about replacing the battery."

"No, really. I'm sorry I snapped at you. You guys took the time to check on me, and I acted like a shrew."

Because she seemed to need it, I hugged her. "We're here for you. But if you feel the need, you could repay our kindness by making those amazing wings the next time we have game night."

"You're so easy. I can always buy you with food," she joked. We'd been through a lot since we'd met right after I moved back to town, and there was a time not so long ago when I wasn't sure if our friendship would survive.

"They're really spectacular wings. Call if you need anything."

"Have you heard from everyone else? Jacy?"

"Brian checked in. They were waiting to hear from Jacy's

folks. Patrea and Chris are good. David's hunkered down at the inn. All the tenants and my parents reported back."

"Good," Neena nodded. "Eddie Mason nailed it when he predicted this storm, didn't he?"

"They should put him on the news."

With that, we headed back out into the weather. An inch of new snow had already begun to fill in our tracks, and it took Drew a minute or two to find the coil of rope he'd left just outside because visibility was worse than it had been.

Back at home, Molly danced through the snow we tracked inside, then ran out and sailed off the front steps when Drew held the door open. The look of doggy surprise she shot back over her shoulder spoke volumes.

"I'll shovel a spot for her while you check in with Jacy. Then, I'm thinking hot cocoa and a DVD."

"You're on." But I took a few minutes to sweep snow out of the hallway and shed my wet clothes first. Finally beginning to warm up, I stood near the heat vent and read through the texts that had come in while we were gone.

We're fine, Jacy had written. *One of the birch trees crushed Wade's swing set.* A photo in shades of blue and black accompanied the text. *And there's another one on the back deck. Brian says it took out two sections of railings, but he thinks that's the worst of it.*

—Tell Wade Auntie will get him a new swing. We have a branch on the garage roof and just got back from Neena's. Drew had to pull-start her generator. Otherwise, we're good. Your folks okay?

—Mom's worried about her garden, but Dad's taking it all in stride. As usual, they've got all the unprepared neighbors over there. The house is full.

—That should keep her too busy to worry. I answered, thankful that everyone I loved most was okay.

News reports called it the worst spring storm in fifty years. Grammy Dupree would have rated it at a solid three-bathtubs on her scale of how much water it would take to get through the storm.

CHAPTER TWO

e woke to blue skies and a snowy wonderland. If wonderland is the accurate term for the aftermath of snowmageddon. Winter wasteland described it better, with bent and broken trees turned to pillowy hills.

While coffee brewed, I checked in with family and friends.

"Momma Wade lost the roof on her potting shed. And Brian says their deck steps are gone, along with two or three sections of railing. They're trying to save some of the birches." I showed him the video Jacy had sent of Brian shaking clouds of white off a bent-over tree and then dragging the top out from where snow trapped it. Freed, the tree swayed up like a dancer while Brian turned and offered a thumbs-up to the camera.

"One down. Fifteen to go," Jacy's voice sounded over the image.

The Evergreen Christmas Tree Farm, Chris and Patrea's place, hadn't fared as well. They'd lost a dozen or so old-growth trees—the kind you generally see in town squares or in front of businesses looking for a little extra splash at the holidays.

We watched the news over breakfast and got our first look at how widespread the devastation was. More than one warehouse in Bangor had lost inventory to a collapsed roof, and several families were now homeless due to the same fate. Downed power lines caused fires that proved extremely difficult to put out because of roads too snowy to navigate.

"Power's not coming back on anytime soon," Drew said grimly. "Could you grab my snowshoes from the back while I suit up? I need to go check on the gym."

"I'll come with you and bring the keys to Jacy's shop. She and Brian are dealing with enough at home right now."

Five minutes into the trip, my calves warned me I might have been too hasty in my decision, but I did my best to ignore them as we made our way toward the center of town. At the first intersection, we stopped to assess the damage. At least one tree blocked the street heading out of town beyond the diner. In the other direction, Curated Collections stood sentinel, with no visible damage to the roof. In fact, the only structure on the street that hadn't survived the storm was the gazebo that had stood in the center of town for more than fifty years.

"That'll make Martha cry," I said, sniffing back a few tears of my own. "And she'll make me organize a fund-raiser to fix it."

"You could donate the money."

"I'd be happy to, but the last time I funded a project, it caused problems between Martha and Bess that somehow ended up being problems for me. I've learned my lesson. It's better to take the long way around in these situations."

"The ladies do love their drama. I should have brought a shovel," Drew said, changing the subject since the snow had drifted in to cover more than three-quarters of the gym's front door. Maybe we can get in through the back."

As we circled the end of the building, Drew stopped short. "That's not good."

"What?" But then, I saw for myself. The gazebo wasn't the only casualty of the storm. "Oh no!" My gloves got in the way, so I pulled them off and handed them to Drew so I could wrestle my cell phone out of the inner pocket of my coat. "Dad," I said when he answered. "I've got bad news."

"Are you okay? Is anyone hurt?"

"Yes. I don't think so. We went out to make sure everything was okay at the gym."

"The roof? That's awful, but Drew has insurance. I'm sure he's covered."

"No." If he kept interrupting me, I'd never get this out. "It's not the gym. It's the lodge. The roof caved in."

The long pause before he spoke worried me. "Dad. Are you there?"

Finally, I heard a ragged sigh. "I'm here. How are the roads? Can I get there from here?"

"I don't think so. We're on foot. Or snowshoes, actually. The plows haven't been out yet. No one has."

"Tell him we'll walk over and send pictures." Drew's helpful nature only made him all the more lovable. My calves begged to differ, but they're not the boss of me, so I told my dad we'd call him back and calculated the shortest route.

Even the shortest route seemed impossibly long but we finally turned the corner and got a good look at what would have been our wedding venue in a few weeks.

Snow humped over a vehicle parked out front, but we barely noticed it as we stared at the damage.

"I don't think we'll be getting married here, do you?"

From what I could see, the side with the deepest snow

had gone first pulling the other half in behind it. The whole thing was just gone. While I snapped a few shots to send to my father, Drew peered in the front window. The way his shoulders slumped told me all I needed to know.

"It's bad," he said while I climbed up a particularly tall snowdrift piled up against one side and looked in the higher window there.

Bad wasn't the half of it. "You've got to be kidding me." Okay, so maybe that wasn't the most compassionate statement to make when you see legs poking out of a pile of debris, but no one could have survived that much roof and snow falling on them, and I'd found enough dead bodies for one lifetime.

"What?" Drew came up beside me to look. "Oh."

I pulled out my phone and called the cops. Well, the cop. Ernie Polk. On his private cell phone. The last thing I needed was for Carole Ann Wilmette to be the only person in Mooselick River to actually make it to work and answer the phone.

"Dupree," Ernie answered wearily as if already knowing what I was about to say.

"Um. I hate to call, but there's been an accident at the lodge. The roof caved in."

"Is that all?"

"Well, no. It looks like someone was inside when it happened."

"Who's dead?" I guess he had known.

"I'm not sure. All I can see is his legs. I didn't go inside." Maybe I'd get points for that.

"Don't. But stick around. I'm heading over."

He hung up before I could tell him the roads weren't plowed. Then again, he probably already knew.

"He says he's coming, and we're supposed to wait."

Expecting to find Drew nearby, I turned just in time to see his snowshoes on the ground and his lower half disappearing through an open window that hadn't been open before.

"Hey," I went over and looked in, but he'd navigated the wreckage to get closer to the man I was sure was dead. "Be careful in there. It's dangerous."

"I had to check, but he's gone."

"Can you see who it is?"

"No." Drew shook his head. "Half the roof fell on him."

From some distance away, I thought I heard the rumble of a snowplow, but a second later, and coming from the direction of the police station, the roar of a snowmobile drowned it out.

Drew popped out the window and had his snowshoes clamped back on before Ernie pulled up beside me.

"Most people take weather like this as a sign to stay the hell home," Ernie glared at me as if all of this was somehow my fault.

"Drew wanted to check on his business. It's not like we broke any laws."

I don't know why I was defending myself. We hadn't done anything wrong. Or I hadn't. Drew sort of broke and entered, but like he said, if there'd been any chance of helping the guy, it seemed like the right thing to do.

"He's in there." Drew pointed his gloved thumb toward the building. "The window wasn't locked, so I went in to see if there was anything I could do, but whoever it is, he's been dead a while."

Ernie took a long-suffering breath. "Did you touch anything?"

"Checked for a pulse. That's it."

Speculating, Ernie looked at the window Drew had gone in and out of. I didn't want to say it out loud, but he wasn't getting in that way. Not without a man-sized shoehorn, some grease, and a minor miracle. "I don't suppose you thought to unlock the door while you were trespassing?" He sounded hopeful.

"I didn't. But I'd be happy to do it now with your permission."

It must have been a long night for him because Ernie looked tired. "Why the hell not? Consider yourself temporarily deputized. Just keep your gloves on. I have to treat this like a crime scene, even if it's an accident."

"Will do." Drew clapped a hand on Ernie's shoulder as he passed. Nimbler than he should be given the amount of muscle he carried, Drew boosted himself up, slithered back through the window, and wasted no time opening the door. "It wasn't locked. I guess I assumed it was without bothering to check."

When I went to follow Ernie inside, he body-blocked me. "Nope. You and your bad luck can stay outside." He didn't send Drew out, though.

Another snowmobile followed the trail Ernie had broken, and I wasn't surprised at all to see my father's face under the helmet.

"You okay?" He said when he saw my face. "I couldn't tell how bad it was from the pictures, so I borrowed Jim's sled."

"It's not just the roof, and it *is* bad." I didn't get more than a few words into the story before he left me standing and went inside. Somewhere behind the building, a tree branch cracked and fell, reminding me that hanging around outside might not be the best thing. I followed my father in and ignored the dirty look Ernie shot in my direction.

As soon as he saw the body, or at least the visible part of it, my father shook his head with pity. "That's Bill Cavanaugh."

The name sounded familiar, but it took me a moment to remember where I knew him from. "Bill, from when we found Delly's hoard? From the bank?"

A colorful character, Delly Harper boasted of a fortune in gold buried on his property. In his will, he appointed my father as the person to oversee the search for it. One of the men drafted to help with the search and share in the proceeds had brought his younger brother-in-law, Bill Cavanaugh, along to help with the search.

Having just removed the man's wallet, Ernie flipped it open and pulled out Bill's license to verify my dad's statement. "It is. How did you know?"

"The shoes." Dad pointed to the natty wingtips under a pair of rubber overshoes that wouldn't have provided any protection against deep snow. "Banker's shoes, we called them. Ribbed him about them some." Knowing him, I could tell he felt terrible about it now.

"Any idea what he was doing here in the middle of a snowstorm?"

Now, Dad shook his head in earnest. "None. But he couldn't have come in alone."

"Why's that?" Ernie's brows shot up.

"Only two of us have a key, and Bill's not the other one."

"The window I came through wasn't locked," Drew explained. "But I figure snowshoes on top of a couple of feet of snow made for easier access."

A dollop of melting snow plopped down from the remaining edge of the splintered roof and landed on Ernie's shoulder. He looked up, then back at the sections of roof layered over the body.

"World's worst game of Jenga," he muttered. "With a nasty prize for the winner." Whatever was left of Bill probably wouldn't be pretty. "But there's nothing I can do about it right now. We need to clear the roads before bringing in anything big enough to move the debris. Probably need a demolition expert to figure out how to shift all of this," he waved a hand to encompass the destruction, "without compromising the scene any worse than it already is."

"Given the storm, how long do you think that will take?" Drew eyed the body, then Ernie.

"A damn sight longer than I want to leave the poor bastard lying there." Ernie scrubbed a hand over his unshaven cheek. "Roads in and out of town are blocked. We've got reports of trees and power poles down in both directions. I can't even get a plow through, and that's just the main roads. Side roads are just as bad, if not worse. We're looking at days to dig out and clean up."

As if the dam had broken, Ernie confessed more. "I've got folks without generators who'll need shelter, and you know what you can't get when the power's off? Gas for your generator. The Gas-n-Go doesn't have backup power to run the pumps, and even if it did, they're cut off until we can get crews in to move trees out of the road. The only place I know of that has a tank and a hand pump is Bennie's. He's got maybe a couple of hundred gallons out at the shop if we can get that road cleared. That won't hold everyone who'll need a fill-up for more than a couple of days, and the preliminary estimate from the power company says we're looking at damn close to a week or more. If," he speared a hand through his brush-cut hair. "We can get the roads open by tomorrow, that is."

The situation sounded a lot worse than I'd expected. Dire, even.

"We've got emergency protocols in place, but we're talking about a situation that goes beyond what we've planned for, and now, this." He pointed to the body. "Couldn't have come at a worse time."

"I've got some demolition experience from my military days." Since Drew rarely talked about his time in service, this statement surprised me as much as it did everyone else. "If you'll trust me, I think I can help—at least with this part of the problem."

I'd already begun rolling around a few ideas to help with some of the rest, but I'd hold off on that until Drew had his say. What followed was a discussion among the men about cables, pulleys, anchors, counterbalance measures, and tools that I wouldn't have understood half of before Patrea had come into my life. Now, I picked up the general gist of the plan that hinged upon getting a plow truck here while my father and Ernie rode the snowmobiles around town, getting the growing list of items Drew said he'd need.

"You want me to drop you at home?" Dad asked me.

"Someone needs to stay here and keep an eye on the body." Ernie's comment held equal parts dare and na-na-na-

na-boo-boo. Apparently, this was my thanks for finding another body, which, technically, I didn't even do. Drew did.

"I'll stay. Just don't be gone too long."

"Back as soon as we can." Drew hugged me goodbye and climbed on the seat behind my dad.

Once the two sleds roared off in different directions, I began putting some of my quickly conceived plans into motion and initiated a group call with my mother and Martha Tipton. If anyone could get the word out, it would be Martha.

"It's Everly, and we've got some trouble. I'll get right into it," I said as soon as everyone picked up. "First, there's been a death in town. Bill Cavanaugh was in the lodge when the roof caved in."

The news elicited a round of sympathy. Once it had passed, I got on to the second issue. "Ernie says it will take days to get the roads cleared of downed trees so the plows can go through. Power lines are down all over the place, and we'll have to pull together to keep people warm and fed until everything is back online."

"In the past, we've opened up the gym at the high school as a temporary shelter," my mother said. "No reason why we can't do that again, and I believe young David has an empty inn. I'm sure he'll do his part."

"I'll call Bess," Martha chimed in. "Her nephew is in charge of the Big Pine Snowmobile Club. He can rally a few members to go out and pick up folks who need a ride into town."

"That's all good. But there's more. We're also facing a potential fuel shortage for running generators because the gas station is cut off right now and doesn't have backup power. Bennie's got a couple of hundred gallons of gas in his big tank and a hand pump. Otherwise, folks will have to make do with whatever they have on hand."

I could almost hear Martha's wheels turning.

"I'll fire up the phone tree and pass the word. We'll tell folks to conserve fuel as best they can. We've faced hard times before in this town. We can pull together again."

It gave me the warm fuzzies—or as many of them as I could muster while standing watch over a dead body.

"We'll need every man who can handle a chainsaw," I said, "along with a few able bodies to help drag away the debris. I'll get in touch with Brian and see if he can handle job safety. They'll be working around the power lines and electricity. We'll need someone to oversee the cutting to make sure no one gets electrocuted. The sooner we get the roads cleared, the better, and it sounded like it would be a while before we could expect any outside help. The main roads out of town are all blocked, and half the state is facing the same situation."

"Got it." My mother's juices always get revved up in the face of disaster. "Just to recap. In order of importance, we'll mobilize crews to clear trees, beginning with those not near power lines or poles and letting Brian take point on those that are. Once the trees are cleared, we'll get anyone with a plow out to help clear the roads."

"Meanwhile," Martha picked up from there, "We'll send the snowmobile club out to bring in anyone who needs shelter and pass the word about conserving fuel."

"That sounds about right. I'll leave things in your capable hands." They hadn't needed my organizational skills after all, but it felt good to be part of the solution. "And I know I can trust you both to keep quiet about Bill. It's best if no one knows until after Ernie's had a chance to break the news to his family."

Technically, that was half a lie. I knew I could trust my mother to hold on to a piece of gossip, but Martha needed a reminder.

"Mum's the word," she said. I hoped she meant it.

Still alone with Bill, I called Jacy next. Once she confirmed that everyone was fine, I gave her a quick rundown of events and asked to talk to Brian.

"Way ahead of you," he said. "I've got six guys up for the job already and three more who will jump in once they get clear. A lot of people have trees down. I tried Drew's number, but he didn't pick up. Now, I know why."

"I'll text you some numbers, too. Friends of his from work. A few more able bodies won't go amiss."

"Good deal. I'll make the calls, then fire up my sled and head your way. I need to talk to Ernie in any case." With that, he handed the phone back to Jacy.

"Listen," she said. "We've got a family on our street with a new baby. They don't have a generator or a secondary source for heat, and I hate the thought of them having to take the baby out in the cold and then bunk down on pallets at the school."

"I can let my mother know. Maybe she can scare up a spare generator."

"Well," Jacy had a better idea. "I was thinking maybe they could use our place, and we could invade yours."

Not a bad idea at all. "We've got plenty of room. You know you're always welcome."

When the thin wail of a newborn sounded in the background, I said. "You're already packed, aren't you."

"Kinda," she said. "Brian got the bad news about the power situation around the same time Ernie probably did, and I know what it's like to have a new baby in the house. Brian already helped drain their water lines and haul all the perishables over here. We'd have pumped up the air mattress if you hadn't said yes."

"You've got a key to my place. Make yourselves at home if you get there before I do. Need any help with transportation?" Not that I had any to offer except the borrowed snowmobile my dad was using.

"All set. I've got bins ready to put in the tow-behind sled. I just need to bundle Wade into his snowsuit, and we'll be on our way. He's very excited to spend the night at Auntie Molly's house."

"Nice to know I rate somewhere behind my dog on the auntie scale."

"I guess them's the breaks." Jacy rang off just as the men returned.

CHAPTER THREE

"We'll be having houseguests for the duration," I informed Drew while he unloaded the supplies, tools, and a folding ladder jammed into the tow sled they must have borrowed from the helpful neighbor, Jim. Carrying a spare body bag he'd grabbed from the station, Ernie listened to what I'd set in motion while they were gone and didn't give me crap for going behind his back to do it. In fact, he thanked me.

And the world did not stop, nor, to my knowledge anyway, did hell freeze over. A major milestone.

"People always pull through in an emergency," he said. "Makes my job bearable when I'm breaking up stupid fights over whose dog pooped in whose yard."

He'd boiled it down to basics, but he was right. Unity, even the temporary type, kept small towns like ours together. The same people who indulged in a heated debate during the proceedings could also work together to put on a community dinner at the yearly town meeting. We'd get through this storm as we'd weathered so many others—together.

"The plow truck will be here in ten. Give or take. Red's driving and he's the best, but he got bogged down in an eight-foot drift over by the grocery store. The automatic chain system doesn't work well in deep snow, so he had to back up and make a few passes to push through."

Already busy fitting a bit into the second of two drills, Drew nodded. "It'll take me that long to rig a couple of pulleys and hook up the cables. We're looking at a lot of snow load on top of a couple of large sections of roof that were already fairly heavy, but if I can hook to something solid, I think we can lift it high enough to pull the body out from under."

He went on to discuss the cable's tensile strength and what would happen if it broke, which would be bad— possibly deadly. Fifty feet of wire cable whipsawing through the air could take out a human in its path and cause plenty of damage to inanimate objects as well.

The ten minutes flew by, and the next five as well, while Red cleared enough snow to get the truck into position. My job would be to sit in the cab with him and relay the orders Drew would issue over the headset built into Jim's snowmobile helmets. At least that meant he had to wear one, which eased a tiny bit of worry. Dad and Ernie—also wearing helmets—would wait in what Drew considered the safe zone and be ready to pull Bill from the wreckage as soon as his body was clear.

OSHA would disapprove, but we'd get the job done if everything went well.

"Go," I told Red when Drew gave the okay. "Slow and steady. Just enough to take up the slack."

Even from the passenger seat, I could feel the strain as the cable went taut. As if he'd done this sort of thing all his life, Red eased off the gas and held the line steady while Drew checked all the connections.

"Good to go. Ease forward about a foot," I relayed the order for Red to follow.

"She's lifting," Drew said in my ear. "Tell him another foot. Easy does it."

"It's lifting. Go another foot. Easy, though." The truck moved forward at a snail's pace. "Six inches more." A moment later, he said, "Stop and hold."

Half of me wanted to be out there to make sure my nearest and dearest were safe, and half of me wanted no part whatsoever of seeing Bill's body. The way the mirrors angled, I couldn't see anything of what went on inside the building, and the back window of the plow truck was blocked by the dump bed full of sand. It seemed like forever before Drew's voice came through the headset again.

"He's out. Go ahead and ease back until I say stop."

The reverse part wasn't any easier since the weight wanted to pull the truck faster than it should go, but Red handled it like a champ.

"Stop. Perfect."

As soon as Red shut off the engine, we both jumped out of the cab, but Drew came out and stopped me from going inside. "Let them finish bagging him up. It's bad enough for your father without him also worrying over you. There was a lot of damage, and it wasn't pretty."

Death never is. At least, not in my experience, so I didn't argue the point. And I could see he'd been right when Ernie and my father carried the body bag out. His face devoid of color, the haunted shadows around Dad's eyes stood out starkly. I went to him and offered what comfort I could with the same kind of hug he always gave me.

"Give me your key so I can lock up, then head on home, Lee. There's nothing more you can do here today."

Why was it that Ernie could call my dad by his nickname when he always called me by my last? Probably because my father hadn't been a pain in Ernie's butt, and I couldn't deny that I had.

Dad nodded. "I'll have to call Max and let him know what happened, and we'll need to notify our insurance agent to get a claim started."

Max, being Maxwell Montayne, leader of—I kid you not —the Benevolent Brotherhood of the Black Bear, Mooselick River's answer to the Elks. As civic organizations went, this one did a lot of good for the community, and my father held the office of second in command.

"Give it half an hour so I can notify Bill's mother before she hears it from someone else. Tell Montayne I've cordoned off the building, and he'll need to clear it with me before anyone goes in. That includes Montayne himself. If he gives you a hard time, you call me."

"Will do, but you won't have to worry about Max going in. He's out of town right now."

I watched Dad ride off, knowing my mother would be there to help him with the first stages of grief. Once he was gone, Ernie turned to Red.

"Good work, Belanger. Looks like you'll be putting in some overtime."

Belanger. Why did that name sound familiar?

"Was that Bill Cavanaugh you just pulled out of there?" Red's voice was gruff with something that didn't sound like sympathy to me. Confused, I flicked a glance at Ernie's face, finding it unreadable.

"Afraid so."

"Feel sorry for his mother." But not for Bill because Red's face had gone hard, and so had his tone.

"The past is past. You remember what time you made your last pass through town last night, Hermon?" Only someone who knew Ernie quite well would have caught the slight edge to the question. I did, but couldn't think of a reason for it at first. Then, it came to me.

Hermon? Red was Hermon Belanger. Now, I remembered where I'd heard the name. He was the father of Grace Belanger, the former real estate agent who'd been murdered by Able Gallow. After she'd been missing for years, I'd found her bones out at Delly Harper's place while trying to track down Delly's murderer. And she'd had a connection to Bill since they'd been dating prior to her death. No wonder Ernie was looking at the man with cop eyes.

"Somewhere between 9:00 and 9:15, I'd say. Not too long after you called and told me to pack it in for the night because there were too many trees down."

"It was around 8:30 when I told you to head home."

Red took Ernie's mild comment as an accusation. "I was halfway to the Ridge Road when you called. I had to turn around, didn't I?"

"Don't get all keyed up. I'm just trying to establish a series of events. Bill's car was plowed in, so he was here when you went through. Did you notice anyone around the Lodge when you went by? See any lights in the windows?"

"God's truth, Ernie, I doubt I even looked at the place. I couldn't see more'n ten feet in front of the plow even with all the running lights on. Seems like I'd have noticed if the roof had caved in, but I'd be lying if I said I was sure it wasn't. It was one helluva long road home, and I had to pull some guy out of a ditch before I made it."

"All right." There wasn't much left to say, so Ernie turned to Drew. "You mind closing that window and locking up for me? I've got to haul the body over to the mortuary before I break Alice Cavanaugh's heart." He didn't seem eager to handle either of those chores. Who could blame him?

"Consider it done. I'll be out with the cutting crews as soon as I can catch a ride with somebody. If you need anything else, just give me a call."

Ernie nodded, then glanced over at me. "Appreciate what you did." Did he mean calling him about Bill or my part in mobilizing the town? Either way, getting a kind word from Ernie was a rarity. Recriminations were more our thing.

"Anytime."

Towing his grisly cargo, Ernie rode off. Before securing the building, Drew called to arrange for one of his buddies to pick him up at our place. "I hate to bring it up again, but we can't get married here. Even if they get a new roof up in time by some miracle."

"Because someone died here." It made perfect sense to me now that he'd brought it up.

"Don't you think it would be weird? I mean, your dad just lost a friend in there, and it wasn't an easy sight. We need to think about it before we consider going ahead."

My mouth dropped open. "Are you saying you want to cancel the wedding entirely?"

"No! I just think we should prepare for the worst-case scenario. From what I could see, I'm not surprised the roof came down. The pole rafters weren't the sturdiest I've ever seen. Probably original to the building, and it's an older one."

Despite all I'd learned from Patrea about old houses, I had no idea what he meant by pole rafters. "Okay," I said, but it sounded more like a question.

"Even if the roof can be fixed in time, we should figure out a plan B. I can't imagine how the building passed an insurance inspection this far north where we're always dealing with snow weight."

The mere idea of changing locations weeks before the wedding was enough to bring on the beginnings of a headache. Did he have any idea how much work had already gone into the planning? My mother would have a fit.

"There's always the inn if David hasn't booked out the date. Let's get past the immediate crisis first, okay?"

Navigating the snow banks Red had left for us on his quest to help retrieve Bill's body ended with me slipping down one on my backside and Drew dragging me up the one on the other side of the street. Two houses down from our turn, his ride whizzed up the sidewalk—a minor traffic violation that on any other day would have been ticket-worthy. Today, I doubted Ernie would care since he'd left a trail there in the first place.

His face ruddy and cheerful when he popped up the visor on his helmet, Kelly Rowe grinned, "Hey, Ev. Nice day, huh?"

"It's pretty. I'll give you that much." I smiled back.

"You okay to get home on your own?" Drew asked as he sat sideways behind Kelly to take off his snowshoes.

I assured him I was and kissed him quickly before he yanked on Kelly's spare helmet. "Be careful out there. I'll have food ready when you're done. There should be enough for you and whoever else might want some." It wouldn't take too long on low heat, and I had several large containers of beef stew in the freezer. "Come home when you get hungry."

e'd been gone less than two hours, but already, my street showed signs of life. Generators hummed, shovels scooped, and snowblowers flung white clouds while people made the best of a bad situation. Only Mrs. Abernathy's place next door to Nina's remained dark and quiet, so I turned my snowshoes in her direction and shuffled up to her front door.

"Mrs. Abernathy," I called out as I knocked. "It's Everly Dupree. Are you okay?" I knocked again.

"Hold your horses," I heard from inside. "I'm coming."

At least she wasn't dead.

She only opened the door a crack. "Make it quick before the last of my heat gets out." It couldn't have been much heat that she was trying to save because she had on several layers of clothes. White hair peeked out from beneath a winter cap, and she wore mittens. Poor thing.

"That's why I'm here. I don't know if you've heard, but we'll be without power for a few days. Do you have a generator?"

"My son has one he brings over if I need it. But he's down in Virginia visiting his wife's folks. Didn't think it would snow this late in the year." Seeing snow in the woods in early May wasn't abnormal for Maine, but getting a storm of this magnitude definitely was. Trees had already started to set on their first tender leaves and while we'd had something of a late spring as it was, crocus and daffodils bloomed.

"No one did," I said while my mind got busy trying to work out a solution. There was one. An easy one—relatively speaking—if I could get Neena to agree to it. "Listen, I have an idea, okay? Working things out might take me a little while, but we'll get you some heat. Or else you can come and stay at our place."

"I'm not leaving my cats in the house alone. They'd freeze to death, and that dog of yours would put the fear of God into them."

Molly liked cats—maybe a little too much for their taste.

"Maybe you could stay at Neena's. She has a cat, too."

The suggestion elicited the elderly version of a thousand-yard stare.

"Okay. I'll figure something out. Just give me a few minutes."

Instead of going home and resting my aching calves, I shuffled across the lawn to Neena's house and knocked on her back door.

"What's up," she said when she answered. "You look frozen."

"I know, but I can't come in with these snowshoes on. Listen," I got right to the point. "Mrs. Abernathy's son isn't home to bring her a generator, and she has no heat."

"That's awful. The poor thing."

"Brian and Jacy are staying with us so her neighbors can use her place since they have that new baby and no generator. What would you think about doing the same? Mrs. Abernathy says she won't leave her cats, but we could haul your generator to her place, and you and Pearl can stay with me.

I've got plenty of extra bedrooms. It'll be like a giant sleepover."

Bless her, Neena didn't hesitate for a second. "As long as we can run a line over to plug in my refrigerator and the pellet stove, I don't see why not. I can set the heat low enough to keep the pipes from freezing." Still, she eyed the snow-filled landscape. "I suppose you have some grand plan for how to get it over there."

I did not.

"We'll figure something out." I turned to see Jacy's snowmobile and pull-behind parked next to my garage. Maybe they would come in handy. "I'll be right back."

Stepping out of the snowshoes, I used muscles I'd forgotten I had, but I was sure they'd remind me of their presence for at least a day or two to come.

"Hey, Jace," I called out when I walked through the door and heard Wade babbling a mile a minute to Molly. "I'm back."

Jacy popped out of the kitchen. "I'm thawing that beef stew you had in the freezer." Had she read my mind? "I figure there will be hungry men here later."

"It was on my to-do list. But there's something else we need to handle, too." I launched into the tale of Mrs. Abernathy, her lack of heat, and what I hoped to do for her. "Do you think your snowmobile and sled could haul the generator over?"

"It might work. Let me get Wade bundled up and we'll go see. Do you think Mrs. Abernathy would watch him while we figure out the logistics?"

"If she wants heat, she will."

She did, and she told us where to find the electric panel. Progress.

A few minutes later, the three of us stood in Neena's garage. "Are you sure we can do this? Maybe we should wait for the men."

"Another comment like that, and you'll have to turn in your girl power card," I told her.

"Says you," she retorted. "You've got someone to deal with spiders and such."

Neena not feeling ready to date again was a sore subject, so I didn't remind her that our friend David seemed plenty willing to battle the creepy crawlies for her.

"The guys are busy, and there's no telling how long they'll be gone, so this is up to us. I think I can pull it easy enough," Jacy decided. "But the generator's wheels are too far apart to fit inside the tow sled. What we need is a toboggan or maybe some skis."

Of all the things Catherine Willowby enjoyed, winter sports hadn't been on her list. A toboggan was something I couldn't provide.

"My folks have one. Or they did when I was a kid. I assume they still do, and we could borrow it," I said. "But if memory serves, it wouldn't be wide enough. We'd need two of them, I think."

"What about a couple of those plastic boat sleds? Hudson bought us a pair for Christmas one year, but whizzin' down hills with a frozen butt wasn't my idea of a grand time. We only used them once, but they're still here somewhere."

Jacy lifted the handles to test the weight of the generator. "That could work."

We found the sleds tucked up in the rafters and showered ourselves with dust when they came down. Neena wasn't the only one who shuddered at what else might have been lurking up there. The faster we got this done, the sooner we could go back to my place and get cleaned up.

It took two of us to tilt each side while Jacy slid the sleds into place. While Neena and I shoveled and packed snow into a sort of ramp, Jacy affixed Hudson's tow rope to the snowmobile. "Here goes nothing," she knelt on the seat and gently hit the gas. The generator bobbled once when the sleds grated over concrete but glided easily enough when they hit the snow ramp.

"Looks like you get to keep your card after all," I grinned at Neena. "And this calls for adding a couple of punches to it."

"What do I get when it's full? My period?"

"I'd rather have a spa day, but I guess you get to pick your own prize."

Between the weight of both the snowmobile and generator, the trail Jacy left was packed down well enough to walk on without sinking. We got Mrs. Abernathy hooked up without the aid of men, but only because Neena knew how. I wouldn't have had the first clue what to do. Then, we ran an outdoor extension cord back to Neena's place to keep the basics running there. She packed a few things, and it was just after noon when I finally walked back through my front door and peeled off my winter gear. A spa day would have been nice, but I'd settle for something to eat and a hot shower. Preferably in that order. My phone rang before I could do either.

"I haven't been able to get in touch with Maureen Abernathy. She doesn't have a cell phone. Could you go and check on her?" My mother didn't bother with a hello.

"Already done. We just got back from hauling Neena's generator over and hooking it up for her. Neena will be staying here."

I could almost hear her relief. "Good. I'll mark that down on my list."

"How's dad doing? He was pretty upset when he left the Lodge."

"You know your father. He can't sit still when he's agitated. He put together a group to check on residents we haven't been able to reach. We've had two more reports of structure damage from snow load or fallen trees. No major injuries so far. Besides Bill, anyway. Such a shame."

"It is."

"Is that your mom?" Jacy came back from checking on the stew she'd left warming. I nodded. "Tell her I just heard from Brian. Half the high school football team showed up for tree-dragging duty, and he's got a dozen guys with chain-saws. They've made good progress. State plow trucks are already rolling through."

Instead of relaying, I put the call on speaker.

"Thanks, I'll update Martha and she can let Miles know. He's got three men hauling the tarps from the Halloween maze over to the high school to set up privacy barriers for those who are sleeping in the gym."

"I've got a couple of camp cots I can send over," Neena offered.

"Same here," I said. "We'll bring them over as soon as we can."

"Great. Talk to you later," Mom ended the call.

"The stew is ready. Our guys, plus a couple of extras, are on their way in for lunch. We should grab ours now while we can."

She didn't have to tell me twice. We got ourselves fed and Wade down for a nap before the men showed up and scarfed down the rest of the stew and an entire loaf of bread.

"The good news is we're clear on the bypass from both ends of town, and the power company is calling in crews from other states to help repair the line damage," Brian announced. "The extra help will get the power back on faster, but we'll see a hike in our rates for the next year or two to cover the cost."

"Snow. The gift that keeps on taking," Kelly joked as he ate and eyed Neena with undisguised interest. Maybe he'd give David some competition if she ever decided she wanted to date again. Or maybe not since she didn't seem to notice him in the same way.

Speaking of David, I had to ask him, "Who's minding the inn while you're out?"

"Miranda Perkins came in with the first wave of people needing shelter and pretty much took over. I'm considering offering her enough money to lure her away from Cappy's. She's used to dealing with people and has the temperament of an army general. Seems like it would be a good fit."

Jacy, Neena, and I exchanged a look. We'd suggested Miranda to him before but maybe he hadn't been ready to let go of the reins. Change wasn't David's strongest suit, and other than one notable exception—buying the inn—he didn't do anything on a whim. Still, since he was considering updating his EMT training, he'd need someone reliable to run the place for him when he was out saving lives.

"She won't come cheap," Jacy warned. "She makes decent tips at Cappy's, but I happen to know she's getting tired of working nights. If I were you, I'd lock her in before she starts looking for something else."

"In other words," I chimed in, "this is one decision you can't think to death or it will be too late."

"You're a pain in the butt, Dupree."

"Right back at you, Barrington." Our relationship ran on the same track as if we shared sibling blood. We teased and exasperated each other, but he had my back, and I had his. "Since we're on the subject of the inn and all, remember when you offered it to us for the wedding? Any chance the offer's still open? Given the extent of the damage, we're concerned the lodge might not be rebuilt in time."

His face gave the answer almost before I finished asking the question. "Sorry. I'd say yes if it were just Drew's family staying, but I booked the rest of the rooms last week."

"No worries. We'll figure something out if they can't get the roof repaired in time."

We could always get married in the town square. Gazebo or not. In the grand scheme, a wedding is just a day. I wouldn't say that to my mother, though.

CHAPTER FIVE

The rest of the day wore on for what seemed like forever. I took calls from Martha and my mother while Jacy and Neena relayed information from the clean-up crews. With only a few minor setbacks, Operation Dig Out Mooselick River was well on its way to being a rousing success. One of the guys on the chainsaw crew had to have stitches in his cheek when a branch sprang back and slapped him across the face. Brian estimated most roads would be at least passable by the end of the next day. Earlier, if the state sent tree services our way.

After a hodgepodge supper, the rest of my expanded household settled in for a movie while Brian put Wade to bed and called it an early night.

We'd made it through the first day of the storm's aftermath. The next couldn't help but be easier.

It wasn't. Some parts of it, anyway.

After breakfast, the men headed back out for another round of tree cleanup while Neena and I volunteered to run our gas tanks over to Pine Tree Auto and see if Bennie could fill them up.

"Looks like the aftermath of the apocalypse out here," Neena said as we navigated around the evidence of how busy the saw crews had been. "It looks like giants played tip the dominoes with some of these pine trees." After we turned off the main road, she pulled out her phone and took pictures while I fought against patches of ice and slick mud.

Bennie wasn't there when we pulled up, but Brandon Sinclair came out and ran the hand pump attached to one of the two large tanks on racks at the side of the garage. Round-faced, he greeted us with a grin plastered above a short but scruffy beard.

"Crazy storm, huh?"

How the man could be so cheerful about it was beyond me. Unless he was one of those eternal optimist types. I didn't know him well enough to say for sure since Bennie did most of the upkeep on my car himself.

"That's one word for it," I said, taking the first filled tank from him and tucking it in my rear hatch while Neena handed him the next.

"I can think of a few choice ones I'd rather use," she said, making him laugh out loud.

"Well, these natural disasters give us a chance to be neighborly, don't they? I'm bunking at the high school, and it's been quite the experience. Nothing like I expected."

"How so?"

"Everyone did their part. People helping people like something out of a Hallmark Christmas movie." He gestured toward a truck parked nearby. "As soon as the roads were clear enough, the guy that runs the Gas N Go donated a bunch of food. Canned goods, whatever was in the coolers and freezers that wouldn't survive. I hauled four loads for him myself."

"That would be Clive Thompson?" I said. This was the first I'd heard of it. "Nice of him."

"Yeah, that's the guy. He said there was no reason to let it all go to waste.The whole town pulls together at times like these. " He switched tanks again. "Really shows you what people are made of."

"Especially when there's a tragedy," I said.

That sobered him up. "Damn shame," he allowed as he set the last can under the spout and worked the pump. "What happened at the lodge. Just awful."

Did he mean the roof or Bill?

When I went to grab the last tank, he carried it to the car for me, secured the lot, and then closed the hatch. "That do you?"

"It will." I paid for the gas, and since another car pulled up, left him to his work.

On the way home, my mother called with the day's first good news. Brian located a generator powerful enough to run one of the pumps at the Gas N Go. Between them, he and the managers hooked it up. With the fuel shortage no longer an issue, the whole town could hunker down to wait out the siege.

We hadn't been home for more than ten minutes when my father called and asked us to meet him at the lodge when Drew got home for lunch. I could tell by his tone what he had to say wouldn't be good news, and it wasn't.

"Do you want the bad news or the worst news first?" Dad looked tired.

"I guess I'll take the worst."

"Bill Cavanaugh was already dead when the roof caved in. He'd been shot and killed. Murdered."

Braced to hear final confirmation that my wedding had to be moved, I hadn't expected that, but it confirmed why the caution tape had been swapped out for the crime scene variety.

"That's awful, Dad. I'm so sorry." I hugged him because he needed it.

"Which brings us to the bad news. Ernie can't clear the building until he and his guys have sifted through the debris for evidence, which, given the damage, could take days. The insurance adjuster's squawking because he's not allowed inside and threatening not to cover us if we don't use an approved company for the demo. The only approved company can't get here for weeks." Frustrated, he shoved his hands in his pockets and stared at what was left of the building.

"Max," he continued, "says they're using that as a loop-hole to get out of paying, and he can put some pressure on them, but it will take time. We'll be lucky to get a new roof on before fall."

Unless we wanted to reschedule, we would not be getting married here.

"I know you had your heart set on us getting married here, but it's okay. We'll figure something out. An outdoor wedding might be nice. Something like when Chris and Patrea got married. I'm sure we can find the perfect location."

He managed a wan smile. "That's not what your mother said."

"Leave mother to me." I'd work her around to whatever decision Drew and I made. One way or another. "You just relax. Let Max handle the insurance company and let Ernie deal with the murder. None of this is your responsibility."

"I was murdered? That must be why I'm still here." It

didn't even surprise me when Bill spoke. Why would it? If someone's dead in this town, their problems become my problem.

"I'd say it is," I said to him and then to Dad, "Bill's here, so it's official. Just remember, I didn't find this one. Drew did." Okay, I'd seen him first, but even so.

"Would it have made any difference?" Despite the gravity of the situation, a hint of a smile tugged at the corner of Drew's mouth.

"Probably not."

Don't think I wasn't tempted to ask Bill who killed him. Making ghosts think about how they died freaked them out. Freaked-out ghosts used up the energy it took to show themselves. Once their energy depleted, they went poof and left me alone for as long as it took to build back up—effectively giving me a break. Still, doing it on purpose seemed manipulative and just plain mean, so I didn't.

"I'm sorry you're dead, Bill."

"Happens to the best of us," he tried to put on a brave face. "How is it that you can talk to me?"

"Just lucky, I guess. These guys can't hear or see you." I repeated Bill's comments so they weren't left out of the loop. "My mom can, but if you approach her in public, she'll ignore you. I will, too, for that matter, so just don't. We'll talk about the rest of the rules later, but if you get bored and want some company of your own kind, go on over and visit Dolly Tibbets. She hangs out at her daughter's salon most of the time. She'll introduce you to the rest of the post-life community."

How he'd cope with Dolly and her chatty nature was his problem.

"I don't want you involved in another murder," Dad put on his protective face. "It's not your responsibility, and it could be dangerous." Nice of him to parrot my words back to me. "Relax and let Ernie do his job."

"I can try." He wasn't happy with my response, but it was the best I had to offer. Being haunted wasn't something a person could simply ignore, at least in my experience. If I could get as good at ignoring ghosts as my mother, things might have been different, but it seemed I inherited my boundary-setting traits from my dad, who had no skills in that department. "But what would you do if someone asked you for help?"

He sighed. "Couldn't this be a *do as I say, not as I do* kind of thing?"

"You can always hope, but what would be more helpful is if you started working on a list of people who might have wanted Bill dead."

That gave him pause. "By people, you mean members of the order."

"I'm afraid so. Given the scene of the crime, I think we have to start there, and it has to be someone brave enough to be out in some seriously nasty weather."

Dad thought a moment, "The only person I'd have left off that list would have been Bill himself."

"He's right," Bill confirmed. "I was having Sunday dinner with my mom. She made me leave when it started snowing, but it got bad before I made it home. It was that wet stuff that turns to ice on your wiper blades and glazes over between swipes."

"Were you planning to meet someone later that day?"

"I don't think so. I can't remember everything. Is that normal?"

Not helpful, but totally expected. "It is. Don't worry about trying to remember."

I repeated the gist of the conversation and said I'd take the car home when my father offered to go back out with Drew to rejoin the cutting crew. Or so he said. It was more likely that he wanted to get Drew alone to hatch out a plan to keep me from working Bill's case.

And then, Bill and I were alone. If I didn't choose my words carefully, he'd follow me home, and I had no doubt he'd come in for a visit, which I really didn't need. At least he didn't need to be fed.

"What am I supposed to do now?" he asked.

"Do you see a bright light anywhere?" One could always hope.

"I don't think so."

One would be disappointed as usual.

"Okay. Well, it looks like you're stuck here until we figure out who killed you. The first thing you need to know is that, along with not expecting me to talk to you in public, you must also respect my personal space. No touching, and no walking into my bedroom unannounced."

Taken aback, he stared at me for a moment. "Who does a thing like that?"

"You'd be surprised." If it hadn't kept happening, I wouldn't have made a rule about it. "Also, I don't give messages to loved ones. Only a few people in town are aware that I can speak to ghosts. I'd like to keep it that way."

I could tell that last one pained him, but he nodded anyway. "Fair enough."

"Good. Now, I've got a houseful. My friend Jacy and her family are there, as well as my friend Neena. They know about ghosts, so if you think of anything that might help me find your killer, you should feel free to come and tell me about it. But be careful, if you think too hard about your death....that will happen," I said as he vibrated and disappeared.

At least I'd have time to update my guests on the current state of events, but he'd be back. They always came back.

CHAPTER SIX

On the third night of the town-wide blackout, Patrea and Chris showed up at our house just after dinner. Theirs had been one of the last roads to get cleared. Laden down with plastic containers, Patrea beat her husband to the door and jammed her elbow against the doorbell until I let her in.

"I've been baking," she said by way of greeting. "I needed something to keep my mind off everything I'm not getting done over at the house. And I know it's not Saturday, but since we're all here, why don't we have a game night? What do you think?"

From over her shoulder, Chris grinned at me as he closed the door behind him. "She already called David and ordered him to come over, so while it looks like she's asking for your opinion, she's not. You might as well go with it."

"Game night sounds fun." I took the containers from Patrea so she could hang up her coat. "It's just the thing I need after the bad news I got earlier."

"What bad news? What's been happening? I've been out of the loop for three days."

She hadn't because we'd talked on the phone at least twice a day, but it was rare for this much time to pass where we didn't see each other in person.

"The big news of the day is that Bill Cavanaugh didn't die as a result of the roof collapse. He was murdered."

"See," Patrea jokingly punched Chris in the arm. "I told you I was missing all the good stuff. Has he made contact?"

"Briefly," I admitted. "Since Ernie's friendly with the order or brotherhood, whatever you want to call it, I might step back and let him solve this one on his own. The worst news is we've lost our wedding venue."

Patrea followed me into the kitchen while Chris split off and headed for the living room to get in on the noisy game Drew and Brian were playing with Wade and his toy cars. Jacy and Neena took their chance to escape and joined us in the kitchen.

"Between the investigation and some issues with the insurance, Dad says there's a less than zero percent chance the Lodge will have a new roof in time for the wedding."

"My mother offered to let Everly get married in her gardens," Jacy said as she popped open the top of one of the containers and selected a nut-studded brownie. "But Kitty wouldn't go for it."

Opening the other two containers, Neena opted for a lemon bar. "I thought Viola was the queen of drama around these parts but Kitty can throw a fit with the best of them. She is not in favor of an outdoor wedding."

"I don't think it was anything personal against Momma Wade," I felt compelled to defend my mother to Jacy. "She and Dad had their hearts set on me following in their footsteps this time, is all. A wedding in those gardens would be something right out of a fairytale. But my dress isn't right for that, and I'd be worried that people would trample some of her rare plants."

"You're right," Jacy admitted. "Momma's gardens are sort of wild and untamed. You'd have to wear something... boho chic to pull off a wedding there. Or pretty princess, even. Your dress calls out for a grand ballroom or someplace elegant. We'd have had to fancy things up at the lodge to make it work if you want the truth."

"That's easy," Patrea snapped her fingers decisively. "You'll get married at the Wentworth. It's the perfect place. You can't deny the decor matches your dress."

"Like they were made for each other, but the house isn't ready, and we only have a little over a month."

"It could be ready in time."

"Only if you let me cover the extra costs." She'd have to pay her crew double overtime, and I didn't want to be the cause of her going into debt.

But I barely got the words out before she shook her head. "No way. This is not negotiable."

"I love that you want to do this for me, but it's too much."

"No, it's not." We'd settled into chairs while we nibbled on baked goods, but now, she pushed her chair back and rose to nearly dance in place. "It's not. I can pull this off, and you'd be doing me a favor."

"How? By sending you to debtor's prison?"

Patrea rolled her eyes. "There's no such place, and I'm not destitute, you know."

We'd never discussed Patrea's net worth. I knew her family was loaded, but she'd never really mentioned her own financial situation, and I wasn't raised to ask those kinds of questions. Besides, she was more excited than she should be. In a moment, I learned why.

"Ever since Neena planted the idea in my head, I've been trying to decide if she was right. The wedding industry is huge, and you have to admit the house would be perfect as a venue. The main bedrooms could double as dressing rooms, and if I add a few more on the third floor, the whole wedding party could stay for the duration. Jacy and Neena could provide period furnishings, which we'd let the guests know are all for sale. David's got the inn for guests to stay, and there's the motel, too. We could advertise it as a small-town destination spot and pull in revenue for the entire town."

"That's nuts," Jacy said.

"It's not, though." Neena jumped right on board. "A mansion in the country would be its own destination for all four seasons. Plus, there's the lake nearby and all those events Martha puts on for entertainment. You'd need a long-term plan for landscaping in case someone wants to hold the ceremony outdoors like you and Chris did. I bet you could do a lot with the grounds to make them nice."

Now, Jacy jumped on board. "Pergolas with climbing vines and fairy lights. Maybe put in a pond and create micro-gardens to offer different options. Do one with all white flowers and another in shades of pink or blue, and have an area like my mother's where everything is all mixed up but works together."

"I'd have to find just the right person to manage the business, but I think it could fly."

Patrea wasn't one to get stars in her eyes over just anything, and she wouldn't jump if she weren't sure she could stick the landing.

"If anyone can make something like that work in a town like this," I selected a second brownie because it was there, "it would be you. But I don't want you taking on more than you can handle on account of me."

She waved my protest away with the flick of a hand. "I won't. You'll be my guinea pig."

"Well, thanks. I guess."

"No," she insisted. "Really. You're primed for this. You've already got catering lined up, and the kitchen is in good enough shape to handle any last-minute prep just as it is. I'll push back the start date for the work I had planned there and focus the crews on finishing the rooms we've already demoed. Some paint and cleaning for the rest, and we're good to go."

"But—" I barely got one word out before she cut me off.

"Don't argue with me. I'm not taking no for an answer. If I have to, I'll make it your wedding present, but I need you to be my trial run."

I know when I'm beaten, and this was one of those times. "I have to run it by my mother first. If she says it's okay, then I guess I'm in. But you have to let me help with the painting and cleaning. And Drew will help Chris with the mowing and clearing of the grounds. Otherwise, the deal is off."

"That goes for me, too," Jacy said. "I'll volunteer Brian for lawn duty. If he argues, he'll have to deal with me, but he won't because he loves Everly, too."

"I'm in for cleaning and painting," Neena declared. "And if you don't mind, I'd like to do a video of my work on the mural and post it on the website you insisted I needed to have. There's good money in restoration work, and I like seeing art come back to life."

Excitement lighting her entire face, Patrea sat back down. "So, we're doing this?"

"I guess we are," I agreed. I might use my mother's approval as an excuse not to burden Patrea with extra work on my account, but there was no way Mom wouldn't want to have the wedding in such a beautiful place. We toasted the deal with wine and baked goods. Just as we should.

We might have squealed a little, too.

Okay, we squealed a lot. Enough to pull the men in from the living room and to see David had joined them while we were busy hashing out the details.

"Those sound like excited noises," Drew said, "and why are you hoarding the baked goods?"

"How would you feel about getting married at the Wentworth?" Our last experience there had been one serious walk on the wild and ghostly side, and it hadn't even been a week since it happened.

When he only blinked a couple of times, my excitement began to leak away.

"You don't want to because of what happened with Charlotte."

"That's not it," he denied. "The house is clear. We saw to that."

I was about to ask for an explanation when he circled the table, pulled Patrea to her feet, and kissed her squarely on the lips.

"Hey, that's my woman you're kissing," Chris protested with no heat whatsoever.

"Sorry, man." And then, Drew turned, grabbed Chris, and planted one on him, too.

"I think he likes the idea." Jacy couldn't have grinned any wider without hurting her face.

"You think?" I laughed out loud.

"It's really not fair," Neena said. "I'm not getting any of that lip action, and I volunteered for painting and cleaning duty."

"Me, too," Jacy declared, earning them both the same treatment.

"Back off," Brian held out a hand when Drew turned toward him. "I'm sure I've been added to the list of workers, but you can thank me with beer."

"Same goes." David's gaze strayed toward Neena, then flicked back to Drew as if he wished he had something to also thank her for. "I'll volunteer for whatever you need, but beer's good. Keep your lips to yourself."

Chris laughed. "I've had worse."

"Really?" Jacy giggled. "I've had better."

"Thanks," Drew said. "But I know you're only trying to protect Brian's fragile ego at my expense."

With the laughter his comment elicited, we kicked off our post-snowpocalypse game night. When I texted my mother the news, she responded with a dozen heart emojis.

Two rounds into Pictionary, the baby monitor issued a spate of happy baby babble. "I've got him," I said since I was closest. Well on his way to being potty trained, Wade wasn't one to let such trivialities as a dirty diaper get him down, so even his happy sounds required an inspection.

When I pushed open the door to the bedroom where we'd set up a temporary bed in a playpen for him, I realized this was not a code brown or a code yellow situation. It was a ghost thing.

"I thought we discussed the rules, Bill," I said to the ghost making silly faces at the giggling toddler, who clearly could see him. Great. Now I had to tell Jacy her kid was like me.

"Sorry. I tried to ring the doorbell, but I couldn't, so I poked my head inside and heard this little guy talking to his stuffed teddy. I only came up for a quick peek."

"You like babies?"

"Who doesn't like babies? I'd hoped to have a family of my own, but I never found the right woman, I guess." The sadness in his tone evoked my sympathy.

"Who are you talking to?" Jacy walked in with the others right behind her.

"Bill's here," I explained.

"Biw," little Wade pointed cheerfully toward the ghost, then chortled when Bill made another face at him.

"I'm sorry," I said as if Wade's exposure to the sight of a ghost was my fault because it probably was since they were drawn to me. "I guess Wade takes after his auntie."

With a flick of her wrist, Jacy waved the apology away. "It's not your fault, and there's nothing to apologize for anyway. Momma says babies and animals can see things we can't because they haven't learned they shouldn't. He'll grow out of it eventually, and if he doesn't, that's okay, too. He's obviously not scared."

Given the peals of bright laughter coming from the child, I couldn't help but agree.

It struck me again how differently we'd been raised. Leandra, who couldn't see spirits, taught her children to be open to paranormal experiences, while my mother, who could see them, pretended they didn't exist—at least until lately, and then only under duress. That was her choice, and I didn't hold it against her, but it couldn't be mine.

Whatever happened with Wade as he grew, he'd be supported and accepted.

"Well, then. I guess you're off the hook, Bill. Was there something you needed to tell me?"

"Yeah. Maybe. I mean, it might not be important, but I stopped somewhere on the way home from my mother's that night. I bought a gallon of windshield wash at the Gas N Go because I was running low."

"Do you know what time it was?"

"Sure, around 7:30. I looked at the clock in my car when I pulled in."

"Did you talk to anyone while you were there?"

"Clive Thompson was working. We didn't have much to say to each other. I can't quite remember other than that he said I was lucky I got there when I did because he was closing soon. I paid and left because I was in a hurry to get home. Hope that helps."

It didn't. "Every little bit, I suppose."

With a final wave at the baby, he said, "See you later, champ," and faded.

"Bye-bye," Wade burbled and waved a chubby hand.

"He's gone," I said, repeating the tidbit he'd come to offer. While Jacy got Wade tucked in and settled for the rest of the night, I called Ernie.

"Who's dead now?"

"Nobody," I rolled my eyes. "I'm only calling to pass on some information that I received from a credible source. Bill stopped at the Gas N Go around 7:30 on the night of his murder."

"How credible?"

"Very. Just ask Clive Thompson, okay? I'm sure he'll corroborate."

"Thanks."

CHAPTER SEVEN

I'd been dreaming about curling my toes into white sand while watching a spectacular sunset with a tropical drink in my hand when a herd of elephants ran past me on the beach. Coming awake, I realized the elephants weren't in my dream. They were in my house. And it wasn't elephants. It was a cat followed by a dog followed by a giggling toddler and his mother, who was only trying to stop the chaos.

This wasn't my first time having little Wade in my house, but Brian and Jacy's parents were a bit proprietary about their grandson when it came to overnight visits, so this was the first time he'd been in my house in the morning—not the same as watching him for an evening.

When the thunder of little feet echoed in the opposite direction, I smiled. When I turned my head to the left, I saw Drew on his side, propped on one elbow, watching me and also smiling.

"This is what it will be like when we start our family," he leaned over and kissed me.

"Minus the cat." I kissed him back. "I think she's actually louder than the dog."

When I walked into the kitchen a few minutes later, Jacy grimaced and poured me a cup of coffee. "Sorry. I tried to keep him quiet, but apparently, the lure of Pearl's tail is irresistible to both dog and child. I made pancakes as penance."

"Don't worry about it. As Drew said, this is good practice, so I know what to expect when it's our turn. I'll take the pancakes anyway, though."

"Auntie! Auntie! Auntie!" Wade pounded into the kitchen and grabbed the hem of my bathrobe. "Up."

Unable to resist, I lifted him into my arms and accepted a series of wet kisses before he wriggled and wanted down again. "Smoochies," he said as his feet hit the floor, and he was off and running again. Probably to give Drew the same treatment.

"There are worse ways to start the day," I grinned and added a dollop of honey to my coffee. "Wade gives the best smoochies. Where's everyone else?"

"Brian left for work an hour ago, and Neena went over to her place to fill the stove. It's surreal that most of the snow is already gone, but we're still in a state of emergency."

"Just one," I said as Jacy pulled a tray of fluffy pancakes out of the warm oven. "You're spoiling us."

She grinned. "Blame Brian. He bartered sex for them."

"I'm sure it was a hard bargain."

"Yes, it was." She settled across from me. "There's been some minor flooding with the quick melt-off, but Brian says if nothing else goes wrong, we should have power back tomorrow, and we'll be out of your hair."

"You're family," Drew said from the doorway. "Our doors are always open."

"Thanks." Jacy rose to fetch him a plate. "I must admit, those old beds upstairs are way more comfortable than I expected."

"Hence the sex pancakes," I said just as Drew put the first bite in his mouth.

He chewed and swallowed, then said. "I don't think I need to know what that means."

Jacy and I laughed.

"Your mom's coming over," Drew warned me. "In about half an hour. I'm supposed to make sure you've put pictures of the house on your laptop because she wants to see them."

"Why do you know this instead of me?"

"She figured your phone would still be in Do Not Disturb mode."

My mother knew me too well. "Okay. Consider me warned."

"Your dad's dropping her off. He asked me to go with him to check out the damage to the gazebo. I think he considered it a mercy invite, but I'd already planned to stop by the gym and check on things. Want to give me your keys, Jace? I'll take a walk through your shop while I'm out."

"That works. Thanks."

Neena returned just as we finished breakfast and helped clean up the kitchen while I dressed for the day. For my mother's sake, I set up a slide show on my laptop, pulling in every photo of the Wentworth I could find. Even with a haze of dirt on the windows, construction debris, and a few cobwebs, the potential for a beautiful wedding was there. Anyone could see it.

"I'm jealous," Neena admitted after Jacy went up to put Wade down for his morning nap. "Only a little, and I'll get over it because I get to wear something fancy and pose on those stairs, too."

"It won't bother you?" I wanted to ask while it was just

the two of us since she was the one most bothered by the ghostly shenanigans that plagued my life. "You won't be weirded out remembering what happened there, I mean."

"It won't. I've made my peace with what happened at the shop, too. Abner wasn't a bad guy or even a bad ghost. He was just irritated because he was stuck between the past and where he wanted to go. It doesn't excuse his behavior, but I understand why he acted the way he did. Charlotte was just plain evil."

And yet, the tone of her voice let me know she still felt uneasy.

"Did I ever tell you how Hudson saved my life?" Maybe now was the time for that story.

"He did? When you were dating?"

"Nope. After he died. Right here in this house. Ray Watson had me up against the door with his hands around my neck. I'd be dead if Hudson hadn't rolled a mannequin head down the stairs like he was bowling for murderers. Remember, you've seen more of the bad side of ghostly manifestations than the good."

When she didn't speak for a moment, I gave her time to think things through. It was still a sore point that I hadn't allowed her to talk to her husband one last time. He'd been my first ghost, and I hadn't handled the situation the way I would have done now, but second-guessing past life decisions doesn't change them.

"Maybe I shouldn't have said anything," I started, then stopped when she held up her hand. Once I got a good look at her, I could see the smile tugging at her lips and the shine of laughter in her eyes. "You're not angry."

She shook her head as a snort escaped. "I'm just picturing it. Bowling for murderers."

"He even yelled 'strike.'"

Now, she giggled. "Did he do that ridiculous dance of his?"

I'd forgotten all about Hudson's victory dance, but I joined her when she rose, thrust her elbows out behind her, stretched her neck out like a chicken, and did an exaggerated two-step.

"If he did, I was too busy getting my breath back to notice, but I wouldn't be surprised." It felt good to talk about his fun side with someone who appreciated it. If her smile was anything to go by, Neena agreed.

"I miss those silly moments," she said, but with more nostalgia than grief.

"He'd want you to be happy, whatever that looks like for you. I know it's true because he told me so."

"I know. I also know you're all hoping I can get happy with David."

"Oh, I think you could definitely get happy with him," I waggled my eyebrows.

"Don't think I haven't been tempted."

That was news to me. "So why haven't you?"

"I loved Hudson, but we can both agree he wasn't what you'd call a deep thinker. He was a lot of fun and good-hearted, and I know he loved me, but," she held her palm flat at the level of her nose, "he was all up here. You know what I mean?"

Oddly enough, I thought I did. "Everything came easy for Hudson. His parents doted on him. He excelled at sports and got decent grades. He'd never lost a family member or even a close friend. He was still...emotionally shiny, I guess."

"Maybe that's what was at the heart of it. He could laugh and play because he didn't know anything worse." Neena nodded, her face pensive. "And I needed that lightness to balance me out. It was why we worked."

"Until you separated, he'd never been tested."

"We separated because we...I...had come to the point where I needed to know there was more to him. That he could go deeper, I guess."

I took her hand because she needed the comfort. "If he hadn't been killed, he'd have shown you he had more."

"I think so, too," Neena sighed. "It's just the opposite with David. He's all about the deep when it comes to me. I know he has lighter places because I see them when he's around you. The way you are with each other. You know?"

"The teasing?"

She nodded.

"Let me tell you, it wasn't easy for us to get to that place. I was not nice to him when I moved back to town. I thought he was taking advantage of my parents. Sponging off them. Plus, he'd stolen my room, and they didn't put his butt on the street for me, so I blamed him."

"Anyone would."

"To make it worse, my mother let me know she'd be only too happy if we got together and I took that out on him, too. He had every reason to dislike me, and for a while, I'm sure he did. The feeling was mutual."

"What turned it around?"

"He showed up for me at a time when I needed someone and proved he was the bigger person. He shared some of his personal stuff, and I vented to him about some of mine. We peeled back the layers and found neither of us was the person the other expected. It took some time, but it led us to the type of friendship we have now. He's family."

"So," Neena smiled. "What you're saying is you're both a lot of work but worth it in the end."

"I guess I am."

My mother showed up and ended any further conversation on the subject, but I figured we were done with it anyway. Whatever decisions Neena made about David and whatever relationship she wanted to forge with him had to be her own.

"Sit here, Mrs. Dupree," Neena vacated her seat next to me then amended when my mother tossed her an arch look, "Kitty, I mean."

"Better. Now, show me some pictures of what Patrea's been doing. Why isn't she here? I called to tell her I was coming and that I would have questions."

"That's news to me, so I don't have an answer," I said.

Patrea showed up a few minutes later with updated photos and a wealth of patience for my mother's endless barrage of questions.

Her photos were newer than mine and showed more progress than expected.

"I didn't know Jerry was so close to finishing the dining room molding. It didn't look that close the last time I was over."

"It goes pretty quickly once the prep work is out of the way. Or so he said, but we'll have to wait close to a month for the plaster to dry completely before any of the repairs can be painted. Something about the alkalinity has to balance for the paint to adhere properly."

When Jacy came back down, she argued for the bridal party to walk down the stairs while I took a position firmly against. "Not in heels. I'll trip. Or you'll trip and kick off the domino effect. I don't want my wedding to be remembered because the bride and her attendants all had to go to the ER."

She remained unconvinced, and I finally agreed to do a trial run and postpone the decision until then. I also agreed to order far too many electronic candles because my mother found some that looked relatively real and insisted we needed scads of them but must observe proper safety protocols.

"More is better," she insisted. "Your dress and the space practically demand romantic lighting. Don't forget extra batteries. Now, for the change of address cards."

I let her choose the wording but insisted we go with an overnight printing company and a simple design for the sake of expediency. "Once the power comes back on, I'll talk to Delia about the flower arrangements. I'll ask her to swap out the table containers for something that goes better with the decor, and I think that does it."

"Not quite." Mom surprised us all by addressing Patrea instead of me. I've taken the liberty of making one or two calls on your behalf. The Select Board meets a week from Thursday. You'll need their approval before moving forward with the plan to turn the Wentworth property into an event space. Be there at seven sharp to speak your piece."

"Okay," was all Patrea got out before Mom rolled over her.

"Expect a call from Barb Dexter. She's a prominent member of the garden club. She'll sponsor you to sit in on their meeting next Tuesday, where you'll ask for advice on which flowers and shrubs will best maintain the historical ambiance. Don't pull that face. You don't have to follow their advice to the letter, but you do need to curry favor with one or two members who hold leadership positions in the historical society."

"Okay."

"Getting the HS on your side is key because if you don't, you'll face opposition with the board since there's significant marital overlap."

"Marital overlap?" Patrea looked at me for clarification.

"Ginger Martin holds the second chair on the Select Board," I said. "Her husband heads up the historical society. It's widely known that she caters to his moods regarding matters of town business. You get him on board—he'll make sure she is, too."

"But that's collusion," she argued.

"Only when it's not working in your favor," Mom said. You'd be better off considering it insurance. Miles Higgins will vote for anything that increases town revenue, which this will. And Clive Thompson will vote however Miles does. Get Ginger in your pocket, show Miles a solid financial picture, and you're a shoo-in."

Stunned, Patrea pressed her palm to her forehead. "That's diabolical."

"That's politics," Mom said mildly. "In Mooselick River."

"I guess I'll talk to Barb when she calls, then." Patrea gave in. "Anything else I need to know?"

"Well," Mom said, putting on her most innocent face, "A

couple of my friends volunteered for cleaning duty when you're ready, but I'd planned to wait a bit longer to spring that one on you."

Jacy snorted. "I bet my mother got in on that one," she said.

"As a matter of fact, it was her idea," Mom admitted. "She put it out on the phone tree once we got past the initial crisis."

"Just how many of these 'couple of friends' can I expect?"

"No more than six or seven. Probably. Ten at the most. A dozen if it's a weekday."

Once the door closed behind my mother, Patrea turned to me. "It's too early in the day for wine, right?"

"Probably." It wasn't even noon yet. "But I have restorative tea and Swiss chocolate—the really good stuff."

Jacy turned on me. "You've been holding out."

"I was saving it for a special occasion, but I think reviving Patrea after getting Kittified counts."

"You mean she's done this before?"

I exchanged a look with Jacy. "How do you think she got so good at it? She's had decades of practice."

Raising her hand, Jacy said, "I can attest to the fact. This was a doozy, though. Top notch. I think I'd rate it a solid eight-point seven on the ten-point scale."

Slumping in her chair, Patrea shook her head. "If that wasn't a ten, I don't want to see one."

"At least this one was for your own good. It's worse if she's mad. One time when one of my teachers accused me of cheating on a test I studied hard for, she ramped it up to an eleven. Principal Thomas showed up in the middle of it and earned himself a nine and a half for his trouble. She never even raised her voice, but I got the A I had earned."

"She should teach a class," Patrea said. She declined the tea but broke off a square of chocolate and then offered the bar to Neena, who passed it along to me.

"And dilute the essence? Never happen," I grinned. "It's not hereditary."

"Isn't it, though?" Tilting her head, Jacy studied me. "Haven't you done the same thing to Martha a time or two? You don't have Kitty's finesse or flair, but you get in the same zone when you put on your organizing hat."

A comment like that might have put our friendship in jeopardy a couple of years before, but my mother and I had mended our fences since then. I found myself flattered by the comparison.

"Maybe so. She was right, though, about all of it. The house is old enough that historical society members might kick up objections if they think you're not being respectful enough. But then, the house also has a history of being a party palace, which might grant you some leeway. I'd make the effort if I were you. At least until the Select Board grants approval."

"Alice Cavanaugh's in the garden club." Jacy blew on her tea to cool it. "Or she was the last time my mother dragged me to a meeting."

"That's Bill's mother?" I remembered Ernie mentioning her name. "I don't think I've ever met her."

"This would have been when I was still in school." After tasting, Jacy added a splash of milk to her tea. "Maybe I'm projecting because of what just happened, but the only impression I can remember of her is that she had sad eyes."

"We should look into her, don't you think?" On any typical day, I'd have grabbed my computer and run a search on the library's newspaper archives, but with cable lines down, that wasn't an option. "Does anyone's phone have good enough Internet to search?"

Not since the storm was the consensus.

"I can call my mother. See what she can tell me if you think it will help," Jacy offered. We'd gone from wedding triumph to tragedy. "Has Bill been back today? Do you think he'll be one of the pesky ones?"

"Not really, but we barely knew each other. Not that a lack of personal history made any difference to the other ghosts I've helped." Amber Hale came to mind. She'd been a total stranger to me, but that hadn't stopped her from showing up whenever and wherever she wanted. Plus, she'd stuck around even after her killer was caught. "And it's early days yet. He's still processing what happened to him. Besides, I told him to find Dolly if he wanted company. Let's not bring Momma Wade into this if we don't have to. As long as Bill doesn't put the pressure on, I'm happy to give Ernie a head start. Maybe he can solve this one without me."

CHAPTER EIGHT

*Y*ou don't really appreciate your daily routines until something comes along to disrupt them for an extended period. Ours had turned into the twice-daily refilling of the generator with gas over at Mrs. Abernathy's, the every other day exodus to the gas station to wait in the inevitable line at the only working pump and keeping little Wade out of trouble. He went from trying to ride Molly like a horse to wanting to touch Pearl's eyeball. Molly tolerated his efforts with enviable patience. Pearl striped his little hand twice. Not that the scratches served as much of a deterrent.

Five days after Bill's death, the power came back on.

"What's that sound?" Jacy spoke into the sudden absence of the noise coming from the generator's engine.

"It's quiet. Blessed, blessed quiet," Neena sighed. "Oh, how I've missed that sound." Not that it lasted long with Wade around. "You know I love y'all, but I'm going up to pack."

You couldn't blame her. We'd been living in close quarters for longer than planned.

While the men went out to get everyone's houses hooked back up to the grid, Jacy checked in with the neighbors staying at hers. Since they were already packing up to go home, Jacy did the same. An hour and a half later, my house felt weirdly empty.

"I need to go turn the water back on at the gym and make sure everything's working. Want to come with?" Drew came out to sit on the back steps while I tossed a ball for Molly. "We'll make it a family outing." He held up Molly's leash.

"A walk sounds good." Temperatures had climbed back up into the mid-sixties, and the sun felt warm. "Why not?"

The topless gazebo and a few bent trees were the only visual signs left from the storm until we got to the gym and saw the yellow flutter of plastic at the lodge. In another day, the whole town would be back to business as usual, except there'd be a job opening at the bank, an emergency meeting to elect a new town treasurer, and the brotherhood would have to find another meeting space.

Drew caught me looking. "It's been a busy few days, but I notice Bill hasn't come around since that one night. Or if he did, you didn't say anything." An unusual occurrence in my experience.

"He hasn't." I nodded toward the ruined building. "He's over there now, though, and I don't know what to say to him. I've been too busy with everything else to even think about looking into his murder."

Turning, I followed Drew inside.

"You could sit this one out," he said. We've got a wedding coming up, and a lot of work needs to be done before it happens."

"We do." Still, I couldn't believe I'd been given the ability to talk to ghosts if I wasn't meant to help them.

Drew sensed my reluctance to commit to doing nothing. "Or not."

"Or not what? Not get married?"

His eyes widened. "Why does your mind keep going there? I meant not sit this one out. Listen, we're all teaming up to get the Wentworth ready, so why don't we team up on this other thing, too? Jacy and Neena are in a good position to chat up their customers, and we all know this town runs on gossip. I'll have to switch off with Riley and do a few more night classes while we whip the grounds over there into shape during the day. What if I drop by the bank and offer a discount on the next round of self-defense classes. Maybe I can get some of Bill's co-workers to sign up and do a class just for them. Women like me. I can get them to talk."

I grinned because if any other man said that, he would have been bragging, but that wasn't Drew's style.

"Then, there's your father."

That one hit me hard. Bill had been a friend, and I knew my dad would want to help, but I'd rather have kept him away from anything that would cause more pain. I sighed, "I know. I can't tell him not to get involved."

"And your mother," he said as he used a wrench to tighten the fitting he'd loosened on Monday to drain the water lines so they wouldn't freeze.

"I get it." I held up a hand. "It takes a village to catch a murderer. Fine. I'll set something up."

But he had one more name to add to the list.

"Don't forget Martha."

Horrified, I froze. "Martha Tipton? Why? You're not suggesting I tell her about my ghosts, are you?"

"No. But Bill was involved in town politics and you can't

deny Martha has an in there. I'm sure you can find a way to use her without letting her know your secret."

It could work, I supposed. I wouldn't be there to see people's expressions when they talked about Bill, but every single one of my friends, including Martha, would know what to look for. Maybe I could pull together a group of sleuths and crack this case quickly. If Ernie beat me to the punch, more power to him.

"Why don't I go talk to her now?" Get it over with since she'd be the hardest one. "Come get me when you're done here."

"Rescue you from her, you mean."

I pulled him in for a kiss. "My knight in shining armor."

Leaving Molly with him, I spent the five-minute walk framing my approach with Martha. An inveterate busybody, she knew everyone and everything that happened in town and used that information to further her own plans. The problem would be turning her focus outside the scope of putting Mooselick River back on the map. Or, I'd need to figure out how to use her single-minded interest in my favor.

By the time I got to the town office, I had the loose beginnings of a plan.

"Hey, Martha. How are things going?"

She stood behind the counter wearing her bifocals for once, scowling while she read through the sheet of paper in her hand.

"Well enough. I was better before I got the estimate for the repairs to the gazebo. My lands, I don't know how we'll pull it together in time for the spring festival. Or if we can at all. The board might vote to tear it down."

She turned the sheet so I could see the number that was

far too close to five figures than I liked. More than the town wanted to spend.

Without knowing it, she'd played right into my hands.

"You know, I already talked to my father about the gazebo. He said the roof didn't actually collapse so much as one of the posts holding it up couldn't handle the snow weight. The roof section came down in one piece that could be lifted back up with something called a telehandler, set back on new posts, and repaired in place. If the town could free up the funds for the materials and crane rental, he and his kids would put in stronger posts to protect this from happening again. He says they should have done that the last time, but he wanted to maintain the historical feel, so he went with the same size as before."

My father taught what used to be called shop class at the local high school but was now called technical education. They'd fixed the gazebo once before but hadn't planned for this much heavy snow. "It might need a few shingles replaced, some of the trim, and a little touch-up on the paint. It wouldn't cost nearly as much as that estimate you're holding."

Frustrated, Martha yanked off her glasses and set them aside. Her drawn-on eyebrows lowered ominously. "That's just the problem. We've lost our treasurer, so freeing up funds won't be easy."

"Lost the...you mean Bill Cavanaugh. Such a tragedy. I'd forgotten he was town treasurer." I laid it on thick.

"His death has thrown everything into a tailspin. We'll have to hold an emergency town meeting to elect someone to take his place. I don't suppose you'd consider—"

"Me?" I cut her off before she could finish that horrifying

sentence, then thought the better of my original plan and pivoted. I could use this to get what I needed without formally enlisting her into my sleuthing group. "Do you think I'd be good at it? Wouldn't it be better to have someone with more experience in financial matters than me?"

Lips pursed, Martha shook her head. "It's a thankless job. We get more contenders for the Select Board positions, but no one wants to handle the money. Too much responsibility for too little pay, I suppose. I practically had to force Bill into running for the position."

"You're not making the job sound enticing," I pointed out. "If I agree to think about it, could you put together some information about the other board members to help me decide? I'd want to know something about their personalities, how they get along with each other, and how they treated Bill. It would be best if you didn't tell anyone we talked about this. You understand?"

When she clapped her hands, I felt terrible because I had no intention of taking over for a man who'd just been murdered. If it turned out that his job here had nothing to do with his death, I'd help find someone to take his place, but it wouldn't be me.

"Got it. I'll work on it from home and email you the dossiers. It will be our little secret."

"Perfect. In the meantime, if I tug on the right strings, I can get the materials to replace the gazebo posts at no cost to the town. If I can't finagle another way, we should have enough in our events fund to cover the large equipment rental. With your permission, I'll make a few calls."

"I knew I could count on you."

She didn't know the half of it. I intended to pay for the

materials out of my own pocket. I'd also pay for the telehandler rental if we could get one here fast enough.

"Same goes, Martha."

Since the exchange hadn't taken nearly as long as I expected, I didn't bother to text Drew as I headed back to the gym.

"You look pensive," Bill said, popping up beside me.

"Just trying to work out my next move. The timing of your death threw a box full of monkey wrenches into my wedding plans."

"Sorry," he said. He didn't sound sorry, and really, who could blame him? "For what it's worth, turning the Wentworth into an event space makes sound financial sense. With the right management, I'd say Mrs. Evergreen is looking at no more than two years to earn a decent ROI. The wedding industry is quite lucrative."

"Where'd you hear about that? And what's an ROI?"

"Dolly," he supplied without hesitation. I should have known. "And an ROI means a return on her investment."

"Are you sure, though? Even in a town the size of Mooselick River? We only have the Bide-A-Way and David's inn for additional guests to stay. That's less than twenty-five rooms altogether. It wouldn't be enough."

"There's room for spillover in Hackinaw. A few camp owners on the lake do weekly rentals, and with the right incentive, I can think of several properties that could be turned into short-term rentals. Lake View Cabins should be up and running by next summer, which is when most weddings happen."

Confused, I stopped walking. "Lake View Cabins? They've been closed for years."

Not just closed but halfway between rack and ruin. There were a dozen or so cabins, if I remembered right, in a scattered semi-circle perched on the hill with a good view of the lake. "I'm not sure I remember them ever being open."

"They will be this year. I approved a loan for Darcy Campbell last September."

"Darcy Campbell? Are you sure?" My memory supplied what little I knew of the woman. She and her husband, Nelson, were Friday-night regulars at Cappy's Tavern. I'd gone to school with Nelson, a cousin to Amber Hale, one of my early ghosts. My one and only personal encounter with Darcy hadn't given me much of a sense of her since she'd been drunk and upset at the time.

"I'm sure. Nelson's a hard worker, so he'll get the place whipped into shape, and Darcy's motivated, too. Her grandfather left the property to her, and even in its current state, it had enough equity that I managed to push the loan through."

"That's...interesting," was the only word that came to mind.

"Mooselick River is poised on the cusp of regaining prosperity. Miles and I discussed it at length over the past few months, and this venture couldn't come at a better time."

"Poised on the cusp?" I repeated because who says things like that?

He kept on talking as if I hadn't spoken. "It was Miles who had the vision for growing the town without losing the ambiance. Clive would have been happy to sign the deal for an outlet mall along the bypass if we hadn't voted him down."

"Outlet mall? When was this?"

"Last fall."

This was the first I've heard of it, which meant Martha hadn't known such a deal was in the works, or she'd have mounted a town-wide protest and put me in charge. Bill went on to explain that putting an outlet mall near the bypass wouldn't pull tourism into the town of Mooselick River. It would do just the opposite. Those places had their own eateries and shops with the goal of keeping people there once they drew them in. Sure, the tax increase would benefit the town, but the established businesses wouldn't get more foot traffic and might even see less.

"All progress is not good progress. That's something Clive hasn't learned yet."

"So you disagreed with him." Maybe this had nothing to do with Bill's death, but as I'd said, every little bit of information helped me get a better picture.

"Vehemently," Bill nodded, his energy beginning to flag. "As treasurer, I didn't get a vote, so all I could do was offer my opinion when Miles asked for it. Thankfully, I swayed Ginger to my way of thinking, and the vote came in at two to one against. The scheme never even got put before the town for a full vote."

He'd gone nearly transparent around the edges, so I got my last question in before he poofed. "Was Clive annoyed with you?"

"Just a little," Bill allowed, and then, was gone.

"Isn't that interesting?" I said to no one.

"Bet your sweet bippy," Dolly piped up from behind me.

"My what, now?"

"Never mind. I'm old, remember?"

When the breeze shifted, I got a whiff of the perm solution and Aquanet that followed the ghost of Dolly Tibbets wherever she went. Still, as ghosts went, Dolly was shaping up to be one of my favorites. She had a cheerful nature, the visual appeal of a tropical bird, and the common sense to know what was what.

"Not for nothing, it would have been nice for people around here not to have to drive to Bangor for decent towels, but he was right. It wouldn't have been good for us at this stage of the town's revival. What your friend is trying to do is a step in the right direction."

"I think so, too."

Dolly nodded in the direction of Jacy and Neena's shop as we passed by. "This town's coming back from the dead, and it wouldn't pay to rush things. Like young Bill says, you can't grow beyond your infrastructure without causing too much stress."

I smiled because until she'd said it, the phrase wasn't one I'd have expected to hear Dolly utter.

"Then again," Dolly winked and tried to give me a nudge with her shoulder, which only ended with her nearly tripping through me and me getting the heebiest case of the jeebies ever. When she righted herself, she finished, "The boy was a two-ton fool for not giving my Mara the money to expand the salon when she asked for it."

"If Patrea's venue gets approved, we'll have to talk her into trying again. She'll need the extra space."

"Damn straight," Dolly agreed, then toddled off when I headed back into the gym.

CHAPTER NINE

On Friday, I woke to a disorienting sound. Silence. Or silence punctuated by Molly's toenails scrabbling on the floor. In all the kerfuffle from the storm, we'd missed her appointment to get them clipped. I added a call to reschedule to my mental list for the day, which also included a trip to the grocery store once I'd had time to assess the sorry state of my cupboards.

Adding a jacket over my pajamas, I tossed the rubber flyer for Molly.

"Have you considered a home equity loan on this house?" Bill popped up out of nowhere, as ghosts are likely to do. "The interest rates are currently stable but low enough to make it worthwhile. Plus, taking out a loan would be a good way to build up your credit score."

"Thanks. I'll keep that in mind."

"A good credit rating is a hallmark of fiscal responsibility. I know you don't think you need a loan right now, but you might later, and then what? You're getting married soon, and I always recommend that newlyweds take credit counseling. Call the bank and set it up. You'll thank me later."

If I had my way, he'd be long gone by the time I got married. Still, his obsession might be a way to get information out of him, and Molly wasn't tired yet, so I kept him talking.

"Who would I make the appointment with? Were you the only loan officer at the bank?"

"With so many online options these days, most banks run with a reduced staff compared to what used to be the norm. There were three of us for a long time—until Martin Walker got arrested and Walter Prescott was promoted from senior loan officer to manager. His first act was to institute a hiring freeze." Before I could ask for clarification, he amended his statement. "I think he only did it to get Agnes Cunningham off his back."

"How so?"

"She lobbied hard for the senior position, but I had more time and experience. It was my job to lose, and she knew it."

Ding. Ding. We had a motive.

"And you didn't think to tell me this before?"

"Everyone knew the job was mine. Agnes didn't stand a chance based on the number of loans I brought in, but she started badgering Walter on his first day as manager, so he called for a complete hiring freeze. There would be no new hires or promotions while he settled into his new position. I took it as a sign to step up my game. It wasn't difficult to edge out the competition."

"You were getting promoted, then?"

Bill rocked back on his heels and grinned. "The announcement would have come at the end of next week, and I had two more loans ready to close by then. I guess Agnes will get the job after all."

"Seems like it. How hard did she lobby for it?"

"Not hard enough to resort to murder, I don't think."

Before I could ask him anything else, he was gone. Fickle things, ghosts.

I played with Molly until she got tired of running and flopped at my feet, then went back inside for a shower that didn't have to be kept short to ensure enough hot water for everyone else. It was heaven, and I felt fully clean for the first time in days.

Over breakfast, I checked my email and discovered Martha had been busy. When she'd said dossiers, she meant full ones.

You would have saved me the time to put together all of this information, Martha prefaced her report, *if you were as involved in the political aspects of running this town as you are in raising money for various projects.*

Pick your battles, Martha, I thought. This is one you won't win. Still, I read on:

Mr. Miles Higgins

Position: Town Board, First Chair

Occupation:

Following in his father's footsteps, Miles became a plumber, eventually taking over the family business, Ace Plumbers, a thriving concern at the heart of Mooselick River for decades. Known for prompt responses, excellent customer service, and Mr. Higgins's friendly demeanor, he's the man for all the town's plumbing needs.

Reading this, I realized Martha might have made a good living in advertising. And also that I hadn't equated the Miles Higgins she described with the man who had rooted out the trouble with the toilet drains at Leo's farmhouse rental the day Patrea took me to see the Wentworth. He looked different dressed for his daytime job than during town functions.

Personal information:

Born in Bangor, Maine, Miles became a resident when his family relocated to Mooselick River in 1976. Both parents are deceased, but Miles has two siblings—a brother living in North Carolina and a sister who lives in Orono. He's been married to Emmaline Tate for thirty-five years last June.

Emmaline Tate. Probably related to Bess. It seemed like half the town was, and that last name couldn't be a coincidence.

The couple has one daughter, Claire Byerson, though I believe she took back her maiden name and goes by Claire Higgins since divorcing her husband two years ago. She must be in her mid-thirties by now. Claire worked at an accounting firm in Augusta after college but took an office management position in Hackinaw last spring. Emmaline watches Claire's son during school breaks. They're friendly people, Martha had written—all of them. A solid family.

Last summer, Claire began dating Brandon Sinclair, a mechanic at Pine Tree Auto. By all accounts, Miles approved of the match, calling Brandon a hard worker and an honest man, but lately, he's changed his tune. Rumor has it that Brandon and Claire split up, so that's probably why.

Very interesting, but I couldn't see how any of that had to do with Bill's death.

Hobbies and other interests:

Miles is an amateur beekeeper. In his backyard, hidden behind neatly trimmed hedges, lies what he calls his buzzing sanctuary—a collection of beehives tended with great care. A charter member of the garden club, Emmaline supported his hobby by designing a garden fit for a queen bee and her hive of workers.

I'm not sure why Martha thought his pastimes were

pertinent, but when that woman paints a picture of someone, she uses every color at her disposal.

Scandal:

I'm adding this even though it is not especially scandalous. It is also old news because people still remember the incident, and you might hear stories about it. The year Miles graduated from MRHS, a group of seniors hid alarm clocks under the seat of the principal's car. He was a stickler for punctuality.

They didn't know that he had to leave early that day, so instead of the alarms going off right as he opened the door at the end of the school day, they went off while he was driving home and caused him to go off the road. He wasn't injured, thankfully. When he saw that the other students were being pressed to name an instigator, Miles went to the principal and confessed that it had been his idea, taking the brunt of the punishment upon himself.

I know for a fact the prank was not his idea, but he spent the entire summer not only mending fences with Mr. Ballentine but repainting his as punishment.

In conclusion, Mr. Miles Higgins is not merely the board's first chair; he's a fine and upstanding man with a rich personal and professional life and a history of doing good things. His commitment to fairness goes beyond upholding the town's bylaws and interests, making him an endearing figure in the community.

As far as his relationship with Bill Cavanaugh goes, I have never heard a bad word exchanged between them.

Mrs. Ginger Martin

Position: Town Board, Second Chair

Occupation:

In addition to her role on the Town Board, Mrs. Martin works at the Mooselick River Public Library. With a deep commitment to childhood literacy, many consider her a pillar of our community.

Ginger Martin was no stranger to me, given she worked for my mother. I'd known her in that capacity for years. She liked to do all the voices when she read to the children.

Since taking a part-time position at the library in 2008, Mrs. Martin has mined the Mooselick River Public Library patrons for gossip like that pursuit was her religion. In addition to talking about her neighbors and friends behind their backs, she regularly avoids participating in any fundraising event and opposes every good idea that anyone else proposes.

Whoops. So much for being a pillar. Tell me what you really think, Martha.

Personal information:

Married to Mr. Curtis Martin, the dedicated curator of the Mooselick River Historical Society, Ginger has lived in this town for her entire life. She is the mother of two grown children, Sarah and Michael, who reside in neighboring towns, and the grandmother of four.

Hobbies and other interests:

Despite vigorous attempts to present a demure demeanor, Mrs. Martin is a fervent trivia aficionado. Every second Wednesday of the month, she sheds her librarian persona to defend her title as the reigning trivia champion at Cappy's Tavern. Armed with obscure facts and a piercing voice, she dominates the trivia competition, earning free drinks and bragging rights. If you ask her, and even if you don't, she will explain that stuffing her head full of random facts is a sign of high intelligence.

In addition to her trivial pursuits, Mrs. Martin is an avid knitter and crocheter who sells her wares locally for spare money. During board meetings, she can be found clacking away with her needles, creating endless scarves and blankets, among other things.

Pornographic pan handle cozies, I wondered.

Scandal:

Three years ago, Mooselick River elected its first female select-man, who promptly insisted we adopt the terms Select Board and Board Chair. Two women were up for the nomination. One an upstanding citizen who constantly demonstrated her willingness to put the town's needs first—a woman of faith with a strong backbone and the guts to do something besides talk a decision to death. The other, a snake in the grass who wouldn't know a fair fight if it bit her on the backside.

My eyes widened as I read. It didn't take a degree in subtext to figure out one of the women was Ginger Martin and the other was Martha. I'd had no idea they were rivals for a leadership position in town politics and hadn't seen that side of Mrs. Martin in any of my dealings with her, but I could see where Martha might be bitter.

Mr. Clive Thompson

Position: Town Board, Third Chair

Occupation:

In addition to his duties on the Select Board, Clive Thompson has served as a volunteer firefighter and has been the store manager at the Gas N Go for more than ten years.

Personal information:

Clive Thompson is a distinguished figure in our community, known for his signature bow ties and friendly demeanor. A confirmed bachelor.

Hobbies and other interests:

An amateur theater buff, Clive Thompson starred in several school plays during his years at MRHS and is quite an accom-

plished singer and tap dancer. On occasion, he can be persuaded to demonstrate his talent at town events and has pressed the board to consider restoring the old theater. This would be no small expense, but it is one that I think we might want to consider in our fundraising efforts. Clive is not the only theater enthusiast in town, and a series of talent shows or plays would certainly draw tourists.

As usual, Martha made a good point. A theater might be an excellent addition to the town.

Scandal:

A few years back, one of Clive's efforts to revive Mooselick River's tourist trade ended in scandal. It all started when Miles noticed a problem with the parks and recreation budget. He went to Bill with an accusation about mismanagement of funds. It was Bill's second year as treasurer, and he hadn't been Miles' first choice as it was.

Miles called for an investigation and quickly discovered that the misallocated funds had been used to finance Clive's latest brainstorm—an ambitious attempt for the town to set a Guinness World Record for the "World's Largest Rubber Duck Collection."

She might say it was Clive's idea, but that scheme had Martha's fingerprints all over it. Funny he hadn't participated in any of the events I'd helped her plan since I moved back to town. Maybe this was why. Also funny, she hadn't described his work or personal life beyond the basics. No glowing terms, no condemnation.

Clive thought we'd break the record if we purchased roughly six thousand rubber ducks. I thought the duckies would be a fun theme for an annual summer fair. We could build a display and show them off. And then, maybe buy new ones each year to maintain our status as record holders. We found a seller on eBay who *would give us a bulk price of $60 per hundred but he could only get us half.*

I did the math. $1800 was a lot to spend on rubber ducks.

When the rest of the board shot down the idea, Clive was supposed to tell Bill not to go through with the order, but he didn't. He said he forgot, but I think he figured he could move forward and put the expense down as a clerical error. He let me think we were still moving forward as well and he was looking for a supplier for the other half when the bill came due. Miles was not happy.

Word got out and people started calling the incident Duckie-Gate. Half the people in town thought it was funny and the other half were outraged over what they considered the misuse of public funds. Either way, the damage was done. The summer fair was canceled because the money had to come from somewhere and Clive almost didn't get reelected that year. He and Bill got into it at the next town meeting because Bill refused to take any of the blame.

So there'd been bad blood between Bill and Clive. Enough to result in murder years later, though? Probably not.

If Ginger Martin turned up dead, I'd have a pretty good idea where to look. Good thing Martha wasn't the violent type.

Nothing in her very long email stood out as a strong motive in Bill's death, nor did any of it inspire me to put myself up as his replacement. I filed all the impressions away in the back of my mind to pore over later, and got started on the rest of my day.

CHAPTER TEN

My checklist for the day included a circuit of all the rental properties to assess storm cleanup. No one had reported significant structure damage, but I'd need to hire a crew to remove downed branches.

On my way back from the farmhouse rental, I stopped at The Delightful Daisy, the only florist shop in town, to talk to Delia James about making minor changes to the design of my wedding flowers.

Against a backdrop of slowly greening grass and storm-bent trees, the colorful flags that flapped in the light breeze seemed even more cheerful than usual. She'd closed up her rustic, three-sided farm stand for the winter, but sprouting things in the greenhouse gave hope for the upcoming season.

"Hey, Delia," I returned her smile. "You must have the best job on earth getting to work with flowers this time of year."

"It's definitely one of the perks. Why do you think I followed my passion? What can I do for you?"

"It's about the wedding. We've had a change of venue."

Delia shuttered her cheerful smile. "I heard about the cave-in at the Lodge. And about poor Bill Cavanaugh. What a tragedy."

"Did you know him?" My crime-solving antenna went up.

"Sure. Standing order for a weekly desktop arrangement of surprise me flowers," she recited from memory.

"Surprise me flowers?"

"So long as I had a vase for his desktop on Monday morning, he wasn't picky about the colors or scents. It gave me a chance to experiment with different designs and still get paid for them. On Friday, like clockwork, he returned the containers and picked up a bouquet for his special someone. Those were not surprise me ones, though."

Ding. Ding. Ding.

"Bill was seeing someone recently? Any idea who?"

"Not for sure." Delia shook her head, then leaned forward to say in a lowered tone, "He didn't bother with cards. But I could tell things weren't going well because he switched over to yellow roses a couple of weeks ago, and then this Friday—nothing."

"Okay." I didn't get it.

"At the beginning of a relationship, he was a dozen red roses kind of guy. Once the relationship hit its stride, he'd switch to whatever his lady liked best. If things went south, he'd ramp it back up with yellow roses. If they stayed together, it was back to the status quo."

"Interesting. So what you're saying is that except for the surprise me flowers, Bill was predictable," I mused.

"As death and taxes. His mother always got a dozen white carnations on her birthday, red ones on Valentine's Day, and pink roses on Mother's Day. Except last month, I think he had two women on the hook."

She had my attention.

"Really?" I drew the word out long while my brain tried to picture Bill as a playboy and failed.

"For a couple of months or so, it was stargazer lilies. Then, one Friday, he shows up and asks for candy stripe tulips instead. He switched right over like it was nothing."

"No yellow or red roses in between?"

Delia shook her head slowly. "Nary a one. First time he ever skipped the roses phase before. Well, until last week, anyway. Last week, he left here with a dozen yellow. I felt bad, you know? Poor Bill."

I leaned on the counter to clarify. "You think whoever he was seeing when he died, they'd had a falling out, but you don't know who it was because he didn't include a card."

Delia slowly shook her head. "But I have an idea who he was dating before Tulip Girl because of the stargazers," she said knowingly. "But it could only have been for one of them this time, couldn't it?"

Was she trying to kill me with the cryptic comments? "Who?"

"Well, it had to be Carlene Nicholson because Grace Belanger was the other one he bought those for, and she's dead."

Wham. Blast from the past, sending a mass of implications flying around in my head. I needed time to think them through, but I'd come here for a reason.

"I guess so. In any case, I wanted to come by with an update on my wedding. We're having it at the Wentworth place. Do you know the house I mean?"

"Are you kidding me?" Her jaw dropped. "I've always wanted to get a look inside that house. How did you manage to fall into that piece of astounding luck?"

"My friend Patrea bought it. She was fixing it up to resell, but she's considering other options. It would be a great setting for weddings and anniversaries. She's letting me get married there to test the theory. And since I am, and the dress I picked out has a similar vibe to hers—1920s inspired in that same cream color, but a different shape—I was wondering if we could change the vases for the table settings."

By the time I finished, I was talking to empty space. Delia had dashed into the back room, where she turned the air blue for a moment.

"What's wrong?" I raised my voice to be heard over the slamming of cabinet doors.

"Someone screwed around with my catalogs." More slamming. This time, it sounded like desk drawers. "There it is."

When she returned with the ordering book we'd looked at when we planned Patrea's wedding, she slapped it down on the counter, sucked a breath in through her nose, and blew it out her mouth.

"Sorry. It's just that every piece of paperwork in this place has been moved around for the past few days. One of the part-timers must have taken it upon themselves to tidy up. Probably didn't understand my system. It may not look organized, but I know where things are if people would just leave well enough alone."

Calmer now, she flipped the book open and looked at me expectantly. "Just the vases? Or did you want to change the flowers entirely?"

I shook my head.

"Just the vases, I think. Something more suited to the

house than those pretty globe-shaped ones we were planning for the Lodge." I described the house for her—colors, moldings, that type of thing.

Nodding, she flipped pages until she found what she wanted, then spun the catalog around and stabbed her finger at the spot. "This one. It's very similar in style and shape to the ones we used for Patrea's wedding but in dark green with gold accents. We'll keep the flowers to those blush colors you already selected and swap out the greenery for white ostrich plumes and a few sword ferns. That will work with the space and your bouquet. It will be perfect."

"I love it. And I'll need arrangements for the foot of the stairs. Maybe the same vases in a larger size on pedestals." Again, I hadn't finished before Delia was already shaking her head. She grabbed the catalog, spun it, and flipped through more pages.

"These." She pointed to an elegant container with a square, footed base flowing upward into a deep but graceful lily-shaped vessel with gently fluted lines. The whole thing was made from what looked like semi-translucent glass.

"These come in sizes of up to three feet tall, and the best part is, they're made from cast acrylic, so they're solid, but don't weigh or cost a ton. I'd fill them with blush trumpet lilies accented with more white ostrich feathers and a few peacock eyes for color."

"I don't even know what trumpet lilies are, but now, I want them. I'd love to take you through the house when you have a day free. We may want a couple of extra arrangements, and it would help if you got a look at the space."

"Just try and stop me. I'd love a chance to go in and take some photos. I'm already considering working up a pitch portfolio and some samples for if and when Patrea decides to move forward."

Her eyes were alight with excitement, and anticipation tempered with determination.

"If your mind hadn't gone there, I'd have been disappointed."

"Oh, don't you worry," something feral crept through Delia's grin. "I've been waiting for an opportunity like this ever since you came to town and got Martha Tipton's juices flowing. Hackinaw can eat our dust."

I wrote her a check for the extra costs and promised to get her into the house as soon as possible. Delia's wouldn't be the only business in town to benefit from Patrea's newest brainstorm. If she...no...if we could pull this off, we could put Mooselick River back on the map in a big way.

More, however, I'd learned something unexpected about the death, or rather, the life of Bill Cavanaugh. Carlene Nicholson's return to town might make more sense if a reconciliation with Bill figured into it, and I had the perfect excuse to call her and fish for details. Given our rocky history going all the way back to some incident in high school that I didn't even remember, there'd be ice skating in hell before I let her plan my wedding. We both knew that, but wondering if I might should be enough to convince her to pick up the phone. And maybe, to take a meeting.

I'd get more out of her face-to-face, so it would be best to invite her to meet in neutral territory. Maybe the inn, or better, I'd ask her to join me for lunch at The Blue Moon. Mabel probably wouldn't spit in her food.

Knowing I'd change my mind if I didn't do it right then, I pulled out her card and punched the numbers into my phone. Carlene didn't answer, which I figured meant she checked her caller ID, so I left a message.

"Carlene, it's Everly Dupree. I'd like to talk to you about my wedding. I'll be at the Blue Moon on Monday if you'd care to join me around noon. Thanks."

Maybe she'd show, maybe not. Either way, I could go for a lunch special and the bonus of supporting local businesses now that the power was back on.

CHAPTER ELEVEN

Still running Martha's email and Delia's information through my head, I roamed the grocery store's aisles. Based on the state of the shelves, I wasn't the only one trying to restock the basic staples. They were out Molly's favorite brand of kibble, too.

When I finally reached the checkout with only about half of what I needed, a single register was open and next to it stood my least favorite cashier.

"Hey, Robin," I said, preparing myself for the expected blank stare. I mean, I'd only worked with Robin Thackery for a short time when I'd first moved back to town. And I'd helped her when she thought she'd be arrested for the murder of our former boss. And I shopped here at least three times a week. No reason for her to remember me, right? Maybe the air didn't whistle between her ears, but it definitely hummed.

"Hey, Everly."

Stunned, I had no response.

"Did you hear? Someone killed Bill Cavanaugh."

"I heard." I watched her miss the scanner with three items and toss them in a bag anyway. "Horrible news."

"Didn't surprise me any." She scanned the next item twice while I tried to keep up with the mental math. Maybe it would come out close enough to spare me a trip to the customer service desk to sort my bill on the way out. "He was shady."

"Really?" I lost track of the scanner math. "How so?"

"He just was. When Spencer died, I tried to get a job at the bank, but Bill told Martin Walker not to hire me."

Smart thinking on Martin's part. The financial needs of Mooselick River would not be best served by allowing Robin Thackery any more access to them than she had in her current job.

"I mean," Robin continued, "who does that to a person and then turns around and asks them out?"

"Bill got you turned down for a job and then asked you out?" My estimation of him dropped a notch. "Right after Spencer died?"

She snapped her gum. "No, last summer."

"You tried to get a job at the bank last summer?" She had me confused.

"No," she spoke very slowly. "He asked me out last summer."

I thought I understood now. The two incidents had been a year apart. Time probably registered differently with Robin than with the rest of the world.

"It freaks me out, you know? To have someone I know murdered almost in my own backyard."

"I didn't know you lived that close to the lodge."

She nodded. "Right behind it. Close enough to hear the roof cave in."

"Do you remember what time it was? Did you hear the gunshot? Was anyone with you? Did they hear anything?" One question at a time was enough to confuse her. Four of them in rapid fire didn't. Go figure.

"Right after the power went out. Everything went dark and then this weird whomping sound. I didn't hear any gun go off, just the roof. No one else heard it because I was home alone." She dropped a pound of grapes on top of the loaf of bread she'd just put in my bag, and I didn't even notice. "All night."

One or more of Robin's answers was a lie. I could tell by how her eyes darted away from my face, and if I had to guess, I'd say it was the last one, but I could be wrong.

"You're sure?"

"Of course, I'm sure. Don't you think I'd know if someone was in my house?"

I wasn't sure if she knew where she was half the time, but she'd confirmed my theory by what she chose to defend. I'd have pressed for more details if someone hadn't loaded the conveyor belt behind me. Holding up the line wouldn't earn me any favors, so I ran my debit card without bothering to look at the amount and headed out the door.

If the roof had caved in at a little after nine, as she'd said, that meant Bill had died sometime before then. It wasn't much to go on, but it was more than I'd had before.

CHAPTER TWELVE

The Saturday after the storm, the Wentworth house stood much as it had before—stalwart and sturdy, with its age showing around the edges. Looking at the property through the lens of it being the place where I'd get married, I couldn't say I minded the ambiance. The stone facade spoke of permanence, come what may—even if what came was a vengeful spirit. At least we'd taken care of that detail already.

"Does it bother you to come back here?" Drew wanted to know.

I shook my head. "Not at all. Does it bother you?" He'd seen some scary stuff in that front hall. I wouldn't blame him if he had second thoughts. When he didn't answer right away, I feared the worst.

"Why would it? Charlotte made a series of pretty poor life—and death—choices. Those are not on you. You set Vanessa free and healed Gloria's spirit here. That has to outweigh any bad energy Charlotte left behind. Getting married here is the best way I can think of to wash the house clean. I'd marry you in a barn if I had to, but doing it here, at the scene of your triumph—in a place owned by someone who loves you, knowing our wedding will kick off something new for her and the entire town? All of that carries weight. The good kind."

"I love how you look at things. I never would have thought to put it into words like that, but you're right on all counts. I want to get married in this house."

"Then let's go in and get it ready." Drew kissed me, then popped open the driver's door. I heard the car coming up the drive even before the nose of Ernie Polk's cruiser slid into view.

"Uh oh," I said. "Here comes trouble."

"Maybe not." But Drew stood with me and watched as Ernie pulled up and exited his car.

"I've got a couple of quick questions," he said to Drew first and then me. "I heard you'd be out here today."

From who? I wondered but didn't ask. "We're getting the place ready for the wedding." I also didn't ask what he wanted, but there had to be a reason if he'd taken the time to track us down.

"You went in through a window to check on Bill Cavanaugh." It was a statement, not a question.

"I did," Drew gave Ernie his best blank face. "It wasn't locked, which I stated at the scene."

Ernie waved that away. "I know. Relax. I'm not accusing you of doing anything wrong. To the best of your recollection, did it look like anyone else had entered the building through that window before you did?"

Drew's eyes widened slightly, then went blank for a moment while he dredged up the memory. After a moment, he shook his head. "I don't think so. There was dust on the sill. I remember noticing it when I checked if the window was latched. But my focus was more on getting to Bill in case there was anything I could do to help."

Nodding, Ernie admitted, "I know, and that tracks. Yours

were the only recent fingerprints lifted from the glass or the sill. It would have been easier if they weren't. Listen, you mind if I talk to Everly alone for a minute?"

At first, I wasn't sure if Drew would leave, but after studying Ernie's expression for a few seconds, he turned to me. "I'll be inside if you need me," Drew ran a hand down my arm and gave me a bolstering look before he walked away.

Your father and I go back a ways." As soon as Drew was out of earshot, Ernie cut off the questions that wanted to pop out of my mouth and pulled my focus in an entirely new direction.

"You're not about to tell me he's a suspect, are you?" It took everything I had to keep my tone from edging into outrage. He'd questioned my mother once in the course of a murder case. Now, my father, too? "What the hell, Ernie? You know Bill and my father were friendly. There's no way he had anything to do with what happened."

"No. It's nothing like that," he shook his head and looked me in the eye. "I got a call from the insurance company. Someone sawed through the rafter supports." He let the implications sink in for a moment before adding, "That's why the roof caved in."

"And you think my father had something to do with it?" My voice rose. "That's even worse."

"Worse than being a murder suspect?" Ernie's brows rose.

"No. But it's just as bad. You can't be serious. Why would anyone do a thing like that?"

"To cover up a murder. Or else for the insurance money. And I didn't say I thought Lee had anything to do with anything."

"For the insurance money? That's ludicrous." It made no sense to me at all.

"It's fraud, is what the insurance company's calling it," he scrubbed a hand over hair grown out a bit from his usual brush cut. "That's a serious allegation."

I picked up on his earlier statement. "If you don't think my father committed fraud, why did you bring him up?"

"Because he has to know who did. Even if he doesn't know he knows, he has to know."

Blinking, I managed to sort out his meaning. "Okay, I get that."

Ernie nodded. "It could be that Bill came in and caught someone sabotaging the roof. Or—" he left the thought hanging.

"Or it was Bill, and someone caught him doing it and shot him to get him to stop." It didn't ring for me. "Seems like an extreme response, and if someone cared enough to kill him to save the building, why wouldn't they have tried to fix the damage?"

Ernie shrugged. "Unless Bill and the killer were in on it together. We didn't find his phone at the scene or in his car."

"I didn't know Bill all that well, but he wasn't what you'd call a physical being if you know what I mean." He'd avoided anything that required actual labor during the treasure hunt his brother-in-law had forced him into. Picturing him sawing away at roof rafters didn't come easy. Or at all, really. Especially not while wearing his work shoes with the rubber pull-ons after eating Sunday dinner with his mother.

"That's why you came looking for Drew. You're trying to figure out how they got in."

"That's the thing. According to Lee, he and Max had the

only two sets of keys to the place, and I couldn't find any evidence of forced entry. All of the other windows were locked, and none of them had been disturbed. The doorknob was wiped clean, inside and out."

He didn't need to draw me a road map to see where this was leading. "So you think it had to be someone who had a key, which leaves Max or my father, which means we're back to you looking at him for murder."

"No," he surprised me. "I'm not. His alibi checks out. Jim and Merline were over at Lee and Kitty's playing cards the night of the storm."

"Max was out of town."

This time, Ernie nodded his head. "His alibi is also iron-clad, considering Max and Viola were visiting his sister in Maryland. They just got back this morning, and he had his keys with him when he got off the plane."

"So, I'm supposed to believe that during the storm of the century, someone got hold of my father's keys, broke into the lodge, sabotaged the roof and/or killed Bill Cavanaugh, then put the keys back without my father knowing?"

"Or," Ernie countered, "at some point prior to the storm, someone got hold of one of the sets and made copies, which they then used to yada yada." He waved a hand instead of completing the sentence. "We only have your dad's and Max's word for it that there were only two sets."

"I can't see why either of them would lie to protect a murderer or a saboteur."

"Me, either. And because I know and trust both of those men, I'm leaning toward them not having knowledge, which brings me right back to where I started, with no suspects and even fewer motives. Bill was in the brotherhood, but he didn't hold an office. He wouldn't benefit from an insurance claim even if the order might, nor did he have a reason to be in the building alone."

"Your job sucks sometimes," I said with feeling. "What did you want me to do?" Because he hadn't come here for no reason.

"Most times," he agreed. "Keep an eye on your father, Dupree. If this is a lodge matter, he knows more than he thinks. As much as I hate to say it, I trust your instincts. Get him talking, and if he says anything that sparks for you, would you let me know?"

"Will do." Especially if there was any danger that might befall my dad. "Anything else?"

"Just that Clive verified the information you gave me. Bill did stop at the Gas N Go at around 7:30 that night. I've also spoken to Bill's mother, but she wasn't sure what time he left her house, so we have no way of knowing if he drove straight there, or what he did between the time he left the gas station."

When Ernie fell silent, I asked, "Did you want the tour? Neena's been working on the mural and I know you were particularly interested in it."

"Another time." He headed back toward his car. "And Everly," he turned back. "It's probably best if you don't say anything to your mother about all of this. No need to get her involved at this stage of things."

"I won't." In an attempt at diplomacy, I held back a smile. He hadn't been on her list of favorite people since he'd brought her in for questioning over the murder of Davina Benet. She'd forgive him eventually, but when was up to her.

Inside, Drew waited with Patrea.

"What did Ernie want?" Patrea spoke first. "Any news on the case?"

"There is. And it's not good."

Because I didn't want to spend half the morning repeating myself, we rounded everyone up and went into the primary bedroom, far enough away that Jerry Kaminski wouldn't hear us talking while he worked in the dining room. If all went well, this was the room where Drew and the guys would get dressed on our wedding day.

"The lodge roof didn't just cave in because it was old. Someone cut the rafter supports. On purpose."

"Before or after they murdered Bill?" Jacy got the question in first, but I could see it in everyone else's eyes, too.

"That's the million-dollar question, isn't it? The insurance company views it as an attempt to defraud them out of a payout. What's more, as far as Ernie can tell, whoever did it probably had keys to the building."

"Didn't your dad say there were only two sets?" Drew frowned. "Is he a suspect? Or is Max?"

I shook my head. "Ernie says not. Ironclad alibis."

Neena nodded. "Max and Viola just got back this morning."

Nodding, I continued where I'd left off. "The working theory is that someone got hold of the keys at some point in the past and made an extra set."

David's left eyebrow shot up. "He's thinking this was premeditated?"

Damn. I should have thought of that and asked for more information. "I don't know. I don't think so. It could be that Bill was the one doing the damage to the supports and whoever came in caught him at it, killed him, and took off."

"Or vice versa," Neena said and I nodded. "But why would anyone cut the supports?"

"To disguise what they'd done," Patrea answered for me. "Or, setting aside the question of insurance fraud because I don't see how anyone stood to gain there, someone carried a grudge against one or more of the members, or the organization in general."

"Or someone didn't want Everly to get married there." Jacy's suggestion came from way out in left field.

"I don't think this had anything to do with me, and I doubt Ernie thinks so, either. He wants me to pump my father for information about who else might have had access to the keys."

"Why doesn't he do that himself?" Chris said. "He shouldn't be getting you to do his dirty work."

"Because he's scared of my mother." I allowed a grin. "She hasn't forgiven him for that Davina Benet business yet."

Unconvinced, Chris wrinkled his forehead until Patrea snorted. "I can't say I blame him. Having experienced Kitty's helpful side, I'd hate to get on her bad one."

"We're having dinner with my folks tomorrow. I was already planning to pry information out of my father, so this just makes it official. Drew made a good point about it taking a village to solve a murder, and how it would help if we all worked together to send Bill into the light before the wedding. I'm asking my parents to get on board with that plan even if Ernie wanted me to be delicate."

"Count me in." Neena was the first to offer, which would have surprised me once, but didn't anymore. "What can I do?"

"Get people talking," Drew answered for me. "It's what

they want to do anyway. You and Jacy are in a perfect position to gather intel."

"He means gossip," Jacy supplied helpfully. "I expect we'll be plenty busy next week. Even if it's just browsers, they'll want to talk about the storm, and about the latest scandal. We'll let them and then report back."

"I'll set up a shared message board and send you all a link," Patrea said, then turned to me. "Get me everything you have already. Names, relationships, theories. All of it."

To that end, I pulled out my phone and brought up Martha's email, which I described to the group even as I sent a copy to Patrea. Operation Who Killed Bill was off to a good start.

Feeling a renewed sense of purpose, I followed the others back downstairs and we got to work.

"Hey, Everly," Jerry Kaminski greeted me when I passed through the dining room on my way to the kitchen for a fresh bucket of water. He didn't say anything else, but I didn't care for the up and down sweep of his gaze, or the fact that for half a moment, it lingered in the space below my neck. What a tool.

"The molding looks fantastic," I said. Keeping the topic firmly on his job seemed like the best way to dissuade him from any attempt at personal conversation. "You do good work."

"So does your mother." He just had to go all cheesy-sleazy with it.

Passing by the doorway, Drew had heard the comment. "Keep your eyes on your plaster, Jerry," he advised in a deceptively mild tone.

I avoided the dining room on my way back, and managed to stay out of Jerry's way for the rest of the day.

CHAPTER THIRTEEN

Sunday dinner could have been more awkward. We could have all suffered random multiple wardrobe malfunctions, for instance, or a case of synchronous incontinence. Otherwise, it was the worst meal I'd ever eaten with my parents.

My fault, of course.

And maybe Bill's, too.

I should have listened to Ernie and ignored Drew because my father was not on board with the mystery-solving plan.

"Leave it alone, Everly," he warned. "Murder is dangerous business, and I don't want you involved."

"I already am, Dad. You know how this works. I don't see where I have a choice. Not if I can help Bill go into the light," I pleaded while my mother and Drew sat silent and unhelpful.

"Tell him I don't blame him," Bill spoke up from close enough that his ghostly chill turned my breath into an icy plume. Seeing the cloud, Dad shot out of his chair.

"He's here, isn't he?"

Wearily, I nodded. "He says he doesn't blame you."

Dad misunderstood. "Why would he? I haven't done anything wrong."

"For wanting to keep Everly safe, isn't that right, Bill?"

Confronted with a ghost at her table, my mother sighed and shook her head slowly. "Why don't you tell him yourself? All it takes is the desire and a little effort."

Bill made the effort. My father sucked in a breath.

"Of course, I don't blame you for that, but you know I meant the other thing," Bill gave my father a level look.

"What other thing? I demanded. "What does he mean?" When my father looked away, I turned to my mother who shrugged as if she didn't know, either.

"Tell her," Bill said, then faded. First-timers never maintained visible form for long. It took too much energy.

His face flushed, his shoulders drooping, my father sat back in his chair.

"I have an extra copy of the front door key, which I gave to Harley Stanfield two years ago last Christmas. We'd ordered paper plates and stuff from that discount place in Bangor, and Max had to take Viola in for an eye exam on the only day they could deliver. I had my last class before vacation, but it was only a half day. When I made the order, the company agreed to come in the afternoon, but they called the day before and said the only available slot was first thing in the morning. Harley said he'd bail me out, but he'd be cutting it close, so he wouldn't have time to pick up or drop the keys off with me after. I figured making him one was easier, so I stopped by the hardware store and took care of it."

"You lied to Ernie." I couldn't believe it. "Right to his face."

"I didn't. Not really. I told Ernie only two people had the key, and that's the truth. I asked Harley to hang it on the hook on the back of the utility room door when he left, and he did. It's in my possession now, so even if I have more than one, Max and I are still the only ones with keys to the place."

"Unless Harley made a copy for himself." While the implications circled in my head, Drew's comment earned a stern look from my father, but he raised no further argument. Someone had murdered Bill Cavanaugh, and according to Ernie, that someone used a key to get into the building. It could have been Harley.

"When did Bill find out what you'd done?" I latched onto the first question that came to mind, only to be met with a puzzled look.

"I don't know. He never said anything to me about it until just now. Harley must have told him." Except Dad didn't seem convinced. "I know I never did. Or do ghosts just know things once they're gone?"

I huffed out a breath. "If it worked that way, every single ghost would just tell me who killed them and make my life a whole lot easier."

If Bill hadn't been talking about the keys, my father must be keeping some other secret, but since his mind had gone right to Harley and the keys, I thought it best to focus there first.

"Were Harley and Bill friendly?" They hadn't seemed particularly close on those few occasions when I'd seen them together at Delly Harper's old place.

"Not really," Dad's forehead finally smoothed out. "They tolerated each other, but that was as far as it went."

"Well, the only way Bill could have heard anything about Harley having keys now that he's on the other side of the veil is if he overheard Harley talking about it after he crossed." I wished now that my mother hadn't encouraged him to show himself, so I could have asked him then and there. "Based on what you're saying, I can't see why he'd hang around someone he didn't like all that much unless he suspected Harley had something to do with his death. Besides, you're the one who brought up the keys, not Bill. Was there something else he thought you should tell me?"

"Not that I can think of."

"Lee," my mother's tone held a warning.

"I didn't have anything to do with that, and you know it," Dad put very little heat into the argument.

"With what?" Clearly, he was holding out.

"I'm not just a member of the brotherhood, Kitty. I hold a leadership position. That comes with certain responsibilities to the organization."

"You can keep your silly passwords, secret handshakes, and whatever else you get up to. I have no interest in breaking into your little boy's club, but Bill is dead."

My parents rarely argued in front of me, and had never engaged in more than lighthearted banter in front of Drew. Mom's tone carried more heat than he'd probably heard from her.

"It's not a little boy's club. We do good things for the community, and I'm well aware that Bill is dead since I had to see the evidence of that up close and in person."

"I'm sorry. I know how hard it was." My mother reached out to put her hand over my dad's. He didn't pull away. Instead, he held on. As fights go, this one might qualify for a speed record.

After a moment, my mother stood to begin clearing our plates. "Drew, would you mind giving me a hand?"

Subtlety is not my mother's strong suit.

"My pleasure."

Under the table, Drew gave my knee a squeeze before joining my mother in the kitchen.

"I'm sorry, Dad. I wish I could leave this alone, but even if I could, I can't look at your face right now and not want to help put Bill to rest."

Agonized, he reached over and gripped my hand. "You don't understand. It's not Bill's immortal soul bothering me so much as remembering what he looked like when we pulled him out of that wreckage. How have you been able to stand seeing things like that?"

"I wouldn't say you get used to it because you don't. It's horrible every single time, but maybe I can get past it easier because of the ghosts. Didn't it help a little to see Bill here earlier? To know part of him lives on and that getting justice will send him to a better place?"

Reaching out, he pulled me from my chair and into his lap like he'd done when I was a child who needed the comfort I would only ever find in my father's arms. Maybe, now that I was grown, I could give him some of that back, so I held on.

"There's nothing worse than realizing you're no longer able to protect your children," he muttered into my hair as he held me close.

"Maybe we can protect each other now. Why don't you tell me what Bill meant?"

Sighing, he let me up. I returned to my chair and waited for the big reveal.

"Three months ago, Harley accused Bill of blackballing his cousin Dale Crawford for membership in the lodge. Dale got into a bit of trouble with the bank over some bad checks when he was younger, and since Bill worked there and wasn't Harley's biggest fan in the first place, assumptions were made, and blame was cast. Bill took the brunt of it."

"You wouldn't be telling me this if you thought Bill cast the deciding vote."

"I don't know who did. I only know Bill didn't because he thought it was me. Even after I said it wasn't. Dale's not a bad guy. I'm not saying he's membership material, but he means well."

Dad thought everyone meant well. At least most of the time.

"You're saying you supported the blackballing." I rested my elbow on the table. "Whether or not Dale got inducted into your club probably isn't a killing offense. Who stood to gain from the insurance claim? Do you have any idea?"

He'd begun to shake his head before I even finished the sentence. "No one. Except for maybe whoever we hired to put on a new roof. And before you ask, at least a few of us would know which supports to cut, but I can't think of a single member who would do such a thing. We're a civic organization, not a bunch of cutthroats. We help the community. We do not harm our own."

But someone had, and now, we had to figure out what to do about it.

"I think we've had enough death on the table for one day," my mother returned to set a casserole dish of warm apple crisp on a trivet. Drew followed behind with bowls and silverware on a tray. "Did you take pictures yesterday?"

Wedding plans lightened the mood until it was time to leave, and I had to ask my father for a favor I knew he wouldn't want to grant. Under protest, he gave me his extra copy of the lodge key and barely a lousy hug goodbye. It hurt not to be in his good graces.

"Give your father some time," Mom murmured when she hugged me goodbye.

"As much as I can," I promised.

CHAPTER FOURTEEN

Knowing if she bothered to come, Carlene would like nothing better than to make me look bad, I showed up at the diner at 11:30 the next day and spent some of that time drinking coffee and chatting with other customers about the aftermath of the storm, which was still on everyone's mind. When Carlene rolled in fifteen minutes early, she didn't look too happy to see me already there.

Hah. Points to me.

Not that I was keeping score, but I totally was.

"What can I getcha?" Thea Lombardi stopped by our table looking surly as usual, but that, I figured, was just the way her face was made.

"Turkey club. Mabel knows how I like it." Since Thea tended to mix up my orders on purpose, I raised my voice loud enough for Mabel to hear me in the kitchen. We'd entered into a lower-level truce since she'd helped me solve a murder, but I didn't trust Thea when it came to food. Feed me mustard instead of mayo once, okay. Twice would not be an option.

"I'll have the side salad." Carlene handed back her menu.

"On the side of what?" Thea wanted to know. Carlene flushed.

"Just by itself with ranch dressing."

"On the side?" Thea asked, and I had to choke back a snort.

Carlene sucked in a breath and then let it out slowly. "Sure. Whatever."

That was when I realized Carlene might not be able to afford lunch. "One check, Thea. This meeting was at my request, so lunch is on me. You're sure you don't want something else to go with your salad?" It was exactly the wrong thing to say.

"If I wanted something else, I'd have ordered it."

"Okay." I met her daggered gaze. She'd used my reduced circumstances against me once, and it made me feel lower than the underside of a snail. I'd feel even smaller now if I gave her the same treatment. "Sorry. I didn't mean to imply anything. I wanted to talk to you about wedding stuff."

Leaning back in her chair, Carlene rested one hand on the table, her nails painted a shade of red that didn't go well with her skin tone. "Do you think I'm stupid?"

Yes.

"No, of course not."

"I have about as much chance of you hiring me to help with your wedding as I do of sprouting wings and flying to Paris to see the sights. I know this. You know this. I don't see why you asked me here."

Sighing, I gave in and offered the only olive branch that would open the door to talking about Bill Cavanaugh. "Listen, I realize we got off on the wrong foot a long time ago, and I don't expect we'll ever get over that, but Patrea Evergreen is thinking about turning the Wentworth place into a wedding venue. I'll be getting married there next month as a test for the idea. As the only wedding planner in town, I thought you might be interested in pitching her some of your ideas."

Her nails stopped drumming on the table.

"Why? So you and your groupies can laugh at me behind my back?"

My mouth opened to accuse her of that being more her style when I realized I'd done just that, and on more than one occasion. Even the fact that she'd started the animosity wasn't enough to mitigate my shame.

"I'm sorry for whatever I did to you when we were kids and for having mean thoughts about you since then. I'd rather just bury the hatchet, and I don't mean in each other's backs. If you're willing, anyway."

I meant it, too. Mostly. Or I did until I saw the calculation in her eyes.

"Consider it buried," she said sweetly. "Now, what's this about Patrea Evergreen and that big old house of hers?"

She was willing to be friendly as long as she got something out of it. Fine. Two could play that game.

"I'd love to set up a meeting between the two of you, but in the meantime, here's what you need to know going in."

In the middle of outlining the basics of Patrea's plans, Thea plunked an overloaded sandwich plate in front of me and a pitiful bowl of salad in front of Carlene. It didn't take a psychic to guess what Mabel wanted me to do. Inside her gruff exterior beat a gentle heart.

"Good grief. I guess Mabel's feeling generous today. I'll never eat all of this and she'll skin me alive if I don't finish it since I gave Thea a hard time about getting my order right. In the spirit of forgiveness, why don't you do me a huge favor and take half."

If you can't beat 'em, kill them with kindness, or else sit on them and squash them like a bug, Grammie Dupree used to say. She tended to mix metaphors and juggle clichés like she'd been born in a three-ring circus. At least part of her pummeled proverb suited the situation.

"I suppose," Carlene said, spreading out her napkin and placing half my sandwich on it. At least neither of us would leave hungry.

We talked about wedding-related things while I tried to find a way to turn the conversation toward Bill Cavanaugh. Other than chiding me for having a mid-week wedding—necessary for some of Drew's family to attend—Carlene had some decent insights to offer. She might actually help Patrea if this whole scheme moved forward. Color me surprised.

"Jolene Stackpole's just looking for an excuse to buy a portable pedicure footbath. I can't think of a bride who wouldn't love to have pretty feet on her big day, and being able to offer mani-pedis right on-site would be a boon to Patrea's business."

"Jolene works for Mara Tibbets, right? Mara's doing the hair for my wedding.

Carlene nodded around a big bite of sandwich. I had to wait for her to chew and swallow before she informed me that Jolene didn't work for Mara outright, but they were business partners of a sort.

"If this wedding venue thing actually flies, they might finally get approved for a loan to expand their services and open up a proper day spa. They've wanted to start one together since they heard the Marlow might open back up."

Bingo. She played right into my hands.

"Really? I didn't know that was even a thing. Why didn't

they get approved before? I know I could use a day of pampering every so often, and it would be nice not to have to drive an hour afterward."

"Bill was dragging his feet. Said we didn't have the demographic in Mooselick River to support such a venture on a regular basis." Those had to be his words, not Carlene's.

"Shortsighted of him, don't you think?" I nibbled on a homemade potato chip and blessed Mabel for making them while I also cursed her for the extra calories. "I'd sign up for a monthly session and I can guarantee a few of my friends would schedule services. My mother, too, once she got over the idea of it feeling like self-indulgence. Seems like a win-win for the salon and the town."

"Would have been if the building hadn't already needed renovations. Bill figured Mara would be better off fixing up what she already had, and when she'd paid off that loan, he would consider giving her money to expand."

"I don't imagine Mara or Jolene were happy about the decision."

"He liked thinking he knew best sometimes." Carlene's tone bordered on speaking ill of the dead. "He wouldn't go higher than forty percent of what Mara asked for and told her she was looking at five years to pay off even that much given the current state of her business."

"I didn't know you and Mara were close."

"We're not. I'm friends with Jolene. She told me all about it. He made it sound like Mara was working out of a room in her house or something. Do or Dye's thriving right now, especially since Mara had the sense to bring Jolene in after that business with Peggy Sullivan. But Bill said all it would take is one single competitor to pop up, and Mara's business could take a hit, so he wasn't comfortable letting her overextend. Too many pitfalls."

Thinking it best to say as little as possible while she was on a roll, I kept my thoughts to myself and only made commiserating noises where I thought appropriate. It worked well enough because Carlene continued her diatribe.

"If she'd have hired the right contractor, I told him Mara could have rolled both projects together for a little less than the amount she originally applied for. All he'd have to do is tack another couple of years onto his projected pay-off date, and the extra business they'd bring in would make it a great investment, but Bill didn't listen to me. What do I know about business, after all? I'm only running one of my own."

I wasn't sure how much solidarity to offer. Dealing with Carlene was like dealing with a new kitten. A gentle touch might elicit a purr or a hiss, depending on their mood, which could change in the blink of an eye. "Exactly," I said, still playing it safe.

"He didn't think being an event planner required any start-up capital." Her mincing tone said she didn't think much of his intelligence and that they might have fought about it. Maybe thwarting her ambitions was why he'd switched from lilies to tulips so abruptly.

"Of course, it would. Marketing materials, a good website, and scheduling software can run a couple of thousand before you even get your first booking."

Carlene rapped her knuckles on the table. "That's exactly what I said."

"I can see where dealing with that type of shortsightedness would be annoying."

"Don't you talk about Bill that way."

Uh oh. I'd gone too far. She'd liked the man enough to date him twice, so I should have known she still had feelings lurking in her vindictive soul. Still, her experience with him made her a good source of information, and I didn't want her to clam up.

"He was a prince among men."

Why was it a hole never opened up in the floor when I needed one?

Because irritation made a poor blanket to cover the misery I could see all over her, I reached across the table to pat Carlene's fisted hand. "He was a nice person who didn't deserve to die."

"No. He didn't."

That she let herself be comforted by me said something about her state of mind.

Based on what Delia had said, I didn't think Bill and Carlene were dating at the time of his death, but I didn't want to set her off, so I went with, "Do you have any idea who might have wanted to hurt him? Was he involved with someone?"

"We weren't that close, and I didn't bother to keep up with his private life." Carlene dropped her gaze to her empty salad bowl so I wouldn't see the tears forming, but she'd been too late. "As to who killed him, it could have been anyone, couldn't it? He was a loan officer at the bank and town treasurer and probably handled the money for that ridiculous lodge of his. Anyone in charge of that much money in a town this size has power. Power always puts a target on your back."

She had a point, I supposed. "People kill for plenty of

other reasons. Revenge. Protection. Love." I left the last word hanging as an invitation, but she didn't bite.

"Like I said, Bill was a good man, but he wasn't my man anymore. I need someone less romantically predictable. You know what I mean?"

"Someone with more than one set of moves?" I offered a knowing half-smile.

"Exactly, and Bill rarely ever changed things up. That's why most women dumped him after a few months," those were Carlene's last words on the subject. "Listen, I appreciate you telling me about this wedding thing."

She didn't look appreciative. She looked like the admission made her underwear too tight, but I kept my face passive. Better to leave things on the best note possible. More points to me. "It's no problem."

There, I thought, argue with that. She couldn't, so I smiled, leaving her with no room to dig in and with the door open if I needed to talk to her about Bill later.

As soon as the door slid shut behind Carlene, Mabel came out of the kitchen with two plates of pie and wedged herself into the seat across from me. We'd talked long enough for the lunch rush to end and give her a break. "You don't look too bad," she tilted her head as her gaze tracked over my face. "Considering."

"Considering what?" I quirked a smile. "Finding Bill Cavanaugh, surviving the storm of the century, or having lunch with Carlene?"

"All that and having to move the wedding besides."

We hadn't had time to discuss the details before. "You'll want to come out and take a look at the kitchen and give me an idea of what equipment to rent. I have a couple of sources

I can tap. You won't have to make do with less than you had at the lodge. I promise."

"I've got sources of my own, girl. You tell Patrea to get her skinny ass in here, and we'll talk about this crazy idea of hers."

Dismay settled over me. "You don't think it will work?"

"Did I say I didn't?" Mabel cocked a brow that I noticed had a little more shape to it now that she had a man in her life who made her feel like making the extra effort. Then, she grinned. "Hell of an idea, you ask me. She'll want to start with pop-ups for the catering until this thing hits its stride and then she'll want to look for a good chef and a regular staff."

"Should I be taking notes?" Instead, I forked up a bite of peanut butter pie and returned her grin.

I probably should have been since she spent the next few minutes outlining a solid plan for what Patrea would need to get her event space off the ground, at least the food side of it.

"By the way, Bill Cavanaugh was dating Claire Higgins right before he died." Mabel dropped that tidbit on me on her way back to the kitchen.

"How do you know that?" I managed to sputter before she sailed through the door.

Popping her head back out, she waggled her eyebrows and said, "Take-out orders."

CHAPTER FIFTEEN

Tuesday, the day of Bill Cavanaugh's funeral, dawned with pea-soup fog that wouldn't burn off until halfway through the day. The damp and dismal morning weather suited my mood as I walked into the hardware store with mist clinging to my hair.

Owner Tim Bennett greeted me with a smile. "You must have known I was getting ready to call you in a minute. Those register vents you ordered came in this morning."

"Fabulous." Even though I'd come for another reason, the shipment arriving was a bonus. "I'll touch base with the tenants and see if they mind me popping in to install them. One more thing off my list."

Not that my list was super long. My boss kept his rental properties in tip-top shape, but every now and then, something weird popped up. In this case, oddly sized floor registers in one of the older homes required Tim to special order them for me.

"I just need you to sign my copy of the receipt." Tim began to shuffle through a stack of paperwork he kept in a mesh tray on one end of the counter. After he'd gone through the stack twice, he said, "I could have sworn I put it right here. It should be on the top of the pile. It hasn't been half an hour since the truck came in."

"I'm sure it will turn up."

"I hope so. Otherwise, I may need to go in for an eye exam. It's been like this since we opened back up after the storm. I keep misplacing paperwork and then finding it filed in weird places. I thought one of the part-time employees might be moving things around, but none of them have what you'd call organizational intentions. They just want to do their shift and go home."

Where had I heard something like this before? From Delia at the florist, that's where.

Then, he offered the clincher. "It's like the place is haunted or something."

The penny dropped. Bill. It had to be. And he had some explaining to do.

It took five minutes before Tim unearthed the order sheet from somewhere, according to him, where it shouldn't logically have been. I sighed as I signed where he indicated, then moved on to what I'd come to talk to him about in the first place.

"Do you recognize this?" I pulled the lodge key out of my pocket and laid it on the counter. It was slightly larger than a regular house key and made from what I assumed was brass.

Tim's gaze flicked to my face, and then his expression shuttered. He recognized the key. "Where did you get that?"

"From my father, and before you ask, he knows I have it. He told me he asked you to make a copy a couple of years ago." I brushed a finger across the words Do Not Duplicate stamped above the code.

"I didn't do anything wrong," Tim said, looking me in the eye, so I knew he was telling the truth. "There's no law on the books that says a person can't have a copy made of a key in his rightful possession."

I held up a hand and kept my voice gentle. "I'm not accusing you of anything, Tim. And I can tell you my father is not under suspicion of anything, either. You can call Ernie and ask him if you don't trust my word on that."

It clicked for him, though. I saw it happen. "You're helping Bill?"

"I am." One of the very few people in town who knew my secret, I'd had to tell Tim about my ghosts when his sister turned out to be one of them. "I need to know if anyone else has a copy of this key."

My hope of pinpointing the killer quickly went poof when Tim scrubbed a hand over his forehead and admitted, "When Max took charge, he put the original key in a safe deposit box for safekeeping and made a copy. From that duplicate, I've made nine more copies over the years."

All I could do for a moment was blink as I took in what he'd said. "Let me get this straight. You're saying there are ten lodge keys?"

He nodded.

"Any of them recently?"

"No." His nod turned to a shake. "The blanks were special orders. I had ten in stock, and your dad got the last one."

"Did you ever make any for people that weren't members of the order?"

Again, his head shook. "And I made every single person sign my log book. That's standard practice. You think Bill's killer used one of those keys." It wasn't a question.

"Maybe. Or Bill had one and let his killer into the building. Either way, it wasn't your fault. With that many keys loose in the world, half the town could have had access."

After a moment's thought, he shrugged. "I guess you're right."

At this point, I could either ask him to show me his log book, which I didn't think he'd do, or let Ernie know what I'd learned. Mindful of my promise to my father to be careful, I went with door number two and hoped I could talk Ernie into sharing that information. Quid pro quo, and all that. It probably didn't matter anymore, anyway.

"Thanks, Tim. I'll just get these register vents out of your way."

Almost everyone in town turned up for Bill's funeral—no surprise, given his job, town service, and activities. Plus, you know, murder tends to bring people out of the woodwork. There's nothing like a good scandal to draw a crowd.

I spotted his ghost standing near the table that held the urn of his ashes. His attention was focused on his mother as she sat in the first pew while Drew and I made our way down the center aisle to a spot halfway along where my folks had saved us seats. I'd rather have stood on the sidelines and watched people's faces, but my father needed my support, and he came first.

When the officiant asked people to stand and share memories, I heard a woman's choked cry from somewhere in the back of the church and thought it might be Carlene's voice. However, I couldn't crane my head around to find out without looking like a jerk.

When Harley Stanfield's voice pitched over the crowd,

my father's body stiffened, and this time, I turned to look— as did everyone else.

"Bill Cavanaugh is dead. He wasn't no saint. Sometimes, people get what's coming to them."

Amid the roar of voices telling him to shut up and sit down, Harley did, crossing his arms over his chest and staring stubbornly straight ahead, which bumped his name right up to the top of my list.

"What's his problem?" I whispered to my father. "That sounded like more than simple animosity."

"Shh. He didn't mean what you think. That's just Harley being Harley."

Harley being Harley put a stop to the memory-sharing portion of the service, and soon enough, the whole thing was over. I followed my folks to the downstairs meeting room. Lined up along walls that hadn't been redone since someone chose to install green paneling sometime in the 1970s, tables groaned with food, and people assembled to offer condolences. Or, in some cases, to wait for something titillating to happen.

Based on the snippets of conversation I heard as I made my way through the crowd, most people expected Harley to be arrested by the end of the day. Funnily enough, it didn't look like Ernie was in any hurry to slap on the cuffs.

"Did Harley just admit to murder in front of God and everyone?" I asked Ernie when I finally got a minute alone with him.

"And make my life easier? No. Harley didn't kill Bill. He's got an ironclad alibi for the time of the murder."

"Really?"

"Really. Bill was shot at fairly close range with a .22 caliber weapon sometime between 8:30 and 9:15."

That probably explained why Robin hadn't heard the gunshot. A .22 wasn't a loud gun, and with the snow muffling everything, the sound might not have carried that far.

"At the time of Bill's death, Harley was clearing the end of our road with his bucket loader so I could get home. If he hadn't, you might have found my frozen corpse sitting in my car on the side of the road in addition to Bill's."

I might not know a whole lot about heavy machinery, but even I knew Harley couldn't drive a bucket loader from where he and Ernie lived to town and back during the coroner's time frame. "What was his beef with Bill, then? Seemed like harsh words to say at a funeral."

"And I'm sure he'll regret them later, but Harley doesn't always think things through. As far as beef goes, my best guess is Dale Crawford had something to do with it. He and Harley are cousins."

I'd heard about the blackballing incident already, so I nodded.

"But this much I can say for certain," Ernie continued. "If Harley ever decided to murder someone, he wouldn't be content to shoot them. He'd want to use his fists."

Another fair point added to the one that put Harley off my list entirely. Still, I made a mental note to look into this Dale Crawford person at my earliest opportunity. Even if he was wrong and only thought Bill blackballed his Benevolent Bear membership, there had to be a reason why he did. And a reason why at least one member didn't want him to join.

Getting to the bottom of that situation might be just what I needed to shed light on Bill's death.

"Since we're sharing and all," I pulled Dad's extra copy of the lodge key from my purse and handed it over. "This is a third key to the lodge, and I have it on good authority that there are at least seven more floating around. You should talk to Tim at the hardware store for a list of names."

"You could just tell me and save me the time."

"Can't because I didn't ask. It's not my place since this is police business."

"Like that's ever stopped you before," Ernie huffed.

"First time for everything." I left him to rejoin Drew and my folks before he could work up a good retort.

Muted conversation punctuated by the occasional awkward laugh, somber clothes, and the scents of potluck dishes combined complete the mood of mourning. People had genuinely liked Bill. That much became apparent as the next hour wore on, and I still hadn't had a chance to speak to him. Given the size of the crowd, he'd probably fade out before I did.

When a late arrival made her way over to offer Bill's grieving mother her condolences and a sympathetic embrace, the mood altered slightly—at least among the tight knot of Bill's co-workers who had formed near the food tables.

From the side, and with her dark blond hair ruthlessly pulled back, I couldn't tell who it was, but when she turned, I recognized the sharp features of Agnes Cunningham, Bill's rival from the bank. I moved closer and listened shamelessly without being too obvious about my intentions.

"I'm so sorry for your loss, Alice," Agnes murmured, her

voice choked with emotion. "Bill was a fine man. He'll be deeply missed."

Alice nodded, her eyes brimming with tears as she squeezed Agnes's hand in gratitude. "Thank you, Agnes," she whispered, her voice trembling with grief. "Bill always said you motivated him at work. You were the reason he put in so much extra time and effort."

While Alice's words sounded like a compliment, they could be taken another way. After all, Agnes and Bill were both in line for the same promotion. "It was the same for me," Agnes replied softly, her voice thick with emotion. I admired him greatly." She patted Alice's hand and glanced around the room to note which other coworkers were there.

With her head bent as if the result of a heavy heart, or else to avoid eye contact, Agnes made her way to the front of the room, where Bill's urn stood surrounded by flickering candles and floral arrangements. Taking a deep breath to steady herself, she approached the urn, her gaze fixed on Bill's smiling photograph.

"Bill," Agnes began, her voice trembling with emotion. "I... I don't know where to start. You were more than just a colleague to me. You were a friend, a confidant, a mentor."

While she spoke in an emotional tone, not a single tear glinted in Agnes' eyes, making me doubt her sincerity. It didn't help her case that Bill still stood nearby and looked at her like she'd sprouted a second head.

"You always had a kind word, a helping hand, and a gentle heart. You went the extra mile with grace and integrity, and I... I will miss you terribly."

As Agnes spoke, the room fell silent, the weight of her words hanging in the air. Mourners who might not be aware of their work dynamic exchanged sympathetic glances, touched by Agnes's heartfelt tribute to her fallen colleague. Others, their co-workers in particular, watched with more skepticism showing on their faces. And as she finished her speech, Agnes placed a trembling hand on the urn, bidding a final farewell to the man she said had touched so many lives with his kindness and compassion.

I wasn't buying a single word of it.

Slightly more believable, at least to my ears, was the short statement made by Walter Prescott. Not to be outdone, he too, approached Alice to offer his condolences, then made his way to the urn. After staring at it for a solemn moment, and waiting for Agnes to vacate the area, he turned to address the room.

"Bill Cavanaugh was the best damn loan officer the bank ever had," Walter declared, his voice gruff with emotion as he stood before Bill's urn. "I've worked with many over the years, but none had the dedication, the ability to see the bigger picture or the willingness to put in the time that Bill possessed. He had a way with numbers, a way with people, that was unparalleled."

Agnes turned her head away as if unable to contain her grief, but from my vantage point, I caught the heated flush that crawled up her face and the fury in her eyes.

Walter paused, his own eyes remaining dry despite the gravity of his tone. "He was like a son to me, always going above and beyond for the clients, for his team, for this entire town. His absence will be felt deeply, not just in the office but in all of our hearts."

With a heavy sigh, Walter turned to reach out and touch the urn gently, as if trying to convey his gratitude and sorrow through the cold surface. "Rest in peace, Bill," he murmured, his voice cracking slightly. "You were a true asset to all of us. You will be sorely missed."

As he made his way to the back of the room, he passed Agnes. She flicked him a glance, but kept her face turned away so he couldn't read her emotions. Probably the smartest way to go.

"That was something, wasn't it? Agnes put on quite a show, but I never knew Walter felt that way about me." An icy chill pebbled the flesh of my arms and raised the hairs on my neck as Bill appeared just an inch or two too close for my comfort. I took a step back. "He certainly didn't act like it when I was alive."

"Thus the great paradox of death," I muttered.

CHAPTER SIXTEEN

With the funeral happening at the church practically next door to my house, my folks naturally stopped in for a few minutes afterward, to sum up our impressions of the event. Molly greeted my father at the door with the full-body wag she reserved only for him and his magic, belly-scratching hands.

He bent to oblige as she flopped down with her tongue lolling. "Who's my good girl? Who's my best Molly?" Both man and dog came away from the encounter with lifted spirits. It was the first time my dad's eyes weren't filled with sorrow all day.

"Anyone want tea or coffee?" I hung up my coat and followed Mom into the living room, where she settled into her favorite chair.

"Nothing for me. The compassion group really outdid themselves this time. I've never seen such a spread at a service, but I suppose they wanted to show Alice how much support she has now that Bill is gone."

Kicking off my shoes, I chose a corner of the sofa and tucked my feet under me while Drew took the other end and spent a minute loosening his tie. When my father trailed in, Molly stayed glued to his side until he sat, then plopped down with a doggy sigh to lay across his feet.

"I noticed Bill's obituary didn't list many close relatives

besides his mother. Only his sister, Althea, and an aunt and uncle in New York," I said. "I also noticed the aunt and uncle didn't show up today. Do you think Alice will move out of state to be closer to them now that he's gone?"

"I doubt it. Not if Althea stays, anyway. Besides, she wouldn't go back if that's where Bill's father still lives. I know she moved here to get a fresh start after ending a troubled marriage. I hope she stays because she feels like one of us now."

It didn't need to be said that Bill's father had not attended the service. The buzz of gossip that surrounded his absence had made us aware of that. If today had been anything to go by, Alice would have plenty of support from her adopted community, so there was that, at least.

"Agnes Cunningham put on quite a show," Drew finally added something to the conversation. "She really should have charged for tickets for that performance, but I think some people bought it, don't you?"

"Walter didn't. Or rather, she took his response that way. I got a good look at her face when he walked past and she was not best pleased. Otherwise, I can't say I learned anything super useful about the case today. Well, other than Harley Stanfield is off the list because Ernie is his alibi."

Dad spoke up, "I could have told you Harley didn't do it. He's all bluff and bluster, that one."

"Even so, I wouldn't defend his choice of actions today." My mother's tone had an edge that indicated she wasn't in a mood to be gracious.

I agreed. "That was a lousy thing to stand up and say at a funeral. He shouldn't have come if all he wanted to do was hurt Alice."

Holding up a hand, Dad stopped us from offering any further opinions. "I'll be the first one to agree with you on that point. Make no mistake. I plan to have words with Harley the first chance I get."

"If there's anything left of him once his wife gets her crack at him." My mother's face remained impassive, but I thought I caught a tiny gleam of satisfaction. "Now, did we learn anything other than substantiating Harley's status as town jackass today?"

"I did," I admitted. "But not at the funeral. I stopped in at the hardware store this morning to pick up an order that had come in." Maybe I fudged my reason for my father a little. Sue me. "One thing led to another while I was talking to Tim, and he told me he'd made more than your one extra key for the lodge over the years."

Dad shot up in his chair. "What? How many?"

I hated to tell him, but I did, "there were seven others, so ten in all."

"Ten?" This time, he shoved his way out of the chair and speared a hand through hair already beginning to stand on end as he paced. When my father gets annoyed, his hair gets poofy. It might have something to do with his blood pressure, but it happens.

"Those were non-duplicate keys. It said so right on them. What was Tim thinking?"

"He says it's not a law and that he's kept a log, too, but as long as the person can present a valid reason, he can make copies just like he did for you. He said every person he made them for was a lodge member, at least. I told Ernie about it already. He'll get hold of the list, but you might be able to get a copy from Tim if you went over there and asked him nicely." I knew I was talking fast, but that was only to calm him down before he did something foolish.

"That means Bill might have had a key, then." My mother followed things to the same logical conclusion I had. "And if he did, he might have let his killer in. Or the killer had a key and let Bill in. I suppose it could play both ways."

"Did Ernie mention finding a key in Bill's possession?" Drew said. "I'd think he would have mentioned it once you brought up the subject."

He was right. Ernie probably would have. "He didn't. What's more, he was surprised to learn about the other keys. I think that means Bill probably didn't have a key on him. Or if he did, it's still buried under the rubble."

Having exhausted his mild fit of pique, Dad slumped back down and, since Molly had circled around to sit with me, kicked his feet out in front of the chair. "That all makes sense. Except for the timing, anyway. I can't understand why anyone would go there during a storm. Especially Bill."

"All he could tell me was that he'd been to his mother's house and stopped at the Gas N Go on the way home for windshield wash because the snow was sticking to his wipers, and he'd run out. We know he didn't go home because his car was still in the lodge parking lot, so whatever sent him there must have happened during that short window."

"If he was meeting someone, they weren't afraid of driving in bad weather," Drew said. "Which leaves half the town."

"Or someone who had a reason to be out in it." Mom looked at Dad. "What about Hermon Belanger?"

"Red?" Dad's forehead wrinkled, then smoothed back

out as his eyes widened. "Oh, right. I see what you're thinking."

"Well, I don't," Drew said. "Want to fill me in?"

My parents have always used a sort of conversational shorthand, but he needed this one spelled out in long words, and so did I. Except once I gave it a second thought, I didn't. "Oh, you're right."

Drew cocked one eyebrow and then shook his head. "I'm not from around here, remember? Elaborate."

"Red Belanger's daughter Grace used to date Bill. You remember Grace, right? The woman whose body we found at Delly Harper's place?"

As soon as the realization hit, Drew picked right up on the context. "The woman Able Gallow murdered."

"Exactly. And not only had Bill been dating her, but if you remember, Able is Bill's brother-in-law. That's another strike against him, isn't it? What if Hermon decided to bide his time and get revenge once the stir died down."

"If he did, he belongs on a stage somewhere because he sure seemed surprised when he found out it was Bill's body under all that debris."

"Drew's right," Dad said. "He did. I was looking right at him when Ernie said Bill's name, and if he was faking surprise, he sure fooled me."

"Add his name to the list anyway," Mom suggested. "We might as well check into his movements on the night. I can ask if people remember hearing the plow go through. Or if they know of anyone else who was out that night. Clive wouldn't have kept the gas station open if he didn't think he'd have a customer or two trying to get in and fill up gas cans ahead of the storm."

"We have a plan, then?" Dad rose. He'd want to get home and change out of his suit and tie. "I'll have words with Harley and Tim Bennett," his tone suggested they might not be kind ones, "and your mother will see if the busybodies kept track of the plow."

The busybodies comment earned him a quelling look, but nothing more. "I was surprised," Mom addressed me instead, "not to see Maryann Payne at the funeral. She knew Bill quite well, all things considered."

All things being her connection to Grace Belanger and the fact that, as a realtor, it was in her best interest to have a relationship with the bank's loan officer.

"Now that you mention it, you're right. It is odd she wasn't there. I'll pop in and ask her about it tomorrow."

CHAPTER SEVENTEEN

I probably should have made an appointment, but I realized it was too late as I slammed my car door. Stepping into the real estate office, I was greeted by the scent of freshly brewed coffee. Owner and agent Maryann Payne looked up from her desk, her warm smile inviting me in. As usual, I couldn't help comparing her to a bulldog in a business suit, but at least she knew better than to try selling me a house. I'd come to discuss Bill Cavanaugh's death and had no intention of letting her pull my focus from that task.

"Well, hello. What brings you in today?" she asked, her pen poised over a stack of paperwork. I wondered if Bill had stopped by to mess with her filing system.

Nah, he probably didn't dare.

"I know I probably should have called ahead, but I was hoping to get your insight on something," I began, lowering myself into the chair opposite her as Maryann waved my protest aside. "You see, I've been trying to piece together some information about Bill Cavanaugh. I noticed you didn't attend his funeral. Given his position as a loan officer at the bank, I would have thought you knew each other."

Maryann's expression softened, a hint of sadness shadowing her features. "I did. Yes. Bill was a good man. Such a sad loss."

And yet, I noticed she didn't explain her absence the day before.

"We worked together quite a bit. You know what it's like in small towns. Bill always went the *extra mile*. If it weren't for his in-depth understanding of the first-time buyer's program, I'd have probably gone under during the lean years. I can't tell you how often he worked his magic to make a dream home a reality for our clients."

"Extra mile?" I'd picked up an odd emphasis on the phrase. "What does that mean?"

Maryann leaned back in her chair, a thoughtful look crossing her face. "Bill Cavanaugh wasn't your typical loan officer. He had a talent for seeing the potential in people, even when the numbers didn't quite add up on paper. A way of understanding their circumstances, their struggles, and genuinely wanting to help them achieve their dreams of homeownership."

Why did everything she said sound like ad copy? I furrowed my brow, intrigued by Maryann's words. "Are you saying Bill took risks on borrowers that other banks wouldn't?"

Maryann nodded slowly. "Mooselick River Bank and Trust is locally owned and operated, but all banks must follow state and federal lending laws. I'm not saying Bill broke any laws, but if you ask me, he may have blurred the lines now and again."

"How so?"

"It's no secret that Bill offered credit counseling to borrowers who needed to increase their credit scores. A few points can make a big difference when it comes to getting a decent interest rate or even getting a loan approved at all." She gestured toward the coffee maker. "Want a cup?"

"Sure. Sweet and light, please."

"Some people just don't look good on paper," she said over her shoulder as she poured a cup for herself and then one for me. "I sent those to Bill specifically because he knew every trick in the book for bumping a credit score."

As Maryann spoke, a new understanding of the man emerged inside me. Clearly, Bill's work went beyond numbers and transactions; he genuinely cared about the people he was helping. Or most of them, anyway.

"Sounds like he was a paragon among bankers. It's odd he refused to give Mara Tibbets a loan to expand her salon."

I'd come to her hoping to find motives for Bill's murder, and instead, she'd given me just the opposite. Thanks for the dead end, Maryann.

"I don't know anything about the business loan side of things," she said after she sat back down. She leaned forward and lowered her voice even though no one but me was there to listen. "But when it came to home loans, I suspect he knew a few tricks that weren't in the books."

"The kinds of tricks that might have cost him more than his job if he got caught?" I asked cautiously. "The kind that could get him into trouble with the law?"

Maryann's eyes darkened slightly before she composed herself. "I have no proof Bill did anything illegal."

I nodded, taking in her words and working through the possible implications as a list formed in my head. "How often did his tricks fail?"

Maryann paused, tapping her chin thoughtfully. "I'd put

his success rate at a solid eighty-five percent. At least in my experience."

"What about foreclosures? I assume you keep track of those." Under the *everyone's favorite aunt* exterior beat the heart of a shark when it came to business. Snapping up a foreclosure sale would be just the thing to make that predator heart go pitter-pat.

"I do, and Bill's numbers weren't any higher than they should be, so I probably shouldn't be saying any of this to you now. All I have are suspicions."

I leaned forward, curiosity piqued. "But you're worried your suspicions might be connected to what happened to him?"

Maryann's gaze grew distant, her brow furrowing with concern. "I don't know. If I had even a shred of proof that his work had anything to do with his death, I'd have come forward." She hesitated momentarily as if debating whether to share more with me. Finally, she took a deep breath and admitted. "There is one thing that has been bothering me, though."

I leaned closer.

"Agnes Cunningham, the other junior loan officer, has been acting like she's my best friend since Bill's passing. She was gunning for the position of senior loan officer when he was alive, and she's become increasingly desperate to prove herself. I find her off-putting at the best of times, and now..." she trailed off and grimaced.

I furrowed my brow at the mention of Agnes Cunningham. Maryann wasn't the first to describe her demeanor as a bit too eager, almost to the point of being ruthlessly ambitious.

"Do you think Agnes could have had something to do with Bill's death?" I asked, trying to connect the dots and failing miserably because I only knew Agnes through what others said about her. Certainly, not well enough to have the first clue what she would or wouldn't do. I'd never met her in person and had only been peripherally aware of her until Bill's funeral, where she hadn't given off the killer vibe. There'd been plenty of feigned grief, but I hadn't sensed triumph or guilt. But then, I'd been spectacularly wrong about spotting killers before.

Maryann shook her head slowly, her eyes filled with uncertainty. "I can't say because I don't know how far she'd go to get what she wants. If you asked me, would she get him fired if she could? That would have been a big fat yes, but murder? I don't know why she'd have bothered."

That struck me odd, so I prodded. "Why not?"

"Well," she tilted her head to look at me. "Killing Bill to get his job wouldn't have done Agnes a bit of good, and if she has half a brain, she'd know that as well as I do."

Since it bore repeating, I said, "Why not?"

"Because, when it comes to the female persuasion, Walter Prescott is the equivalent of an eight-year-old boy."

My brows shot up. "Huh?"

"Boys rule, girls drool. He thought it then, and he thinks it now. Especially when it comes to women in business. Agnes won't get that promotion while he has anything to do with handing it out. I'm not a betting woman, but I'd still put money on him bringing in someone from outside the bank now that Bill's death is forcing his hand."

"Why didn't he just promote Bill when he had the chance?"

Maryann's expression never changed, but she lifted one hand to rub her fingers together. "Money, of course. Why would he give either one of them a raise if he could get two people to work harder by dangling the carrot?"

"Rude."

"To say the least. In any case, all I can really say about Agnes is that she's known to be ruthless in her pursuits and that I wouldn't put anywhere near the same trust in her as I had in Bill, and we'll have to leave it at that."

A shiver ran down my spine as I realized the gravity of Maryann's words. Could Agnes Cunningham's ruthless ambition have crossed a line that led to tragedy? And all for nothing?

"Will you call me if you think of anything else that might help lead to Bill's killer?"

Maryann paused, weighing her words carefully. "How about this? If you keep me in the loop, I'll keep you in the loop, but if I hear you've been casting aspersions on Bill's character, I'll deny we ever had this conversation."

She kept a friendly tone, but I knew a warning when I heard one. I nodded in agreement, understanding the delicate nature of the situation. "Deal. I don't want to smear his name or undo any of the good he's done by calling attention to what we both know is mere speculation."

Maryann smiled gratefully, her eyes reflecting a mix of determination and concern. "Nicely done. If you ever decide to take up a career in politics or sales, you could use that diplomacy to good effect."

"It's interesting that you'd lump those two pursuits together." I couldn't hold back the tiniest of smiles.

"You can't have one without the other." She winked at me.

As I thanked Maryann for her insight and made my way out of the office, my mind raced with newfound possibilities. Where else might he have compromised his values if Bill had cut corners at work? Were his values compromised at all? He'd done nothing but help people. Was Agnes Cunningham any better? And would she automatically get a promotion now that Bill wasn't there to stand in her way?

One way to find out, I supposed, would be to take Bill's posthumous advice about applying for a home equity loan. I didn't have to go through with it if I didn't want to, but he was right about the effect it would have on my credit score, and it would give me a chance to learn something about Agnes Cunningham.

The day after I visited Maryann's office, I fitted my key into the front door of Curated Collections, Jacy and Neen's combination second-hand/antique store and art gallery. The bell above the door tinkled softly to announce my arrival, but the shop wouldn't open for another two hours yet. I wasn't there to work. I was there because Dolly Tibbets woke me from a sound sleep and told me to come.

The familiar scents of oil paint, wood polish, and old things greeted me. The cozy atmosphere enveloped me even in their new building, which was cavernous compared to their first place. That was all Jacy and Neena's doing. They both had an eye for creating enticing vignettes out of their wares, and the warmth of their displays made people feel at home. People who feel at home spend more time browsing and also buying. This was the heart of their success.

As I passed shelves of vintage trinkets, the whisper of shuffling papers drifted to my ears. Bill was here, and as Dolly had warned me I could, I was about to catch him in the act.

"Hello there, Bill. Whatcha doing?"

Startled, Bill turned to find me watching him as he removed a sheaf of paper from the printer. He furrowed his brow, scanning the room before his gaze settled on me. Anyone else would have had the sense to look guilty. Bill was not blessed with that much sense.

Dismissing me, he turned back to his work. Above the printer hung an antique mirror in an elaborately carved frame. Reflected in its glass, Bill's features were obscured by a soft, ethereal glow. Huh. Maybe that was how ghosts looked to other people. Mostly, I saw them as they'd been in life—solid and regular with just a hint of fading around the edges. An interesting observation that had nothing to do with why I'd come.

"Bill!" I spoke loudly enough to interrupt what he was doing

"I'm busy," the ghost responded, his voice echoing through the room.

"I can see that for myself. What are you doing?" Besides using up all your energy for the day, was the part I didn't say. No wonder he hadn't been bothering me like my other ghosts did.

"Generating a cost/benefit analysis as the basis for a loan

application," he said in a tone that suggested I'd asked a question that only Captain Obvious could answer.

"Why?"

Bill hesitated, his form beginning to go transparent in the middle. "This is a growing concern, certainly, but any business of this caliber could be enhanced with an infusion of working capital. It takes money to make money. Everyone knows that."

I raised an eyebrow, intrigued by his formal tone. "Okay."

Bill sighed, his increasingly incorporeal form shimmering with frustration. "And I've been sorting out one or two minor issues in their filing system if you must know. A messy office is a sign of messy business practices, though this wasn't one of the more egregious offenders."

I blinked twice before I responded. This was not normal ghost behavior. Or maybe it was. I mean, I've only dealt with a few of them, so how would I know for sure? Except his actions reminded me of someone I'd worked with at my ex-husband's charitable foundation—a woman who, once she started something, couldn't stop until it was done.

"Can you stop for a minute? There's a question I need to ask you."

Bill shook his head sheepishly. "Not if I want to finish."

Thinking I should be used to my weird life by now, I still marveled at the absurdity of the situation. "I think you've been haunting local businesses, rearranging things to your liking. Am I right?"

The ghost nodded this time, his body fading a little more while his hands remained busy with the papers. "That's about the long and short of it, I'm afraid."

"Well, I must say, Bill, that's certainly a unique hobby," I remarked, a smile tugging at the corners of my lips. There were worse things he could be doing. "But it's time to end your paperwork-rearranging escapades, don't you agree?"

He stopped and looked at me like I'd grown a second head. "Can you think of a more productive way to spend my afterlife?"

"Several of them, actually. Besides, what you're doing is not only intrusive, it's rude."

Crestfallen, Bill dropped his gaze to the floor. "I was only trying to help. Now that I'm gone, Walter won't have any choice. He'll have to put Agnes in charge, and she's a stickler for going by the book. Sometimes, you have to trust the person, not the numbers."

If I wasn't mistaken, he'd just confirmed what Maryann Payne had said. "Tell me the truth. Did you ever fudge information on loan documents?"

He didn't look away, which both surprised me and earned my respect. "Credit histories are not the only indicator of someone's willingness or ability to repay a loan. I may have been too lenient sometimes, but my track record spoke for itself. Only one of my home loans over the past five years has even come close to ending in foreclosure."

"Okay." That hadn't been my burning question for him, so I asked it now. "Did you ask Tim to make you a key to the lodge? I know a few spares were floating around." He hadn't had it on him when he died, but the killer might have taken it.

"No, I never did."

With that, he opened Jacy's top desk drawer, extracted a sticky note, slapped it on whatever document he'd been holding, and then winked out, leaving me to wonder who he meant. A person in danger of losing their home might be looking for someone to blame. The banker who loaned them the money might be a target.

In my admittedly narrow experience, revenge was a strong motive for murder.

CHAPTER EIGHTEEN

Usually, the atmosphere at the bank exuded an air of quiet efficiency, but today, as I stepped through its doors, a sense of mourning overlaid the calm, yet still seemed somehow forced. The polished wood counters barely gleamed under the subdued, almost flat light of a single fixture. At least the lone teller greeted customers with a warm smile as she went about her business.

I waited my turn and asked to speak with Agnes Cunningham, the loan officer. As I waited, I couldn't shake the feeling of unease that had settled in the pit of my stomach. Despite what I had told the teller, I wasn't here for a loan. I was here to beard what might possibly be a killer in her den.

When Agnes finally emerged from her office wearing a professional but friendly expression, I put on my best smile and greeted her warmly. "I'm Everly Dupree. Thanks for taking the time to talk to me, Ms. Cunningham. I appreciate it."

"Call me Agnes, please." She shook my hand and gestured for me to follow her into her office. As we settled into our seats, I couldn't help but notice the framed photograph on her desk, a smiling portrait of Agnes and her late co-worker, Bill Cavanaugh, taken in front of the bank's vault. Interesting.

"It's my pleasure. Now, Everly, what can I help you with today?" Agnes asked, her tone polite but businesslike.

"I'd like to apply for a home equity loan," I said, taking a deep breath and meeting her gaze steadily.

She arched an eyebrow in surprise. "A home equity loan? May I ask why?"

I hesitated for a moment, carefully choosing my words. "Not too long ago, Bill Cavanaugh advised me that taking out a loan would benefit my credit rating. Since I respected Bill's opinion, I thought I should follow his advice. Especially now that he's gone."

Take that, Agnes.

"You do agree with him, don't you? About building my credit, I mean. I thought it might be fun to redecorate the house." I replied cryptically, not wanting to reveal too much too soon.

"Of course." Agnes nodded thoughtfully, opening one of her desk drawers. Unguarded for the moment, her expression took an almost feral glee before she composed her features.

Feigning dismay, I said, "Or maybe I should put it off a bit longer. As you mentioned at the funeral, you've lost a significant person to the bank. My new drapes can wait until you've all had time to recover. I'll just go now. So thoughtless of me. I can come back later."

I rose, and she just about fell out of her chair when she did the same.

"No. Don't go." She caught me before I got to the door, took my arm, and led me back to the chair. "It's fine. It's true we've lost a pivotal member of our team, but Bill would want us to continue serving the good people of

Mooselick River. Come back, and let's fill out an application, shall we?"

It wasn't easy, but I only rolled my eyes internally. "If you're sure this is a good time."

"None better," she assured me. "Bill would be glad to know you took his advice."

"I suppose he would," I allowed, letting her settle me back in the seat across from her desk.

"Very well, let's get started on your application then," she said, opening a cabinet door revealing a series of paperwork cubbies. "You'll need your last four pay stubs for income verification, proof of insurance, and this year's property tax statement unless those are all in escrow—in which case, you'll need your most recent mortgage statement."

Living in a town the size of Mooselick River and working at the only bank, Agnes couldn't help but be familiar with the unorthodox way I'd purchased my home. She probably knew all about the account funded by my ex-mother-in-law, too.

"I don't have a mortgage on the house, but I can provide you with the insurance and tax information."

"That's good." She sounded distracted as she pulled papers out of their slots, frowned, and slid them back in.

"Is something wrong?"

"No," her laugh sounded forced. "It's just that someone has rearranged all the application forms. I can't imagine why."

I could.

Soon enough, she found what she needed. Instead of handing the paperwork to me to fill out, she picked up a pen and printed my name on the first line. "First, we'll start with your basic information. I understand you're getting married soon. Weddings are so expensive these days."

So, she did know something about me. Did she think I was borrowing money to fund my wedding? But then, she assumed I had a mortgage, so maybe she was unaware of my recent windfall. I wondered if bank gossip didn't extend to large deposits. Not that the why mattered as long as I could get her talking. "Yes, they are. It adds up quickly between the flowers, the catering, and the dress, even if you're not going for something splashy."

And I wasn't. I'd done that the first time, and that wedding day never quite felt real. This time, with Drew, we wanted warmth and family. An intimate ceremony—as intimate as you could have with a good chunk of the town wishing to attend—and we hadn't gone overboard on spending. But Agnes didn't need to know that, so I let her think whatever she wanted as she pelted me with questions and filled out the application herself.

Did she do that with everyone? Or just me?

The next few minutes were a blur of questions, numbers, and financial jargon as Agnes meticulously reviewed the details with me. Despite the seriousness of the situation, I couldn't help but admire her professionalism and attention to detail. Still, every time I mentioned Bill's name, she pulled the conversation back to my application.

As we neared the end of the process, Agnes looked up at me with a hint of concern in her eyes. "Given the unusual circumstances of your home purchase and the rising real estate values, you've accrued a lot of equity in a short time. If you were to sell the property, you'd be subjected to a considerable capital gains tax."

I gave it another shot. "Maybe that's why Bill suggested I take out a loan. He might have thought it would be a good idea to close up the gap."

"I think not. Bill would be fully aware that's not how it works. The tax is calculated on the difference between value and acquisition costs. You paid nearly nothing for a house that now holds considerable value."

"It's a good thing I have no intention of ever selling it, then."

"Yes, well, it looks like your personal information is all in order. I suppose I should have asked before. How much were you looking to borrow?"

She caught me off guard. I expected her to give me an opening to discuss Bill's death by now, so I hadn't thought that far ahead.

"Based on the current market value, you could access as much as two hundred thousand. Are you sure you'd be able to repay a loan of that size given your salary?" she asked gently.

Assuming her desk computer had access, I found it strange that she hadn't checked my current balance. If she had, she wouldn't have been worried—and she'd have known I didn't need a loan to buy new drapes. I hesitated for a moment and decided since subtlety hadn't worked for me, I'd pull out my hammer. "Well, Agnes, the truth is, I'm not interested in a loan. I'm here to ask you about Bill."

Agnes's brow furrowed with confusion. "Bill? What do you mean?"

I took a deep breath, steeling myself for what was to come. "After discovering his body, I find myself carrying a sense of responsibility around his death, so I've been doing some digging into his movements on the days before his murder. I can't help wondering if there's a connection between his work and what happened to him. As his closest co-worker, I thought you might have insight on any possible motive. Your heartfelt words at his funeral made me think you might know why someone wanted to harm him."

Agnes's eyes widened in surprise, her expression shifting from confusion to concern. "I...I don't know what you're talking about, Everly. Bill was a dear friend and colleague who perished in a horrible accident. Why would anyone want to harm him?"

I held Agnes's gaze, searching for any sign of deception. "I'm not sure, Agnes. But it's fairly obvious someone did. I think you or someone else at the bank might hold the key to unlocking the mystery."

As I spoke, the weight of my words hung heavy in the air, and the silence stretched between us as Agnes processed what I had said. As I watched her carefully, I couldn't help but wonder if I was finally getting closer to uncovering the truth behind Bill's tragic demise.

"I'll tell you the same thing I told Ernie when he came around. I don't know anything."

Except she did. I could see it all over her. The way her shoulders stiffened and her face closed off, but not before a flicker of fear widened her eyes.

"Maybe not. Still, stepping into Bill's shoes might be more difficult than you think, and if you do, you could be putting yourself in the same kind of danger. I'd be careful if I were you."

She might not be ready to talk now, but I hadn't said

what I said as a mere ploy to get the truth out of her. If she wasn't the murderer, she really could be in danger.

"I'll be fine. No one here would lay a finger on Bill. Or on me. That much I can tell you with absolute certainty. I'm sorry, but you've wasted my time and yours on a foolish mission."

Not surprised by her stubborn refusal to see the possibilities, I repeated, "Just be careful," rose, and headed for the door. I heard the aborted loan application hit the trash can before I turned the knob.

Maybe one of the other members of my little sleuthing group would have better luck breaking through Agnes' shell. Letting go and letting someone else do what I considered to be my work didn't sit all that well, but with only two weeks left to go, I was needed at the Wentworth if we hoped to have it ready in time for the wedding.

Back in my car, I logged into Patrea's message board app to add a quick update and noticed a note from Jacy. *Lots of talk about the funeral, but nothing we didn't already know.*

I'd already passed through town when Patrea called to ask if I could pick up coffee on the way. In a stroke of good luck, I saw Clive Thompson through the window when I pulled into the Gas N Go. From behind the counter, he was deep in conversation with a man around my age that I didn't recognize and it seemed like they weren't happy with each other.

Whatever was going on between them stopped when I walked in, but the air still vibrated with tension.

While I filled the seven cups Patrea had ordered, the tone between the two men changed. Laughing together, they seemed pretty chummy as they talked about the storm, which was still a major topic of conversation and probably would be for another week at least. It all felt false to me.

"I can't complain," the customer said, his voice loud enough to carry across the store. "Between the board letting me clean up what fell in the roads and folks paying me to cut up and haul off blow-downs around town, I've cut pretty near fifteen cords of firewood without having to pay for stumpage. That storm was the best thing that's happened to my bank account in years."

"Just goes to show something good can always come from something bad."

"Sure does. Catch you later." The guy took his bag of stuff and left while I doctored my coffee and filled the two empty cup-holder slots with enough sugar packets and creamer cups for everyone else.

"Looks like things are mostly back to normal here." I put the two cup holders on the counter.

"Or whatever passes for it," Clive winked at me.

"Who was that? Does he sell firewood?"

"Sure does. That was Dale Crawford. His number's on the board over there," he said, pointing toward a corkboard studded with notes listing things for sale or wanted.

Dale Crawford, cousin to Harley Stanfield and past purveyor of bad checks. Interesting how chummy he was with Clive.

"Thanks." I paid for the coffee and tried to think of something to ask him that might help in my investigation. "I heard you kept the store open until nine on the night of the storm. That was a nice thing to do."

He shrugged off the praise. "I knew people would need

gas for their generators. No big deal. I've got a 4x4, and I don't mind driving in snow. It was the least I could do."

"Still, it must have been a nasty drive once the plow stopped running. You could have been stranded." I slipped my wallet into my purse and picked up the drink holders.

"Here, let me get the door for you." Clive came around the counter, made the gallant gesture, and followed me out to open my car door. "I'm the kind of guy who likes to serve his community."

"So I see. Thanks for the help."

"Anytime."

Leaving me with no real proof of whether he might be Bill's killer, Clive went back inside, and I drove away.

Proof or no proof, something felt off with him.

CHAPTER NINETEEN

he meeting room of the select board looked exactly like what it had once been: the classroom of an elementary school, complete with a green chalkboard on the far wall. Patrea Evergreen, poised and professional, stood in front of a schoolroom table, her eyes fixed on the trio of board members seated before her. Less than a dozen people occupied several rows of seating, including our little group of six, plus Martha and her cronies. It wouldn't be like this when it was time to elect a new treasurer, but tonight's meeting had no bearing on that topic.

"Good evening, esteemed members of the select board," Patrea began when it was her turn to speak, her voice carrying no hint of nerves. She'd done her homework to get two board members on her side. Well, in Ginger Martin's case, Kitty Dupree had been the one to put in a good word since the two women worked together at the library. Plus. Satisfied with Patrea's plans for a sympathetic renovation, Ginger's husband was firmly on board. Emmaline Higgins, Miles's wife and head of the garden club, had also given her stamp of approval, so Miles shouldn't put up much of an argument. This meeting was nothing more than a formality.

Letting her gaze travel from one to the next, Patrea aimed her opening statement at Clive Thompson. "I come before you today with a proposal that I believe will benefit our community and breathe new life into the local economy."

I could tell she had her work cut out when Clive Thompson leaned back in his chair, his face twisted with skepticism. Gone was the genial man I'd spoken to earlier in the day. "And what, exactly, did you have in mind, Mrs. Evergreen?"

Patrea squared her shoulders, meeting Clive's gaze head-on. "As I'm sure you know, I recently acquired the Wentworth property and would like to transform it into an event space for weddings and other special occasions." Moving forward, she handed each select member a copy of her proposal.

Setting his aside, Miles Higgins, the head of the board, leaned forward with interest. "As I've done some work at your place already, I've heard a fair bit about your proposed venture. I think it sounds like a wonderful idea, Mrs. Evergreen. The Wentworth house has been sitting vacant for far too long and, in my opinion, is perfectly suited to a venture of this nature. My wife was quite impressed with your plans for the grounds."

Pragmatic to a fault, Ginger Martin nodded in agreement. "The historical society has also endorsed your efforts, in no small part because you've indicated you'll maintain as much of the home's authenticity as possible. As far as the town goes, I can see the potential for increased foot traffic to our other businesses. Weddings always draw a crowd; those visitors will need places to dine, shop, and stay."

Clive, however, remained unmoved, his expression stern as he addressed his fellow board members. "I fail to see how turning the mansion into an event space will benefit the town. As you just pointed out, Ginger, such an endeavor will bring excessive traffic and disruption to the surrounding neighborhood."

Considering the surrounding neighborhood consisted of mostly empty fields and a couple of farmhouses too far away to hear anything short of cannon fire, his objection wasn't terribly valid.

"I don't believe I mentioned traffic or disruption, Clive. And I certainly did not use the term excessive," Mrs. Martin retorted.

Patrea took a deep breath, maintaining her resolve. "With all due respect, Mr. Thompson, if you review my proposal, you will see I've already spoken to my neighbors, who are completely on board with the plan. Based on those discussions and their endorsements, I have plans in place to address those specific concerns. I will ensure that events are held at appropriate times, parking is well-organized, and noise levels are kept to a minimum."

Clive considered Patrea's words for a moment before speaking. "I'll need some time to think it over, Mrs. Evergreen. I'm not ready to give my approval just yet. In case you weren't aware, we are in the middle of a crisis. Our treasurer has been killed, and his death has opened our little government to no small amount of scrutiny. This isn't the time to splash out on new ventures. We need to get our affairs in order first."

Miles Higgins shot Clive a disapproving look, his features stern. "Clive, we can't afford to delay this decision indefinitely, nor is our lack of a treasurer a reason to do so. Mrs. Evergreen has not asked for funding." He glanced at Patrea for confirmation.

She shook her head. "All I'm asking is for the board to verify there are no zoning or other regulations to preclude such a business."

"Just so, and as I understand it, a private wedding will be held on the property in a matter of weeks."

"There will," Patrea confirmed. "Assuming I am within my rights to open a home I own to a friend for that purpose."

I think Miles Higgins would have come around the table and patted her on the head if he could.

His tone genial, Miles continued. "Mrs. Evergreen has put forth a sound plan, and the potential benefits for our town are undeniable. As I know of no zoning issues, I say we allow her to move forward with this opportunity before it slips through our fingers."

Ginger Martin chimed in, her voice tinged with impatience. "I have to agree with Miles on this one, Clive. We can't let fear of change hold us back. The Wentworth property is a gem waiting to shine again, and Patrea's proposal is our ticket to revitalizing it and putting more money in the town coffers as a result."

Clive's brow furrowed as he felt the weight of the room pressing in on him. Miles and Ginger had valid points, but he was a man set in his ways, cautious by nature, and for reasons of his own, I suspected, refused to give in. "I still have reservations," he began, his tone hesitant. "We need more time to consider this from all angles before making a decision that could impact our town for years to come."

Patrea held Clive's gaze, her eyes unwavering. "I understand your concerns, Mr. Thompson. But I urge you to trust in the potential of this project. I know you want the best for Mooselick River. Your record of activities in that respect stands for itself. You have worked tirelessly in the past to create prosperity in our fair town. I only ask that you let me attempt to do the same."

Something in her tone suggested she wasn't asking for permission now but putting him on warning.

Clive folded his arms, his expression dubious. "But what about the added strain on our local resources? More people means more demand for water, electricity, and emergency services. Can our town handle the increased pressure that hosting events will bring?"

Patrea continued to meet Clive's gaze, her voice steady. "I've already considered those factors, Mr. Thompson. In my proposal, I've outlined plans to work closely with the utilities departments to ensure we can meet the venue's needs without putting a strain on town resources."

When he would have said something else, she rolled right over him. "Additionally, I plan to hire extra security and coordinate with emergency services to handle any issues that may arise during events. We're talking smaller weddings here, with under a hundred people including guests and participants—intimate affairs for those who want that cozy, small-town experience. Not stadium events hosting thousands. I don't recall anyone complaining when tourist buses started rolling into town twice a week during the summer."

Miles Higgins leaned forward, his tone earnest. "Clive, I understand your concerns, but we have a real opportunity to bring growth and prosperity to Mooselick River. The benefits of having a thriving event venue far outweigh the challenges you're speculating might exist. I think we should put this to a vote right now."

Ginger Martin nodded in agreement, her eyes alight with enthusiasm. "Think of all the jobs that will be created, Clive. The local economy will receive a much-needed boost with an influx of visitors spending money at our businesses. This could be a turning point for our town. After all our efforts, this could be the thing that puts us back on the map."

From where I sat, I could only see Martha Tipton's face from the side, but my vantage point was good enough to see fever-bright red staining her cheeks as she vibrated in her chair. Whether it was Ginger Martin or Clive Thompson causing her distress, I couldn't tell for sure. My money was on Ginger, who hadn't lifted a finger to help during any recent town event Martha had planned. Don't say anything, I thought hard in her direction. This wasn't the time for her to push. She must have heard my mental order because she clamped her mouth shut hard enough to bunch the muscles in her jaw.

Clive rubbed his chin thoughtfully as if weighing the arguments in his mind. He took a deep breath, his decision still hanging in the balance. "I appreciate all of your input, truly I do," Clive began, his voice measured. "Not to speak ill of the dead, but this board is still dealing with an issue of mismanaged funds. Until we have regained the trust of our constituents, I think this should be put before the entire town, not just the Select Board."

"You bite your tongue." Martha jumped out of her seat, fastened her hands on her hips, and gave Clive a withering stare. "You know as well as I do that the board approved the money to replace that old, broken-down wheelchair ramp. Just because we didn't take your suggestion and go for the cheap repair so we could spend the money on benches for the Veterans Memorial doesn't mean the funds were mismanaged."

Nose in the air, Clive said, "That was not the first time Bill Cavanaugh took it upon himself to release funding that wasn't approved by the entire board. Now, if you don't mind, I'd like to keep this discussion to the topic at hand."

Never mind that he'd been the one to bring it up.

If Martha could set a man on fire with merely a glance, Clive would have needed the fire department, but she sat back down. I could only imagine how much restraint it took for her to keep quiet. He'd been an ally of hers at one time, and this stubborn stance of his must rankle. Mentally, I took half the money I'd put on Ginger Martin back and put it on Clive's side. Both of them had made Martha's list tonight.

Patrea's brow furrowed slightly, a hint of anticipation in her eyes. Clive continued, his gaze sweeping across the room. "I want detailed projections on how this venture will impact our town's infrastructure. I want to see comprehensive plans on how you intend to mitigate any potential strains on our resources and community services."

The room fell into a thoughtful silence as Clive's request hung in the air, the weight of his words settling over them. Patrea nodded slowly, a determined glint in her eyes.

"I understand, Mr. Thompson. I will provide you with everything you need to make an informed decision. I wouldn't want to put you at odds with your fellow board members or the town."

Miles and Ginger exchanged a knowing look. Anyone with even the slightest understanding of human nature could see the silent understanding passing between them. It was two against one, and if Patrea called for a vote right now, it would go her way but cause disruption among the board members.

Seeing the same thing I did, Patrea nodded, allowing disappointment to flicker across her features. She'd give Clive the rope to hang himself, but the determined glint in her eye was as good as a warning. Thompson was in for more than he expected if it was paperwork he wanted. He'd tossed a gauntlet down in front of the wrong woman.

"Of course, Mr. Thompson." She kept repeating his name. A courtroom tactic if I ever heard one. "I appreciate your consideration, and I'm more than willing to work with you to address any concerns you may have."

As the meeting adjourned, Patrea left the select board room, catching my eye and giving me a nod. I caught up with her outside.

"Martha hasn't talked you into running for treasurer, has she?"

"No," I shook my head vehemently. "Not even close."

"Good." Patrea's eyes glittered with something between humor and fury. "Tell her I want the job, and I mean to get it, so she'd better have my back."

"Consider it had." Martha had come up behind Patrea without her noticing. "You have my full support."

Clive was in for a surprise come emergency election day. Newcomer or not, Patrea had not only married into one of the oldest families in town, but she'd made something of a name for herself by helping folks who needed legal help, whether they could afford it or not. She'd be good at the job, and with Martha's support backing her, I didn't see anyone else standing a chance.

"Any idea who else is running?" Patrea slowed her steps to match Martha's.

"So far? No one but you." Grinning, Martha pricked Patrea's bubble and patted her on the arm. "But you never know. Maybe Clive will talk Walter Prescott into throwing his hat in the ring." With those final words, Martha headed for her car, leaving the six of us standing together.

"Did we just uncover another possible motive for Bill's death?" Jacy kicked things off.

"Seems like a stretch to me," David said, standing next to Neena as he often did. "Unless the entire town was in on it."

We discussed possibilities for a few minutes until the three board members exited the building and interrupted the conversation.

"I don't think this is getting us anywhere," I finally said once they'd each driven off. "We can't discount anything at this point, but we need more information. Drew's got self-defense class tomorrow. A couple of the women from the bank signed up, so he'll see what he can learn from them."

"Jacy and I will keep our ears open at the shop," Neena said. "Maybe we'll finally hear something juicy. So far, we've come up short. People have been talking about the storm more than the murder. I think that's almost sad."

When David put a hand on her arm to console her, Neena almost absently rested her other hand on his for a moment. The pace might be glacial, but I'd eat my shoe if they didn't end up together. "I haven't been much help, either. Miranda's still working out her notice at Cappy's, and it's too early in the season to hire full-time cleaning staff, so I'm a one-person show at the moment. All my guests are from out of town, and the only time I get a break is when one of the part-timers handles the desk along with cleaning."

"You're stuck in your own little oasis, aren't you?" Patrea teased.

"Feel like it sometimes," he muttered.

"Most of our downtime is spent preparing things for the wedding." I felt like Bill wasn't getting my best efforts. His timing hadn't been great, but I couldn't exactly blame him for that. Almost two weeks into the investigation, we'd all stalled out. If something didn't turn up soon, I'd have an uninvited guest at my wedding.

"Don't blame yourself for that." Drew must have followed my thoughts. "We're doing the best we can, and as far as I'm concerned, our wedding takes precedence. It's Ernie's job to track down killers, not yours."

"The place is coming together," Chris said. "The lawn looks like a lawn again, and the house is almost ready for paint and—"

"Bill's not getting any deader." Brian cut him off in his haste to show support. "Tomorrow could be the day this whole thing pivots for us."

It was the best I could hope for. "You guys are the best." I felt so much better now.

CHAPTER TWENTY

"I have news." Dolly walked through my kitchen wall, bringing a chill to air now perfumed by the faint odor of perm solution and hair spray that always hovered over her. "Big news. I may have cracked the case."

Wouldn't that be nice? Between final dress fittings, getting the Wentworth ready, and preparing for the Spring Fling event over Memorial weekend, I'd given less thought to Bill's murder than I should have. Plus, he hadn't been nearly as pushy as other ghosts.

Even now, I should already be on my way to the florist to approve the vases that came in the day before. Bill definitely wasn't getting my best work.

"Tell me all about it."

Excited, Dolly began to talk and then shook her head. "Easier this way." Before I could work out what she intended to do, she'd already stepped so close that her features blurred, and then basically dove inside me with her icy, slimy, ghostly self.

"What are you doing?" I said out loud.

"Show not tell. Duh," Dolly's voice reverberated through my body as she pulled up the memory of what she'd seen, showing it to me as if I'd been her head the entire time.

I hated being possessed in this way because it felt like a violation of my free will, but I found the process fascinating.

The narration played through my head as if I was listening to an audiobook while I watched the action occur—weird but cool.

"I appreciate you squeezing me in like this," Edie Baker said, lifting her chin to let hairdresser Mara Tibbets attach the plastic cape around her neck. I know you don't usually open this early, but it's the only time I can get here this week."

Morning sun filtered through the windows, casting shadows across Mara's face.

"It's no problem. Happy to do it. Don't you worry about a thing. We'll get you fixed up in a jiffy."

The scents of beauty products lingered in the air, mingling with the gentle strains of jazz music playing in the background. Mara Tibbets, the bubbly hairdresser with a flair for gossip, ushered Edie to the shampoo sink.

Edie settled into the plush leather chair at the shampoo sink, closing her eyes as Mara massaged the suds into her hair. The week's stress began to melt away as she breathed in the calming scents of lavender and eucalyptus.

"Just lean back, honey. Is the water too hot?"

"No," Edie sighed as she felt Mara's strong fingers press and play over her scalp. "It's just right. I can't tell you how much I needed this today. My hair is out of control. I've let it go way too long, but I've been so busy working extra hours at the bank."

"It's that busy over there?" Mara worked in conditioner.

"Since the hiring freeze. We lost a teller, but Walter refuses to relent and take on anyone new."

Neither woman sensed the presence of resident ghost

and Mara's mother, Dolly Tibbets, who prided herself on never missing a hint of hot goss.

"What the heck is hot goss?" Dolly's voice overrode the narration and echoed through my head like a gong.

"Gah," I said out loud, "It means hot gossip."

"Oh." She fell silent again, thankfully, as the narrator continued.

Dolly quite relished her role as ghost spy. Since she'd stayed behind to keep watch over her daughter, helping Everly with her investigations gave the ghost something fun to do. If you couldn't whoop it up in the afterlife, Dolly thought, what was the point?

"Damn skippy," Dolly agreed at a headache-inducing level.

"Hush up, or I'll miss the good stuff," I warned her. This whole business of hearing her thoughts through the voice of the dreamlike narration threw me off kilter, but I didn't want to miss anything.

"If you ask me," Edie continued once Mara had finished rinsing. "He instituted the freeze to keep Robin Thackery from applying again. Can you just imagine putting her in charge of anyone's money?"

"I'm pretty sure that would trigger a run on the bank."

Now, Mara stood behind Edie's chair, scissors in hand, ready to work her magic. In the mirror, she confronted Edie's suddenly apprehensive expression.

"There are worse things that could happen, and I think they have. I know something, Mara," Edie whispered, glancing around nervously to ensure they were alone. "It's about Walter Prescott, my boss at the bank."

Mara's eyes widened with curiosity as she leaned closer,

eager to hear every juicy detail. "Tell me what happened, Edie. I promise I won't breathe a word to anyone."

Taking a deep breath, Edie launched into her tale of intrigue. "About a week before Bill died, Clive Thompson came to see him, and they got into an argument. I couldn't hear what it was about because they took it behind closed doors, but there were raised voices."

"Really?"

"It gets worse. Now that Bill is dead, Walter decided to run for town treasurer and bribed Clive Thompson to influence the election."

That didn't jibe with what I'd heard after the town meeting.

Mara gasped in shock, her hand flying to her mouth to stifle the exclamation. "No way! Are you serious, Edie?"

Edie nodded solemnly, her brow furrowed with worry. "Dead serious. Clive came to see Walter the day before yesterday and I overheard them talking. They were in Walter's office this time. It's more private than Bill's was."

"And you're certain there was a bribe involved? It couldn't have been something else"

"I don't see how it could have been anything else. Clive told Walter that he thought Bill had done something wrong and that they needed someone decent for the job. Someone who understood what it meant to work with key members of the board and had influence with some of the more prominent people in Mooselick River. Someone like Walter. Then, Clive said he could be instrumental in helping Walter get elected. And then, I heard Walter offer Clive a thousand dollars and Clive didn't even hesitate to accept. I don't know what to do."

Mara shook her head in dismay, her scissors forgotten as she processed the bombshell revelation. "That's just despicable, Edie. And to think, Clive Thompson seemed like such a respectable man. His mother must be spinning in her grave, but why would he do such a thing? Doesn't he have enough influence already? He's been third chair for the past four years."

"I don't know. I only overheard the conversation in pieces because a customer took our last penny rollers, and I had to get some from the storage closet to restock. They're stored all the way in the back, and you can't hear anything from there. I didn't dare to linger near the door for too long."

"Did they know you were there?" Mara said as she combed out a section of Edie's hair and made her first snip, sending strands to the floor.

"No. I held my breath and didn't move a muscle."

"Good. Men who are willing to take money for favors are willing to do worse if you ask me."

At that, Edie sucked in a breath, her wide eyes meeting Mara's in the mirror. "You don't think either of them had something to do with Bill Cavanaugh's death, do you?" She shivered at the notion.

If Mara didn't, Dolly certainly did. Everly would just about pee her pants when she got a load of this information.

"I am not in any danger of peeing my pants," I interrupted the retelling to assure her.

"If one of them did," Mara said, "it had to be Walter, right? If he's angling for Bill's position in town business, it seems like he had more reason to want Bill out of the way."

"Could be. I just don't know. It's enough to make me think I ought to be looking for a new job, except with Bill gone, Agnes should step into a promotion, which leaves room for a new loan officer, and I've got seniority. I'd hate to leave a job just in time to lose a promotion. But do I want to work for someone with so few scruples?"

Given her own difficulties with the bank, Mara hesitated to offer an opinion. If Edie moved up, maybe her chances of getting that expansion loan would improve. Still, if Mara offered encouragement at this point, Edie might decide her motives were suspect later. Worse, Edie might be in danger.

"I think you need to be careful. Someone's already dead, and what you heard might have had something to do with it. Maybe you should go to the police."

Every ounce of color leached from Edie's face. "I can't. It's too dangerous. I'll just forget I heard anything, and you need to do the same. If you don't, I'll deny everything."

Dolly Tibbets hovered nearby, listening in on their conversation. That cat, she thought, was out of the bag already. Even if Edie didn't know, she'd pulled the drawstring.

Mara paused for a moment, her heart going out to Edie as she pondered the gravity of the situation. With a reassuring smile, she placed a comforting hand on Edie's shoulder. "No one will hear a word about any of this from me. It's in the vault." She mimed turning a key in front of her lips. "What's said in the salon stays in the salon."

"Okay. I trust you." But Edie looked conflicted, her eyes clouded with uncertainty as if she wished she'd kept her mouth shut. "If anything happens to me, I want you to go to the authorities."

Mara squeezed Edie's shoulder gently, her gaze filled

with empathy. "Nothing will. We won't ever speak of this again, and no one will ever know."

As Mara spoke, her fingers deftly continued their work on Edie's hair, combing, snipping, and shaping. The rhythmic motion of her hands seemed to soothe Edie's nerves, offering a sense of calm amidst the storm of emotions swirling within her.

Mara's declaration lasted less than three minutes when she opened her mouth and brought up the subject again. "I'm not voting for Walter Prescott if he runs for treasurer."

"Me, either," Edie agreed. "I'd vote for the devil himself before I did."

"It might be time for Clive Thompson to make his graceful exit from town politics, too. It's obvious he can't be trusted."

For the first time since she'd unburdened herself, a smile flirted around Edie's lips. "No. He clearly can't."

"Then we'll just have to make sure neither one of them gets elected to any town office again, won't we?"

"We?" Edie wondered. "What can we do to stop them?"

"Plenty. It's time we got a few more women involved in what goes on around here. Martha Tipton has an appointment on Wednesday. I'll put a bug in her ear, and she won't even know it was me who did it."

"But you said you wouldn't tell anyone what happened." Edie was halfway out of the chair when Mara grabbed her arm and eased her back down.

"And so I won't. Just a gentle nudge in the right direction should do it. All I have to do is suggest someone else for treasurer—someone who is already in her good graces. Then, I'll do the same when it comes to Clive. You know they don't get along the way they used to—not since Duckie-Gate, anyway. You leave it to me. I know just the right button to push."

"You're a little bit scary, I think."

Laughing, Mara reached for the blow dryer. "Then it's a good thing I have the town's best interests at heart, isn't it?"

Still hovering to scoop up every single detail, Dolly's heart swelled with pride. Martha Tipton might think she was the only force in town. Martha Tipton would be wrong.

Once Edie left the shop, Dolly blinked out to find Everly and report what she'd overheard. If she felt a pang over betraying Edie's confidence in Mara, Dolly reasoned that her actions were for the greater good. One man was already dead, and she didn't want poor Edie's name to be added to the tally.

With the recitation over, Dolly shook me off like a dog shakes off snow and stepped away. I didn't appreciate the sensation and let her know.

"Never mind your delicate sensibilities," she waved my protest away. "What do you think about the information?"

"I think it bears more thought, and I'm late for my appointment, but it should help to know that Martha is already ahead of the game. She asked me to run for treasurer. I declined, but Patrea decided she'd like the job. I suspect Walter's gonna need more than Clive in his corner."

Dolly's arrival made me later than I'd planned to leave to meet Patrea at the mansion, so I put off adding notes to the message board until I'd had a chance to tell her everything I'd heard while it was all still fresh in my mind.

It would be just the two of us and the crew today since

the guys all had work and so did Jacy and Neena. With any luck, they'd hear something to help move things along today.

CHAPTER TWENTY-ONE

JACY AND NEENA

While Everly headed toward the Wentworth, Jacy's ears picked up the name of a woman suspected to be Bill's latest paramour.

As she slipped into the center of a round rack of vintage dresses, Jacy found Neena already there, poised and waiting to catch every morsel of gossip being exchanged between the two women nearby. Their voices carried a mix of shock and intrigue, blending with the rustle of hangers sliding along metal racks. But the excitement in their tone was unmistakable.

"What are you doing here?" Jacy mouthed. She'd been discreetly eavesdropping on customers all day but, so far, hadn't heard anything useful in solving Bill Cavanaugh's murder.

In response, Neena tilted her head and rolled her eyes in the direction the voices were coming from, then put her finger to her lips.

"I feel so sorry for poor Claire Higgins," one of the women said, making a slight effort to lower her voice. Jacy assumed neither woman was a regular shop customer because she didn't recognize their voices.

Delighted at their luck, Jacy and Neena listened in on the nearby conversation. Claire and her doomed love life were among the possible motives for Bill Cavanaugh's death. But at this point, she and her friends could only speculate that the two had been involved.

"Oh, I know, it's just dreadful," the other replied, her voice tinged with sympathy. "To lose Bill Cavanaugh in such a tragic way... And after they'd only been seeing each other for a few weeks. That girl is downright unlucky in love, I tell you!"

Finally, Jacy thought, we have verification that the two were an item. She had seen them together a few times around town, but hadn't realized they were dating until after he'd died. They certainly hadn't given off the lovey-dovey vibe. But then, you never knew, did you? Still waters run deep."

"After that business with Brandon Sinclair?" the first woman continued, her tone dropping to a scandalous stage whisper. "You'd think she'd have been more careful about jumping back on the dating bandwagon. Maybe he had something to do with the...you know what."

Jacy frowned at the mention of Brandon's name. From what she knew of him, Brandon seemed like a nice enough man—maybe not the sharpest pencil in the pack, but a decent guy.

"Brandon? You mean you think he had something to do with Bill Cavanaugh's murder?" the second woman asked, sounding intrigued.

"Well, rumor has it that he blamed Bill for foreclosing on his house," the first woman explained, her voice tinged with excitement. And you know how Brandon gets when he's angry. He's been telling anyone who will listen that Bill was out to get him—first, because the bank wouldn't give him more time to catch up on his payments, and then, later, for dating Claire."

The second woman gasped in shock, her hand flying to her mouth. "Goodness gracious! Do you think he would have...?"

"I wouldn't put it past him," the first woman replied darkly. And get this: Ever since Brandon and Claire broke up, he's been sleeping in the office at Pine Tree Auto Repair, where he works!"

Her companion shook her head in disbelief. "It's positively scandalous! And poor Claire got caught in the middle of it all. Who would have thought Bill Cavanaugh would get mixed up with the likes of her? You know she quit that fancy job she had? Just up and walked out without even giving notice."

Jacy could think of many reasons a woman might quit a job without notice—sexual harassment and not being paid what she was worth, to name two. Maybe Claire hadn't had a good reason, but perhaps she had. That didn't mean Claire and Bill were a match made in heaven, but she didn't see leaving a job as quite the character flaw the two gossiping women did. She also didn't see why Brandon should blame Bill for his financial woes, but maybe there was more to the story.

"I heard Claire and Bill were already on the outs when he died," the first woman continued, her voice tinged with sympathy. "And they hadn't been dating all that long, but you know how it is with rebound relationships."

The second woman's voice turned somber. "But which one was rebounding?"

"Why, both of them. You knew Bill and Carlene Nicholson got back together right after she came slinking back to town, but it didn't last long."

Their conversation trailed off into murmurs as the gossipers moved on to inspecting a rack of blouses, leaving Jacy and Neena to ponder the tangled web of relationships and secrets that seemed to be unraveling before their very ears. As they waited for the two women to take their purchases to Judy, the cashier at the front counter, Neena whispered, "Who was that? I didn't get a look at them, did you?"

Her head shaking, Jacy admitted she hadn't. "I had no idea Bill and Claire were getting serious."

"What are you doing in there?" The dresses parted to reveal newly-hired and indispensable employee Judy Jackson's arch stare. "Aren't you a little old to play hide and seek?"

Jacy's heart skipped a beat at Judy's sudden appearance, guilt coloring her cheeks as she scrambled for a plausible excuse. Neena shot her an amused glance, biting her lips to keep from laughing.

"We were just...pricing these dresses and noticed a problem with the rack," Jacy offered with a forced smile, hoping to divert any suspicion and keep the two gossipy customers from discovering they'd been overheard. "Everything's just fine. We have it under control. You go on ahead and wait on those customers. We'll be done here in a minute."

Judy's eyes narrowed as if she could see right through their feeble attempt to cover up their eavesdropping. "Uh-huh. I'll get right on that," she quipped sharply before turning away to assist the two women who had approached the counter to check out.

As they waited another minute to make it look like they'd fixed something, Jacy leaned in closer to Neena, her voice barely above a whisper. "It looks like Brandon might have had a motive."

Neena nodded. "Or two of them."

Jacy frowned thoughtfully, piecing together the snippets of information they had gathered. "Or else Claire was caught in a love triangle between Brandon and Bill."

"Or maybe Bill was caught in one between Claire and Brandon," Neena said, then frowned. "Wait, that's not what I meant."

Once the two customers had left the building, Jacy and Neena crawled out of their hiding place and joined Judy near the checkout counter.

"You tend to hear things," Jacy said to Judy. "Even if you don't pass them on. Is there any buzz to support the theory that Bill Cavanaugh and Claire Higgins were getting friendly before she split up with Brandon Sinclair?"

"I had my suspicions," Judy admitted with a knowing smile, her eyes glittering with hidden knowledge. "Claire and Brandon were doing very well before everything went south. People thought he bought that house because he planned to propose, but they split up before the ink was dry on his mortgage papers. Maybe he did propose, and she didn't want to get married again. Some people don't after a bad divorce."

She leaned in closer, ensuring Jacy and Neena were thoroughly captivated by her revelations. "Or she didn't want to because Brandon has a temper when something doesn't go his way. He also can't take responsibility for his own actions. According to him, Bill Cavanaugh pushed through a loan that he would never have been able to afford."

Neena frowned. "I wouldn't have figured Brandon for being a hothead the way he's always smiling."

Jacy nodded her agreement. "Same here. Are you sure?"

To her credit, Judy paused a moment to think. "You know, I've never seen any evidence of his temper. Honestly, I wouldn't be able to prove or disprove the theory. Not first-hand, anyway."

"What about Claire?" Neena said. "I know of her, of course, but I've never met her. What's she like?"

Judy shrugged. "From what I've heard, she's like any spoiled rotten brat who grew up and hit a few surprises when exposed to the harsher realities of life. And that her parents would have done her a favor if they'd said no every so often. But, again, this is all hearsay."

"You haven't met her?"

"Once or twice, but I haven't spent enough time with her to form an opinion. Still, everyone agrees she was in an abusive marriage, and no one deserves that. I'm sure it took some guts for her to walk away."

"I'm sure it did," Neena said, leaning her elbow on the counter.

"My sources haven't said much about how things were with her and Bill. I only know a little about how things were with Brandon because my neighbor likes to talk, and Brandon lived two doors down from her until he lost his place."

"Oh," Jacy said. "I knew that. I just forgot that I knew it."

Grinning, Judy said, "Mrs. Tucker called their relationship a recipe for disaster waiting to happen. Claire seeking solace in the arms of someone who seemed different but carried his own baggage, and Brandon hoping to find redemption in someone who embodied everything he yearned for but couldn't truly have."

Neena snorted. "Sounds like a soap opera."

"Those would be Mrs. Tucker's obsession. She sees herself as one of the soap opera divas who dangles everyone like a puppet on a string, except no one pays her any attention, and even if they do, she's far too obvious to get away with anything. She lives in her imagination a lot."

"Are you saying everything you just told us is BS?"

But Judy shook her head. "I don't think so. The two women you were spying on just now had similar things to say, even if the language wasn't as dramatic. You want drama, you should have been here when Millie Nicholson came in yesterday. According to her, Carlene got caught in the crossfire of Bill and Claire's romance. Carlene came back thinking she and Bill could make a go of it this time around, but Claire got her hooks in him, and poor little Carlene got her heart broken...again."

As Jacy and Neena absorbed Judy's words, they realized they could have just asked her for the latest gossip instead of hiding in the racks and eavesdropping. It would have saved time and the embarrassment of being caught.

"You have to love this town with all the drama lurking

beneath the surface," Neena grinned. "It's what makes life interesting."

Jacy nodded in agreement, her mind racing with all the new information they had just learned. None of it seemed overly helpful, but then, you never knew what piece of information would tip the scales of a case.

Before they could delve deeper into the subject of Claire and Bill, the bell above the shop's entrance chimed once more, signaling the arrival of a new customer. Jacy and Neena exchanged a knowing glance, silently acknowledging that their day was far from over as they prepared to assist the newcomer.

Since they'd learned nothing else of note, Neena sent Jacy home at closing time and stayed behind to update the murder message board.

CHAPTER TWENTY-TWO

The morning after Jacy and Neena dropped their gossip bomb on the message board, we planned to meet at the Wentworth. I'd just put my car in gear when my phone rang, and the bank's number appeared on the screen. I couldn't have been more surprised.

"Hello?" I answered.

"This is Walter Prescott calling for Ms. Dupree."

"This is she." What did he want?

"It's come to my attention that you recently met with our loan officer. May I ask why you didn't follow through with your loan application? Was there a problem with Ms. Cunningham's performance?"

Nosy. Still, he'd given me the perfect opening for a face-to-face meeting. According to Dolly, he was in cahoots with Clive Thompson over being made the next town treasurer. Not if I could help it.

"I'd rather not discuss this over the phone," I said, letting my tone suggest there had been a problem. I'm heading out for the day, but I can make time to meet with you at your office. If you'd like me to drop by, we can talk."

Drew had left an hour earlier, taking Molly with him. With the shop in Judy's capable hands, Jacy and Neena would meet us after dropping Wade off at Leandra's. Other than David, who'd had to bow out because of a last-minute booking, it was all hands on deck for mulching and bedding in the last of the annuals, which would make my wedding venue sparkle with color.

There was a pause on the other end of the line, and then, "I'm not in my office at present. Would it be possible for you to meet me for coffee at the new bakery? I can be there in five minutes."

Did he not want Agnes to know we'd spoken?

"Sure. I'll head right over."

"See you then." He rang off.

I texted Patrea to tell her what was up and got back a series of emojis suggesting she'd like me to bring baked goods and coffee. I texted her a thumbs-up and drove to the bakery.

Once dreary and almost wholly vacant, the town center now bustled with activity. The front window at Knit Up featured their best-selling product. A dozen pots rested on racks designed to elevate the handles, which were covered by a veritable rainbow of crocheted cozies—pornographic cozies, no less. Whether they were intended to look like that, I couldn't say, but they had certainly generated conversation.

When I chose a table from those few that ranged around the front of the bakery, Walter hadn't arrived, so I took a moment to chat with the owners, Leland and June Cobb. I'd gone to school with Leland, who went by Landy, as opposed to my father, who went by Lee, making it easy to keep them separate.

I went to the counter and put in my coffee order and a larger one to take to the rest of the group at the Wentworth. "I'm meeting someone, so if you could hold off on the to-go order until I give you the signal, that would be good. How's Landy's dad doing?"

"He had his final treatment at the end of January," June smiled as she swirled foam into my latte. She'd added pale pink tips to her platinum hair and let it grow out a bit over the winter. Still, she reminded me of a charming pixie. "The treatments were hard on him, but his latest PET scan came back clean. I think having us here was a big boost for him."

"Family is everything," I said as I paid for my latte and smiled back at her. "How's business?" I had a vested interest since having the town run smoothly kept Martha Tipton off my back. "Are you stocked up and ready for the Spring Fling?"

The event was just days away, and I'd had to bow out of most of the organizing this time around. Thankfully, Martha had decided to do a reprise of the event from the year before, so hadn't needed me, anyway. I wasn't even planning to attend.

"We sure are," Landy said, joining his wife. "If it's as busy as Aunt Patty says, we can put some money back against the lean months. I really want to make a go of it here."

Walter arrived just then, so I didn't have time to outline any of the ideas that had been niggling in the back of my head. It might be time to start an association for local business owners to discuss ways they could promote each other. In a town the size of Mooselick River, there wasn't a lot of room for competition, and as Grammie Dupree used to say, if one life preserver is good, two is the next best thing to a raft.

With his mincing gait and stocky frame, Walter reminded me of David Suchet's portrayal of Hercule Poirot—minus the mustache and cane, of course.

While he ordered, I returned to my chosen table and waited for him to join me. Once we got the pleasantries out of the way, I said, "Thank you for meeting me, Mr. Prescott. You asked about Ms. Cunningham's performance. Did you have specific concerns?"

"Please, call me Walter." He took a hurried sip of his coffee, then winced when it burned his tongue. "I'd like to keep this informal."

"Okay," I nodded and waited for him to answer the question.

"As you know, Bill Cavanaugh died recently."

"Yes. Tragic. What were you doing when it happened? Do you remember?"

He looked at me as if he thought me ghoulish for asking, but I needed to know.

"I was doing what any sensible person should do on a night like that. Staying inside out of the weather and working on a jigsaw puzzle. I find them quite calming."

"With your wife? Does she like puzzles, too?"

"Normally, but my wife wasn't feeling well, so she took some nighttime cold medicine and went to bed early."

If that stuff worked on Mrs. Prescott the same way it worked on me, he could have left the house and come back without her being any the wiser. Walter had no alibi. Before I could probe further, he pulled the conversation back to his intended topic.

"In any case, Bill's death opened up a potential position at the bank. I intended to promote him to senior loan officer. Now, I'm forced to decide between promoting from within or hiring someone outside the bank. It would be helpful if you could tell me more about your experience. Agnes—Ms.

Cunningham, that is, can be a bit aggressive at times. Some people find that type of behavior off-putting."

It was easy to see that he lumped himself in with those people, so I went with my gut and took the opposite position to see what he'd do.

"That wasn't my experience at all. In fact, I found her to be quite deferential. And thorough. She explained how much equity I could expect to borrow against and then expressed concern over my ability to make the payments given my current income should I borrow the maximum amount."

Why did he look pained?

"So she advised against the loan, and you chose not to move forward?"

"Not exactly, but I suppose it might look that way." I leaned forward. "We both know I didn't need a loan, don't we, Walter?"

Now, his face flushed, and he swallowed hard. On one hand, he wanted information, but on the other, he didn't want to annoy someone who might be considered an asset to the bank.

"Yes, well, you can see why I might have questions. I wouldn't want you to think it necessary to take your business elsewhere."

Finally, we were at the crux of the matter. To give myself time to figure out how to use this information to my advantage, I picked up my latte and watched him over the rim as I sipped and swallowed.

"Is it true Clive Thompson is putting his weight behind you for the position of town treasurer?"

Eyes widening, he let it show that I'd caught him off balance.

"I intend to put my name in the hat," he finally admitted. "But I wouldn't say Clive is a factor in making that decision."

Tilting my head but keeping my gaze locked on his face, I gave him a measuring look until his eyes flickered away.

"So you didn't offer him an...incentive to back you over someone else?"

This time, when Walter tipped up his coffee cup, he drank like a drowning man gasping for air, which he then was because the coffee was still on the hot side. Gasping, he held up one hand, so I waited until he was finished spluttering.

"Wherever did you get that idea?" If his face got any redder, I feared he might need medical assistance, but he still couldn't look me in the eye.

"It's not true, then?"

"Of course, it's not true. Clive asked me to run because he thought I'd be the best man for the job. Reluctantly, I agreed."

I leaned back in my chair, caught owner June Cobb's eye, nodded that she should get the rest of my order together, and then tapped one finger on the table. "You made what appeared to be a heartfelt speech at Bill Cavanaugh's funeral. It seems odd that you'd be so quick to throw in with someone who leveled some fairly serious accusations against him during his time in office. Unless your speech was just an act."

"How dare you say such a thing to me? Bill was a good person. Decent, honest, and kind. The type to go above and beyond for our customers. A true man in every sense of the word." Walter found his courage again.

"And yet, Clive accused him of misappropriating town funds," I kept my tone mild.

"Why the sudden interest in town affairs? I'm well aware Martha Tipton implied the job of treasurer was yours for the asking. Did she send you here to psych out the competition?"

"You called me, remember?" My coffee had cooled enough to drink freely, so I drained the cup. "To answer your question, I had no problem with Agnes Cunningham or anything else related to the loan process at the bank. I merely chose not to follow through with it for my own reasons. As you well know, I don't need the money."

Reminding me of a fish in a tank, he opened his mouth several times and closed it again but declined to speak.

"And," I continued, "You should know I have no intention of running for treasurer. Despite what you may have heard, Martha only asked me if I'd consider running. I turned her down flat. My friend Patrea, on the other hand, is quite keen to be elected. Martha's influence, along with any I might possess, will be directed toward her."

With that, I left him sitting there, retrieved the bag of pastries and carry holder of coffees I'd paid for, and sailed past him. He'd told me a great deal more about himself than he realized.

Back in the car, I considered what I'd learned so far during the drive to the mansion. Lost in thought, I didn't register the presence of flashing blue lights until I was halfway down the driveway. When I did, I floored it. Spewing gravel, I pulled up next to Drew's truck, jumped out of the car, and headed for the cluster of people standing at the foot of the front steps. My heart kicked in my chest.

"What's wrong? What happened?"

"It's okay," Drew said, though his expression looked carved in stone. "No one's hurt."

"Speak for yourself," Jerry Kaminski said, speaking loudly as he stepped toward Drew, forcing Ernie Polk to shoot out a hand and stop him. "I want that dog put down. She bit me."

"Nipped you, you mean." Unlike Jerry's outraged tone, Drew kept his voice low and even. Almost a growl. Anyone who knew him well could tell he was in a dangerous mood. "Barely."

Fear receding, I looked toward Molly, who sat calmly nearby. "Are you saying Molly bit you? My Molly?"

Hearing her name, she came to me, executed one of her whole-body wiggles, and rubbed against my leg until I reached down to pet her.

Jerry's face froze. "She's your dog?"

"Yes." My forehead wrinkled in confusion. I looked at Drew for answers, but with all his attention focused on giving Jerry the stinkeye, he didn't notice. "She's my dog."

"Not his?" Jerry pointed toward Drew.

"I guess she's ours, but she was mine first. What's going on here?" I nudged Ernie since no one else seemed inclined to talk.

"Jerry says Molly attacked him, and he thinks she should be put down for aggression." Even Ernie couldn't make that statement believable since he knew as well as I did that Molly was the sweetest lover dog you could ever meet.

"Attacked is a strong word, I suppose," Jerry walked it back.

Next to me, Drew stiffened, but he didn't say anything.

"Tell me exactly what happened," I ordered.

When Jerry opened his mouth to speak, Patrea stepped forward and talked over him. "Jerry showed up a little while ago looking for a trowel he'd possibly left here when he finished the job. When he didn't find it, he decided to wait around until you got here because he thought you might know where it was."

"How would I know where it was? I didn't use his tools."

Letting an elegantly arched eyebrow convey her inner thoughts, Patrea said, "Be that as it may, while Jerry was waiting, he took it upon himself to help Drew spread mulch around the rosebushes. Things were said, I guess, and Jerry raised a rake and walked toward Drew in what Molly took to be a menacing manner. She barked a warning, but when Jerry continued to advance, she tried to grab him by the leg of his pants and pull him back. Apparently, she miscalculated and nipped his calf."

Half of me wanted to bite him myself, and the other half wanted to give Molly a treat and tell her next time to go for blood, but I knew Ernie wouldn't take it well if I did either of those things. Instead, I opted for damage control and killing with kindness.

"I'm sorry, Jerry. Truly, I am. Molly's never done anything like this before." Ignoring the sound that came through Drew's clenched teeth, I stepped forward and laid my hand on Jerry's arm. "Can I see? How bad is it?"

Over Jerry's shoulder, I caught Ernie rolling his eyes. I totally agreed.

Mollified, Jerry pulled up his pants leg to reveal a hairy calf that sported a small red mark. "Oh, that's just awful. I'm so sorry. I don't know what got into her. Molly's usually so gentle. She couldn't have known you meant Drew no harm."

I kept making a big deal about the injury and profusely apologizing until he patted me on the shoulder.

"It doesn't even hurt. Don't you worry your pretty head for another minute. Honestly, I feel much better knowing you have a dog around to protect you. We won't bring it up again."

"I take it you don't intend to press charges?" Ernie deadpanned.

"No. Of course not. It was just a misunderstanding," Jerry laid on so much smarm his tone was thicker than Grammie Dupree's gravy.

He didn't look quite as pleased when Ernie turned to Drew. "What about you? Do you want to file for attempted assault? I'd say you have plenty of witnesses."

But Drew shook his head. "I'm good. If that trowel turns up," he paused and pinned Jerry with a look, "I'll make sure it's returned. Personally."

It wasn't exactly a threat, but it was definitely a threat.

"I guess that's settled," Ernie said, reaching down to scratch Molly between the ears and then looking at Jerry. I'll follow you back to town. See that you don't come to any more harm."

Neatly boxed in, Jerry headed for his truck.

"Keep your hands clean, Parker," Ernie warned before he followed.

"You don't need to worry about me," Drew slid an arm around my waist, not just for Jerry's benefit. "I know how to brush off a fly without using a swatter."

Ernie nodded and made good on his promise to follow Jerry back to town.

"Well, that was interesting," I said. "I've got coffee and snacks."

Giving me a squeeze, Drew let a smile tug the corner of his lips up. "I hope you got an extra muffin or something. Molly needs to get the taste of jackass out of her mouth."

We got to work while, across town, my mother had an encounter that added to our investigation.

CHAPTER TWENTY-THREE

KITTY

Her mind dwelling on murder when it should have been on work, the cozy confines of the town library didn't offer Kitty Dupree its usual comfort as she shelved books. It was too quiet today—if too much quiet in a library were possible. She had always loved working here, surrounded by the musty scent of old paper and the endless rows of knowledge and stories. Today, she had more on her mind than books.

Between Bill's death and Everly's wedding plans changing, Kitty's mind churned constantly, making it difficult to focus on the restoration work waiting in her office. Three weighty tomes of historical significance needed their bindings preserved for inclusion in a Portland museum exhibit. She should have had them finished and shipped out today, but one still needed her undivided attention.

It certainly didn't help that Ginger Martin was late for work again. No doubt she'd breeze in with some excuse about town business taking up her time, and with the lack of a treasurer right now, the excuse would be genuine. Even so, you don't take a job if you don't intend to do it to the best of your ability. These were words Kitty lived by.

As she reached for a stack of books, the hushed tones of

Althea Gallow's soft exclamation reached her ears from the neighboring aisle.

When Kitty rounded the corner, Althea stood in front of the new releases section. Long, wispy locks in desperate need of a hair appointment fell over the woman's face as she flipped through the latest in a long-running futuristic mystery series. Ever since Althea's husband, Able, had been sent to jail for the murders of Grace Belanger and Delly Harper, she'd stopped taking care of herself. Seeing the poor woman so reduced tweaked Kitty's heartstrings.

As if sensing another's presence, Althea turned and caught Kitty's eye. She offered a timid smile and held up the book she was scanning through.

"Hi, Althea. How are you today?"

With the hint of a newfound sparkle in her eyes, Althea beckoned Kitty over to her side. "Have you read this series yet? I've been waiting for the newest book to come out," Althea exclaimed, her voice filled with excitement. "It's by one of my favorite authors. I thought it might take my mind off my troubles. Reading often does now that it's just me in the house."

Kitty stepped closer, her curiosity piqued. She examined the book cover adorned with intricate designs and cryptic symbols hinting at the enigmatic tale within. "No. But that series has been on my list to start. I've heard great things about it. Do you think it's worth recommending?" she asked, eager to hear Althea's opinion.

"Oh, absolutely!" Althea nodded enthusiastically. "If this one is like the rest of the series, the plot twists will keep you on the edge of your seat, and the way the author weaves clues and red herrings together is simply brilliant. You have to try it," she insisted, her enthusiasm both rare and infectious.

As they continued their conversation, Kitty couldn't help but wonder about Althea's other reading preferences. "Do you like other genres? Or is it only mysteries you enjoy?" Kitty asked, genuinely curious.

"I used to read romance novels when I was younger, but lately, it's the whodunits I can't seem to get enough of." Althea paused for a moment, a thoughtful expression crossing her features. "These futuristic ones are entertaining, but I also have a soft spot for historical mysteries with a touch of the supernatural. There's something enchanting about unraveling secrets from the past or delving into what might be that takes me out of everyday life."

If a touch of sadness stole over Althea's features, it was only to be expected, given the rough patch she'd been going through lately.

Kitty smiled to herself, grateful for the small moments of connection she shared with the library's regulars. These small interactions made her job so fulfilling, and she couldn't imagine being anywhere else.

"Speaking of mysteries, I do hate to bother you, Kitty, but I have something I feel I should tell someone, and you always treat me...the same as you ever did," Althea lowered her voice to speak urgently, her eyes going wide with concern.

The change in Althea's demeanor was both abrupt and upsetting. "What is it, Althea? You seem quite distressed." More than she had at her brother's funeral.

Althea glanced around cautiously before moving closer,

her voice barely above a whisper. "I saw something last week that's had me terribly worried ever since."

A quiet woman to begin with, Althea had practically become a ghost since her husband's arrest the previous fall. She'd dropped out of sight except for the occasional trip to town for groceries and a stop at the library. Kitty wished she could do something to help, but every attempt ended the same way—with Althea skittering off like a scared rabbit.

"What did you see?" Kitty encouraged.

"I don't know if it's my place to say anything, but I stopped in at my favorite diner for a bite after my doctor's appointment in Bangor, and I saw Walter Prescott having lunch with Carlene Nicholson. This was the week before the storm, and it looked like they were up to something."

"Up to something?" Kitty's brow furrowed with concern as she processed Althea's words. "Walter Prescott? The manager of the bank? What could he possibly be up to with Carlene Nicholson?" One thing leaped to mind, but Kitty had trouble with that particular mental image given that Walter was married, at least ten years too old for Carlene, and not at all her usual type.

"I don't know the man all that well," Althea shook her head, her expression troubled. "And I wasn't sitting that close, but it didn't look innocent, Kitty. They were huddled together, speaking in hushed tones, and Carlene had a mischievous glint in her eye."

Kitty's mind raced with possibilities as she considered the implications of Althea's revelation. "Do you think Walter could be cheating on his wife?"

Again, Althea shrugged. "Maybe. But don't you see? They're both connected to my brother. He used to date the

Nicholson girl, and Walter Prescott was his boss. You don't suppose they were plotting to do away with him, do you? I know I shouldn't jump to conclusions, but it looked awful funny to me."

As she heard Ginger Martin arriving for work through the back door, Kitty placed a comforting hand on Althea's shoulder. "I'm glad you came to me with this. I'll keep an eye on Walter Prescott and Carlene Nicholson. If I find out they had anything to do with Bill's death, you can be sure I'll do whatever I can to uncover the truth and put a stop to it."

Still clutching the mystery novel to her chest, Althea nodded gratefully, her eyes shimmering with unshed tears. "Thank you, Kitty. I didn't know who else to tell. People don't look at me the way they did before..." she trailed off since they both knew what she meant. "They figure I should have known what Able was like, and maybe they're right."

"Now, Althea," Kitty reached over to put her hand on the distressed woman's shoulder. She'd have offered a comforting hug, but Althea went stiff with only a simple touch. "You can't go back and second-guess yourself just because you weren't looking for evil where you had no reason to think you'd find it. What Able did, well, it didn't have a thing to do with you. I know that, and so do most of the people in this town. The decent ones, anyway."

The rest of them should be ashamed for putting this poor woman through more than she'd already been forced to endure.

After swallowing hard a couple of times, Althea nodded. "I appreciate that. More than I can say. But Kitty, just be careful. Maybe it's because of Able, or maybe because I've read too many books like this one, but it's bad enough my brother is dead. I don't want anyone else to get hurt."

Kitty squeezed Althea's shoulder reassuringly. "I'll be careful." Since Althea seemed to have exhausted her conversational needs for the day, she bobbed her head and then carried the book to the counter to be checked out. After she'd gone, Kitty grabbed a pad and paper to make notes on what she'd just heard, which, once she put it down in black and white, wasn't all that much. She should have asked more questions.

She'd just tucked the note into her pocket when Ginger walked in.

"I know. I'm late, but it couldn't be helped. Town business, you know. I swear, if it's not one thing, it's two others. I don't know how I find the time to manage it all. There are just not enough hours in the day."

"I suppose not," Kitty said, allowing a hint of annoyance to color her tone. "But this isn't a volunteer position, Ginger. I expect you to arrive on time for your shifts. If you cannot fit the library into your busy schedule, I can always offer your job to someone who can."

Ginger's look said, how dare you, but her mouth said, "I've already apologized once."

"Did you? I must have missed that amid your list of excuses. In any case, I have urgent work in my office. You'll need to finish re-shelving the returns. Please check to make sure none of them are on the holds list for another patron before you do. If you need me...well, please don't."

Leaving Ginger staring after her, Kitty retired to her office before she could give in to temptation and fire the woman. Years they'd worked together in harmony—right up until Ginger got elected to the Select Board and decided she was too important for menial tasks anymore.

Before she got out her bookbinding supplies, Kitty went online to update the murder message board but decided her news was better delivered in person, so decided to stop at Everly's house on her way home.

CHAPTER TWENTY-FOUR

"I'm sorry to drop by unannounced," my mom said when she walked through my front door on her way home from work. "I had some restoration work that took longer than expected, and Ginger was late again, so I haven't had a chance to call. But I have news, and it seemed better to tell you before...well, in person."

After declining my offer of coffee or tea, she perched on the edge of her favorite chair in my living room. Tension showed itself in the way she fidgeted with the collar of her blouse.

"You remember Althea, dear? Althea Gallow." Mom began, her brow furrowed with worry. "Well, she approached me in the library, looking as troubled as ever."

I nodded, my curiosity piqued. "Yes, I remember her. Until Bill's funeral, I hadn't seen her since what happened with Able. Even before her troubles, I remember her as quiet and reserved."

Mom sighed, her gaze distant as she recalled their conversation. "Indeed she is. But today, she seemed even more distressed than usual. She told me she saw Walter Prescott having lunch with Carlene Nicholson in Bangor a few days before the storm, and it looked like they were up to something."

My eyes widened in surprise at the revelation. "Walter Prescott and Carlene Nicholson? That's unexpected." Walter's name seemed to be popping up a lot these days. "Did she get close enough to hear anything?"

She shook her head, her expression troubled. "No, but Althea seemed convinced it wasn't innocent. She's worried they might have been involved in something sinister, especially given their connections to Bill."

My mind raced with possibilities. "I don't know Mr. Prescott well enough to talk to him about his personal life, but I can pin Carlene down and see what she has to say about it. She pops in at the Wentworth place every couple of days because she's hoping to get a job with Patrea if the wedding venue scheme goes forward."

"Okay," Mom nodded in agreement, a determined glint in her eye. "You handle her, and if she doesn't spill the details, I'll give Walter Prescott a poke. After all, he's on the library board, so it wouldn't be difficult to find an excuse to get in a room with him."

"Just make sure it's a room with a safety exit. If he's involved in Bill's death, he could be dangerous. I don't want you getting hurt."

Apparently, when a daughter expresses concern, it gets a mother's dander up. Or that's how it works with mine.

"Give me a little credit for having decent people skills and an ounce or two of common sense."

Whoops.

"I do, Mom. No one knows that better than me. I didn't know Walter was on the library board. How well do you know him?"

"Well enough to say I can't see him as a killer. The man will pinch a penny until it cries, but I just can't work my way around to a mental image of him pulling a trigger, much less hacking roof rafters to cover up a crime. He's a paper-pushing, number-crunching, bottom-line kind of guy."

Thinking back to what others had said of him, I realized all that played for me, but there was one other factor to consider. "Can you picture him and Carlene Nicholson together? You know, romantically?"

She shrugged—or maybe she shuddered. "Given the age difference, I wouldn't have said so, but you never know."

"That's my point. You never know what a person is capable of until they show you. Take Brandon Sinclair, for instance. According to the notes Jacy and Neena added to the board today, he has a wicked temper when things don't go his way."

"No, he doesn't," she looked at me like I'd sprouted a second head. "Who told them that?"

"The notes say they heard it from Judy, who heard it from her neighbor, Mrs. Tucker."

Mom snorted. "I wouldn't put much stock in anything Gladys Tucker says. She's never seen a molehill she couldn't talk up to be a mountain."

"He had a right to be upset. According to Maryann, Bill had a habit of pushing loans through even if the numbers weren't on his side. If he did that to help Brandon get his house, and then Brandon couldn't keep up the payments, I could see where he might be upset. And that's before you add on that Bill dated Claire after she broke things off with Brandon. That's strike two."

"He's not a lodge member."

I found her response frown-worthy. "I don't see what that has to do with anything."

"Tim says he only made keys for lodge members. If Brandon wasn't one, he wouldn't have a key."

"He wouldn't need one if Bill got there first and let him in. Did Dad have any luck getting that list from Tim?"

She shook her head. "He said the log book turned up missing."

I wrinkled my nose. "Where did we land on the plow truck timeline?"

"Nowhere good if Red was your prime suspect. I have three reliable reports that track his progress through town. He wouldn't have had time to stop, kill Bill, *and* sabotage the roof. Also, another of my sources confirmed the stranded motorist story. Red pulled her husband's car out of a snowbank."

He hadn't been high on my suspect list, and this didn't entirely bump him off, but it pushed him all the way to the bottom.

Citing the need to get home, Mom left a minute or two before Drew came in with takeout from Bertino's. The spicy red sauce and garlic bread scents reminded me how many hours had passed since lunch.

"Was your mom here?" After planting a quick kiss on my lips, he carried the bags to the kitchen, set them on the table, and sent Molly into ecstasy with belly scratches.

"She stopped by with news." I gave him a quick rundown while I set the table, then settled across from him and dug into a tub of spaghetti and meatballs. Drew wasted no time following my lead since he had to be back at work in an hour.

"Long day for you," I said as he pulled a large order of salad from a second bag, which he then balled up and lobbed toward the trash can before dividing the greens into two bowls.

"Not so bad. Riley handled the gym for an hour, leaving me to finish the week's paperwork, but she has plans this evening. You'll be happy to know that I was able to get two women from the bank to sign up for tonight's self-defense class. I'll do my best to charm information out of them."

"Better go easy on the garlic bread, then." I grinned at him.

"Not that kind of charm," he grinned back. "I save all that for you, and if we're both suffering from garlic breath, we'll cancel each other out."

"I don't have any plans tonight. Should I come to class with you?"

"To save me from wanton bank women?"

I snorted out a laugh. "I think you can handle yourself."

He shook his head just as my phone rang. When I got up to retrieve it, I saw Martha Tipton's name on the screen and nearly hit the ignore button.

"She'll just call again." Drew read my mind. "You might as well take it."

Sighing, I answered. "Hi, Martha. What can I do for you?"

"You have to meet me at the town office. The Spring Fling…it's all a disaster. Say you'll come. I need you."

Always the drama with this one.

"I've had a long day, Martha. Can't we meet tomorrow?"

"It has to be tonight," her voice went up an octave, edging quite close to what I considered shrill. "Say you'll come."

"What's the problem? At least give me some idea. Maybe I can fix it from here."

"No. You can't. It's awful, I can't even tell you. It has to be tonight. Meet me in an hour. Say you'll come. You just have to. I can't do this without you."

I'd had enough experience with Martha to know the perceived crisis probably wasn't that bad, but she wouldn't let up until I agreed, so I did and hung up. "Looks like you're on your own with the wanton women after all."

Drew reached across the table to pat my hand in consolation. "So I heard. I'm sure you'll sort it all out in no time."

Since I had to leave before he did, Drew offered to put the dishes in the dishwasher so I could shower off a few layers of sweat and grime from stripping wallpaper in the downstairs powder room at the Wentworth.

"Remember, you don't put plates in front of bowls, or they won't get clean," I said on my way to the bathroom.

"I know." He waved me away.

He didn't know. His approach to loading the dishwasher lacked even a basic level of common sense or logic, but at least he tried. I'd fix it later, I decided as I stepped under the hot water.

When I got to the town office, Martha's car was already in the lot, which didn't surprise me. In Martha's estimation, being on time meant being at least fifteen minutes early. Hoping whatever had happened would be easy to fix, I went inside and headed for the meeting room.

"Surprise!"

The chorus of voices took me off guard. For a moment, I couldn't take in what was happening as I surveyed the beaming faces turned in my direction.

My mother was there, as were Jacy, Neena, Patrea, and Leandra, plus Judy from the shop and June Cobb. Bess Tate's face split into the biggest grin I'd ever seen her wear. Patricia, Martha's other partner in crime, clapped her hands. There were others, too. Barb Dexter, Mabel, Thea, and several of Leo's tenants smiled back at me. These must have been Riley's evening plans. The room was packed with women.

"You didn't figure it out, did you? We've been so careful," Martha said, hugging me and beaming. "Happy Bridal Shower."

"I hadn't a clue," I answered truthfully over the lump that rose in my throat. "You totally pulled it off."

My first instinct was to say this hadn't been necessary. It wasn't my first wedding, but when I saw the joy on all their faces, I realized it *was* necessary, for them, anyway. They'd come together to show their love and respect. Tossing such a kind gesture back in their faces would suck all the joy away, and I wouldn't do that.

"I'm overcome." I gave them the truth and gave it to them with tears to prove it.

"Enough with the sob-fest," Bess Tate declared. "This is a party. Let's whoop it up."

She had a good thirty years on me, but I was under no illusion that if there were a whooping it up contest, Bess would put us all to shame. Two seconds later, she proved it when she raised her voice, "When's the stripper coming?"

Scandalized, Martha rounded on her. "This is a bridal shower, not a bachelorette party. Have some dignity, Bess."

"You have some dignity," Bess retorted. "I'd rather have some hot-diggity."

Pinch-faced, Martha announced her intention to ignore Bess for most of the evening—a plan that lasted through playing a few bridal games but went spectacularly awry during the opening of gifts.

During Pass the Bouquet, a version of musical chairs, Bess hip-checked Martha and knocked her out of the circle. Martha let it go. She also let it go when they were on the same team for creating a toilet paper wedding gown, and Bess "accidentally" tossed a handful of iridescent glitter in Martha's hair.

Wearing the winning gown, I sat in a chair decorated with streamers and silk flowers to open gifts. I'd already sniffled over Martha's handwritten recipe book and waggled my eyebrows at Leandra, who gifted me a collection of herbal massage oils. Jacy, Neena, and Patrea got squeals and hugs over the two-day couples spa retreat they'd chipped together on. And I cried full-on when my mother presented me with the locket she'd worn on her wedding day.

"This one," Bess grabbed the gift Jacy had planned to give me next and substituted another. "It's from me."

I untied the ribbon, opened the deep purple box, and peeled back the tissue paper to reveal a set of truly scandalous undergarments. The panties, if you could call them that, basically consisted of some ribbons in a crisscross pattern held together with small metal rings. The bra defied the definition. It was nothing more than the under-wires held together with more ribbons and a narrow silk strap that I assumed was meant to cross over the nipple area.

"Hold it up," Bess ordered as heat burned across my face. I was blessed—or maybe cursed—with the pale skin that goes along with being a natural redhead.

When she wouldn't relent, I did as she said, and Martha gasped. "Where did you get that?"

A mental image of Bess Tate wandering around a shop that sold such wares was more than my imagination could stand and still allow me to keep a straight face. Humor edged out embarrassment as the scene played out in my head. At least she hadn't bought me a set of edible underwear. Or worse, something battery-operated.

Next to me, Jacy let out a soft snort, and I assumed she'd gone there in her head, too.

"Frederick's of Hollywood," Bess said in a tone that implied Martha was an idiot for not jumping to a natural conclusion. "Had to go online because they stopped sending catalogs."

"You went online?" I couldn't tell if Martha was stunned by the action or the results.

"I know how to use a computer," Bess defended herself with acid on her tongue. "You want to get someone in the baby-making business you've got to prime the pump a little. Once Drew gets a load of her in this, we're looking at a done deal."

Quivering with silent laughter, Jacy handed me the final gift in an attempt to change the subject. This one was from Patricia.

Unfortunately, a collection of the famous panhandle cozies did nothing to improve the mood.

"Why did you get her a set of willie warmers?" Bess demanded. "Don't you know he needs to keep his goods cool if they want to get pregnant?"

The words fell out of my mouth so quickly that I heard them along with everyone else. "Wouldn't fit anyway."

Jacy lost it. I lost it. My mother tried to hold on, but lost the battle. Laughter screamed through the room as Martha chided Bess for her dirty mind.

CHAPTER TWENTY-FIVE

*D*REW

While Everly attended her surprise bridal shower, Drew prepared for the evening's self-defense class.

One of only two women who'd bothered to show up at all, Agnes Cunningham was eager to participate. The other, a younger woman named Jada Hall, whom Agnes had dragged along with her, loudly complained that her feet hurt and she'd rather be at home watching TV.

"Hush up, Jada," Agnes ordered. "Hasn't losing one co-worker this month taught you anything? You need to be able to protect yourself if someone comes after you."

Unconvinced, Jada rolled her dark eyes toward the ceiling. "Like who? I haven't done anything worth getting murdered over, and you know it."

The evening couldn't be going better, Drew decided. In his guise as the affable instructor, he stood at the front of the room, his easy smile radiating warmth while he ruthlessly planned out how to mine these women for the information he needed. This team approach to the case had been his idea, and he intended to do his part well. If these women knew anything about Bill's death, he meant to hear about it before they went home.

"Agnes is right, you know. Even in a town as safe as this one, it's good to know how to handle yourself." He gave Jada a moment to absorb, then said, "Let's begin. Since this is your first class, we'll work on some basic techniques. By the night's end, you will have begun to build inner strength and confidence."

Letting her breath out in a huff, Jada looked like she had more to say but didn't offer another argument. Having taught plenty of these classes, Drew recognized the spark of interest she'd tried to hide with her actions and handled it by turning to her companion.

"Agnes, why don't we start with you? Can you tell me a little more about what made you decide to take this class?" Drew inquired gently, his eyes filled with curiosity as he observed her poised stance.

Agnes shifted slightly, a contemplative look crossing her face before she responded, "I...we both work at the bank, and I thought it might be a good idea to learn some self-defense techniques. You never know when that kind of knowledge might come in handy, right?"

Nodding, Drew acknowledged the practicality of Agnes' decision and probed deeper. "Have you ever felt as if your life was in danger, either at or outside your workplace?"

Both women shook their heads, which he noted with interest.

"Not really, but you never know what might happen," Agnes said, her eyes shadowed by something he thought might be worry. "You'd know all about that, I suppose."

With a reassuring smile, Drew moved into the demonstration portion of the class, explaining and leading the women through the various methods for countering a face-to-face attack.

"Bring your knee up as you grab your attacker's shoulders and pull them down into the blow. You're aiming for the space just below the ribcage."

"I always thought you should aim lower. You know, hit them where it counts. In the...misters." Despite her earlier protest, the information triggered Jada's interest.

"Despite popular belief, a blow to that area won't fully disable a determined attacker, and while less statistically likely, you might be facing a woman. Knocking the wind out of them is the better option, but if you can't hit just below the solar plexus, the crotch is a good second choice. Hit hard in whatever area you can, and make it count."

"Okay," Jada said and nodded. "Got it."

"Use your voice," Drew added. "Say no, and say it loud." He strapped on a practice pad that covered him from shoulder to just below the area Jada had mentioned. "Agnes, if you'd like to go first."

He encouraged her to begin, and as she launched into the motion he'd shown her, her movements were fluid and confident. For a beginner, she executed strikes with precision, showcasing unexpected strength and grace but also a measure of anger. The woman, he judged, had hidden depths. Enough to kill a man? He wasn't sure, but she went at the exercise with single-minded purpose.

Jada fell silent as Agnes surged forward, the sound of her strikes against the practice pad echoing through the space. Drew watched intently, impressed by her control and focus. Well into her middle years and a bit soft around the middle, he hadn't expected her to display this much power. Probably driven by anger. Or she was highly motivated to learn. Or, more likely, it was a combination of both.

As she finished the series of moves he'd shown her, Drew

offered words of praise that had Agnes turning to him with a satisfied grin, her eyes just a bit feral.

"That was fun," she said. "I didn't expect it to be."

"I'll never be able to do any of that," Jada said, her voice filled with genuine dismay. "You have to be mean to go after a person that way. I'm just not like that."

Self-satisfaction dropping away, Agnes stepped forward, frustration evident in the set of her shoulders as she studied her co-worker. "Suck it up, Jada," she said with a cold smile before stepping back to let Jada have her turn.

Drew watched closely as Jada moved into the exercise, her initial efforts weak and halfhearted. "It might help if you think of someone who has hurt you. Picture an enemy as your attacker," he encouraged gently.

"Some of us don't go around making enemies, you know." But exasperation fueled her efforts, making them slightly more effective.

"Some of us don't have a choice," Agnes said bitterly.

"Maybe I should picture your face," Jada told Agnes, who responded with a thousand-yard stare.

Seeming resigned, Jada managed to score enough decent strikes that Drew let her off the hook and moved on to the next exercise, where he switched from the full-body practice pad to ones that only protected his hands.

"This time, Jada, I want you to use your fist. Not like that," he said when she made one and jabbed it at the pad on his left hand. "I want you to use the back of your fist and swipe down. In a real-life confrontation, you'd aim for the bridge of your attacker's nose. A blow there can make the eyes water. It's harder for them to hurt what they can't see clearly. The downward swipe generates more force and reduces the damage to your hand, allowing you to fight longer and harder. "

"I don't want to fight at all," Jada muttered but managed to land several decent hits before Drew let Agnes tag in.

"What about you? Can you picture someone you'd like to take down?"

Agnes nodded, her gaze narrowing with focus as she called up an image. "My boss hasn't promoted me to senior loan officer, even though he promised me the job months ago," she admitted, her frustration evident in her voice. "Take that, Walter Prescott."

Drew nodded in understanding, urging her to be specific. "And how does that make you feel, Agnes? What specifically bothers you about it?"

Agnes hesitated for a moment before responding, her voice tinged with annoyance. "It bothers me because I've worked hard for this promotion and know I deserve it. But Walter seems to overlook my contributions, and it's frustrating."

Drew listened intently, making mental notes as Agnes spoke. Walter Prescott was one of the suspects in Bill's murder, so he had every intention of prying more information out of Agnes. The easiest way, he figured, was to get her to air her grievances.

"Channel that frustration into your fists," Drew encouraged but noted she was still holding back. Her strikes weren't what they could be. "What else is bothering you? Is there someone else you could picture?"

"Does it count if that person is me?"

"Not especially. Beating yourself up will only weaken you in a confrontation. Why would you do that?"

Frustrated, she blew out a breath. "Fine. If you must know, I feel like it's my fault Bill Cavanaugh is dead."

When Drew's eyes widened, she amended. "I'm not saying I killed the man. I'm just saying I wished something would happen to get him out of the way so I could get the job I wanted. Now, he's dead, and I feel like it's karma or something."

On the spot, Drew switched up his plan for the rest of the class, grabbed a pair of padded gloves from the nearby storage basket, and offered a quick lesson in the proper delivery of jabs and uppercuts.

"Jab, jab, uppercut," he repeated as Agnes ran through the exercise. After several rounds, she seemed to let go of whatever held her back and went at him with a vengeance. Tears shone in her eyes.

"Who are you picturing now?" Drew asked quietly.

"Bill Cavanaugh."

"Why?"

"Because he went and got himself killed before I could prove I was the best woman for the job."

When she'd finished, Drew judged she'd dropped much of her emotional baggage and enough information that he had trouble seeing her as a suspect. Walter Prescott, however, was still on the list.

Drew turned his attention to Jada, who was waiting less than eagerly for her turn. "All right, Jada, you're up," he said with a smile, settling his practice pads back in place.

Jada stepped forward, her eyes flashing with something he couldn't quite read as she strapped on the gloves.

"What did you hope to take away from this class, Jada?

Why did you come?" Drew asked, his curiosity piqued as he guided her in using the proper form.

"Agnes made me."

When Drew merely cocked an eyebrow, she paused for a moment, adjusting her stance before replying, "Well, the same reason Agnes did, I guess. I'm a teller at the bank, and since there are only two of us, I work a lot of hours, so there's always the risk of a robbery. Mooselick River may be a safe town, but you never know when things might take a dangerous turn."

Her voice held a note of challenge as she lifted her fists and locked her gaze on Drew's raised left hand. She scowled as if picturing something that evoked emotional weight.

"Who will you battle today?" Drew asked quietly.

"Walter Prescott." She jabbed hard enough for leather to slap against leather with a resounding noise.

Jada's frustrations bubbled to the surface with each punch, her words spilling out in a torrent of anger. "That man is a misogynist and a philanderer," she declared vehemently. "He's perfectly willing to work a person to death to keep from hiring more help just because he's a cheapskate. I don't like him. I don't trust him, and I know for a fact he's done something shady."

"You're in a safe space here," Drew said slowly, his face a mask of concern. "Go ahead and let it all out. You'll feel better if you do." Drew gently urged, sensing that pushing too hard wouldn't reveal the secrets lurking beneath Jada's claims.

Jada's punches grew more forceful as she vented her frustrations about Walter Prescott, her anger fueling each strike against the practice pads. Sweat sheened her rich brown skin. The sound of her blows reverberated through the room, a physical manifestation of the pent-up rage she had been carrying.

As she continued unleashing her fury, Jada's words came out in a rush, her voice filled with anger and resentment. "I overheard something yesterday," she began, her tone tinged with uncertainty before quickly shaking her head. "But it was nothing important, just office gossip."

But as she threw another powerful punch, her resolve hardened, and she couldn't hold back any longer. "The truth is, Walter would rather promote an unqualified man than a woman with more experience," she confessed through gritted teeth. "I heard him talking to someone on the phone. He's taking applications for the position he promised Agnes, but I didn't want to tell her because I knew she'd be upset."

As she got into it, her fists flew with increased precision and strength, each strike punctuated by a fierce determination to prove herself. With each hit, Jada could feel the weight of all the times she had been overlooked and underestimated.

"I'd like to punch him," Jada admitted with a steely glint in her eyes, her voice laced with defiance. And with that declaration, she poured all her frustration and pent-up rage into her final, most powerful punch. The sound of her fist connecting with the padded practice pad echoed through the room, a testament to her newfound confidence and inner strength. "But this helps."

As she stepped back, taking deep breaths to regain her composure, Drew offered a smile filled with understanding and encouragement.

"We all experience frustration at times. Exercise helps us productively channel that energy."

"If I had more time, I might consider signing up for some classes," she responded. "I had no idea beating the heck out of something could feel this good."

"It's good to find an outlet," he said, genuinely impressed by her performance. "But I want to remind you that self-defense isn't just about physical strength. It's also about understanding your emotional triggers and learning to focus them on something positive. We make time for the things we find important."

Jada nodded, her face flushed from the exertion, but her eyes still burning with determination. "Thanks," she said softly. "I'll remember that."

"Is that true?" Agnes broke the mood with a shrill question. "What you said about Walter trying to hire someone outside the bank?"

Jada's voice trembled with a mix of sadness and determination as she answered, "I know I should have told you before, and I'm sorry, but from what I heard, he's got three interviews lined up this week. I know how hard you've worked. It's not right what he's doing."

"He won't get away with it," Agnes promised.

If Drew had any doubt that Agnes was capable of murder before, he didn't once he'd seen her fury grow cold. "Don't do anything rash," he said gently, touching her shoulder. "One murder in this town is enough."

Agnes shrugged off his hand. "Oh, I have no intention of killing him. Not that he doesn't deserve it. There are better ways to take down a man like Walter. Like you said before, hit him where it hurts."

This had not been Drew's intention. He'd meant to elicit clues, not provide a motive for someone else getting hurt.

"How can I help?" Jada was ready to cast her lot in with Agnes. This couldn't be good.

"Let's not get hasty," Drew tried to repair the damage he'd done, but it was far too late.

"We take him down from the inside, that's what," Agnes spit the words out. "Expose all his dirty little secrets. Or let him think we will. Whatever works."

"Well," Jada said. "There's something else. I have been noticing some strange behavior from Walter lately. He's been acting more secretive than usual, often leaving the bank early without any explanation. He could have more to hide than just his hiring practices."

"We should talk to Edie. She's nosier than a hound dog and sick of being worked like one, too. ."

He'd started a war of sorts. From the sounds of things, Walter probably deserved one, but that didn't make Drew feel any better about his part in kicking it off. There were two sides to every story. Perhaps Agnes wasn't as good at her job as she thought. Maybe she didn't deserve the promotion, so Walter hadn't given it to her.

"We should have brought her with us tonight," Jada said, dropping her gloves in the basket and turning to Drew. When's the next one of these classes?"

"Um. If you like, I could do one tomorrow night and keep it private." He'd have to shuffle some things with Riley and use the hot yoga space, but keeping ahead of this developing situation would be worth it.

"The bank closes at six tomorrow," Agnes considered. "I

can make that work. You in, Jada? I'll get Edie here. We can work out our plans while we work out our bodies."

Jada barely hesitated. "As long as part of the plan involves ending the hiring freeze, I'm in. We need at least one more full-timer behind the counter."

It hadn't occurred to them that Walter might be Bill's killer, and if they poked him too hard, the same thing could happen to them, Drew thought. He weighed the need to solve one crime against the possibility of instigating another and came up with a bad taste in his mouth. At least they considered him harmless enough to discuss their plans in front of him. He needed to keep it that way for now.

Double agent Drew Parker reporting for duty.

CHAPTER TWENTY-SIX

Three days before my wedding, the Wentworth house bustled with activity. Another week had passed without any new clues to Bill's murder, but I'd been a bit preoccupied with my upcoming nuptials. A month of good weather erased any lingering aftereffects of the storm that broke a one-hundred-year record for snow in May.

In return for putting up a series of signs designating the types of plantings used, the garden club went way beyond the mere giving of advice and turned the front of the house into a showpiece. An anonymous donation to the club might have been involved, but what Patrea didn't know, I didn't intend to tell her.

When my mother predicted a dozen women might show up to help clean and prepare for my wedding, she underestimated by a few. Car after car rolled up to park on the lawn Chris and the guys had worked so hard to win back from its meadow state.

"Here comes the bucket brigade," Patrea said, fussing with the drape she'd just finished hanging in the groom's changing room. She twitched the material one last time, tilted her head to survey the results, and stepped back. "Looks good, don't you think? Or maybe we should have gone with the burgundy in here."

How she could remain so calm in the face of all we had

left to do was a mystery to me. This was the only room with window coverings. They'd been delivered the week before, but we'd had to wait for the painters to finish before installing them. Then, in addition to a final clean and polish, we had several truckloads of furniture to haul in and arrange.

And yes, I did recognize that I might be having a case of the bride jitters because, normally, this type of organization falls right in my wheelhouse.

"No, save the burgundy for the other bedroom. This goes better with the woodwork." When I stepped closer to touch the material, I looked out the window at the many women piling out of their cars. Brigade? I think she brought the entire army."

"I'll take it," Patrea laughed, heading down to meet them. Since Jacy was helping Neena with the final bit of cleaning on the living room mural, they beat us to the honor.

"I thought you said you were only bringing a few women," I whispered in my mother's ear when I hugged her hello.

"Many hands make light work," she whispered back.

She wasn't wrong. They didn't even wait for Patrea to give them the grand tour but split off into groups and swept through the place like the tide rolling over beach sand.

"Who did the outside windows?" Martha cornered Patrea in the dining room.

"Ah. A company called Crud Busters. They power washed the entire exterior, including the glass."

"Did a good job. Got a card?"

Patrea grinned. "I'll have Everly text you their information. It was quite satisfying to watch."

Less than an hour later, I followed Jacy's mother, Leandra Wade, from room to room as she waved around a smoking bundle of white sage. I'd stopped her from salting doorways and windowsills, but she wouldn't be swayed against the smudging or against placing a small crystal in every room.

"Are you sure this is necessary?" I asked for the second time.

"Cleaning a house's energy is just as important as washing its floors," she insisted, wafting the stinky smoke into every corner. "You never know what psychic echoes might lurk in a house this old."

You could have knocked me over with the feather she was using to direct the smoke when we walked into the dining room, and I saw Robin Thackery handing a drapery swag up to Carlene Nicholson, who stood on a step ladder. What were they doing here?

"Hey," I blurted, "I didn't know you guys were here."

"We were late," Robin admitted breezily.

"Her fault," Carlene's tone wasn't light at all. "The place is coming together."

"It's fully lit," Robin agreed, snapping her gum. "Like on fleek."

Above Robin's head, Carlene rolled her eyes at the slang.

My lips twitched, and for the first time ever, Carlene and I had something in common. "Okay, well. Thanks, I guess. I'll tell Patrea you approve."

"Oh, I do. I'm booking this place for my wedding." Robin handed Carlene the next panel. "If it ever opens. I've heard it might not."

"From who?"

Shrugging, Robin stared into the distance for long enough that I couldn't tell if she was thinking about her answer or had powered down entirely. Meanwhile, Carlene snapped her fingers for the final swag panel, so I handed it up to her and watched as she clipped the hooks into place.

"How does it look?"

"Almost perfect. Just nudge that middle panel to the right by half an inch."

Once she had, Carlene dismounted the step ladder and joined me to view the results from below.

"Dale Crawford," Robin finally dredged up a name. One I had an interest in. "He heard it at work."

"And where's Dale working these days?" I'd only clapped eyes on the man once, but she didn't need to know that.

"Well, he sells firewood, but that's mostly in the fall, so he's been picking up short shifts at the Gas N Go. Harley Stanfield got him the job, I guess."

Putting two and two together, I came up with the actual source. Clive Thompson. This didn't bode well for Patrea.

But Robin wasn't finished, and her next sentence nearly made me choke.

"To make up for turning his balls black."

"Who did what to what?" If I hadn't been suffering from mild shock, I'd have caught on faster.

"You should know all about it," Robin looked at me like I was slow. "Your father was one of them."

Now, Carlene did choke on a laugh but it finally clicked for me. "You mean the membership vote at the lodge." It really clicked. "Are you saying Harley blackballed Dale?"

She nodded, leaving me stunned. How could that be right? Hadn't Harley been upset with Bill because he thought

Bill blocked Dale's membership? Wasn't that why he made a nasty comment at Bill's funeral?

If that wasn't the case, Harley must have had another reason for his outburst. Plus, why would Harley cast the negative vote for the man he was supposedly trying to sponsor into the club in the first place? None of this made sense.

"Don't believe everything you hear," Carlene cautioned Robin. "Clive Thompson thinks he has all the power, but he can't hold out forever. The rest of the board will force a vote if he doesn't stop dithering. Almost every business in town would benefit from what Patrea intends to do here, and anyone with half a brain knows it."

"How?" Robin scoffed. "By jamming up our roads with cars and making the police department work overtime to break up drunken brawls."

"That just goes to show what kind of weddings your friends have. This will be a classy place."

Now it was Robin's turn to roll her eyes. "Weddings mean booze, and booze brings out the worst in some people. It doesn't matter how much they're paying for the champagne."

She might have a point.

"I'll tell you the same thing I told Walter Prescott the other day. Part of planning any celebration is making sure you have someone on hand whose job is to keep things running smoothly. Hire the best, and they'll keep track of the guests."

"What were you doing talking to Walter Prescott about wedding planning?" Robin did my job for me, so all I had to do was wait for the answer. "He's already married."

"Really?" Carlene deadpanned. "I hadn't noticed since I've only known his wife my entire life. Sylvia is my mother's closest friend. I consider her an honorary auntie. If you must know, I'm helping Walter plan something special for their anniversary."

That would explain the lunch in Bangor, I supposed. And even at her worst, I didn't think Carlene would poach on a woman she considered family. Not to mention the age difference.

"Walter's not a fan of having an upscale wedding venue in town?" I checked to see if I'd read between the lines correctly, and Carlene had been trying to convince him the idea had merit.

She waved her hand dismissively, picked up a table runner that matched the drapes, and smoothed it into place on the ornate mahogany buffet table set against one wall. "He's been listening to Clive. They're thick as thieves, the two of them. He'll come around once the board gives the okay."

My next question slipped out before I had time to consider what her reaction might be.

"If you're so close with Walter, why didn't he step in and force Bill to approve your loan?"

I should have just bitten my tongue right off. Carlene spun to face me, her eyes blazing. "Did I say Bill turned me down?"

Hadn't she? I thought back to the conversation at Mabel's diner. She'd said Bill didn't think wedding planning required start-up money, not that he'd denied her a loan.

"You're right. I'm sorry. I just assumed—"

"Well, don't," she cut me off, and our delicate truce

ended—at least temporarily. At some point, she'd decide she needed me to be on her side with Patrea and make nice again, but until then, I chose to work in another room.

But first, I stopped by the kitchen to refill my water bottle and found Chris and Brian already there.

"What's up?"

"Trouble with the mower," Chris guzzled half his drink. "One of the brackets on the deck needs welding. We'll have to run it out to Pine Tree and see if we can get Bennie to look at it."

"If Brandon's there, bring up the subject of Bill. See if you can get him talking. We need to know where he was at the time of the murder. I've had conflicting reports about his temper. If you could get him to talk about his breakup with Claire, it would help."

"You know men don't pry into other men's feelings, right?" Brian cocked an eyebrow, but he had a twinkle in his eye.

"Do your best, and let me know how it goes. I'm heading out now to spend time with Drew's folks. They wanted to come a day early to save us from having to pick his sister and her husband up at the airport tomorrow."

"Will do." Brian waved me off. "I'll update the message board with whatever we find out. Go have family time."

Patrea reiterated the order when I told her I was leaving.

"Get out and stay out until the rehearsal. We've got this, and you're officially relieved from work duty. Go be a bride now."

"But the florist," I started to say.

"I'll handle it. Go." She practically shoved me out the door.

CHAPTER TWENTY-SEVEN

C**HRIS AND BRIAN**

Dust plumed out from behind his utility trailer when Chris turned down the dirt road to Bennie's garage and swerved to dodge the worst potholes.

"Bennie's cleaned the place up some since I was here last," Brian said, pointing out the brand-new wooden fence that hid the rusting wrecks that once marred the view on the right-hand side of the garage. A second section of the new fence backed a short line of vehicles up for sale.

Chris pulled into the section designated for customer parking. With the weather holding nice, Bennie and Brandon worked with the overhead door open.

"What's up?" When he saw them coming, Bennie wiped his hand on a rag and offered it.

"I've got a bracket on this mower deck that needs welding. You got a minute to help me out?"

Bennie glanced back at the car he'd been working on. "I'm tied up right now. Got a customer waiting to pick this one up, but I can have Brandon take a look for you."

"Sure. I don't think it'll take too long."

"Hey, no problem." Bennie went back inside, and after a minute or two, Brandon hauled out a portable welder.

"Where's the trouble?" He said after the three men had exchanged headbobs for greetings.

Chris led him to the trailer and pointed to the faulty mounting bracket. "She took a beating taming the lawn at the Wentworth."

Brandon climbed up on the trailer to better examine the damage.

"We've been getting the place ready for a wedding," Brian added. "Rush job because of what happened at the lodge."

Both men watched Brandon's reaction, but he barely registered the mention of the murder scene.

"Shame about that," he said, running a finger along the damaged bracket. "I hope they build it back. My father was a member before he took off. I remember going to the Christmas parties when I was a kid. I got a Duncan yo-yo in my stocking one year. I learned how to rock the cradle and walk the dog. Wonder whatever happened to it."

"I had one of those," Chris said. "But I know what happened to mine. I knocked a framed photo off the wall trying to learn how to make it go around the world, and my mother confiscated it."

"Fun times." Brandon jumped down from the trailer. "Looks like this will weld up easy. You want me to reinforce the other bracket while I'm at it?"

"Sure. Sounds good."

"Hey, is that Bill Cavanaugh's car over there on your for-sale lot?" Brian mentally patted himself on the back for noticing the perfect segue to turn the conversation back to the murder.

Again, Brandon's expression showed no signs of distress or guile. "Sure is. It's not up for sale yet, but his mother said she couldn't drive it, so she had us pick it up once the cops were done with it. Soon as it clears probate, we'll sell it for her. Or Bennie will, anyway. I'll be gone by then."

"You're leaving town?" Brian's radar lit up. "What for?"

"Love," Brandon's reply did not suggest he planned to go on the lam. "I met a woman online, and we're moving in together on the first. We found a nice little house in Fairfield. It's a rental with an option to buy and big enough to raise a family. Kendra has a daughter from her first marriage, but I've always wanted one of my own."

Brian could relate. "I haven't hardly had a decent night's sleep since Wade came along, but I wouldn't trade fatherhood for anything. We're talking about trying again."

Brandon grinned when he reached for the welding helmet he'd balanced on top of the portable welder. "I'm a prime example of how everything happens for a reason. If I hadn't lost my house, I'd probably be married to the wrong woman, but I got lucky this time. Kendra's everything I thought I would never find. She wants more kids."

With that, he donned a helmet and gloves, fired up the welder, and set about the business of fusing metal to metal. As predicted, the job didn't take long, and as far as Brian and Chris were concerned, they'd pried all the information out of Brandon that they could.

While Chris drove back, Brian updated the message board.

CHAPTER TWENTY-EIGHT

"Wake up, Everly!" A voice interrupted my sleep. I might have ignored it as part of a dream if Dolly hadn't followed up by poking her finger into my forehead. Between the slimy chill and the scent of perm solution that followed her everywhere, I had no choice. I opened my eyes to see her hovering next to the bed.

"What?" She'd better have a good reason for waking me up.

"You'd better come. It's Bill."

"What's wrong with him?" It wasn't like he could get any deader. Maybe this could wait until morning.

"He's over at the town office, and I think all his pins fell out."

I didn't have the brain power to follow her metaphor at two in the morning. "Pins?"

Lit from whatever light a ghost carried within, Dolly's face bobbed a bit as she looked at me like I'd lost a few pins of my own. "Wig pins. You know, as in he's wigging out."

Resigned, I slid out from under the covers. "Define wigging out."

"Same as before, with all the paperwork. But it's worse this time. He's muttering and mumbling and won't listen to reason."

"Okay," I gave in. She'd haunt me until I did what she wanted. Might as well get it over with.

"What's wrong?" Drew's voice emerged from the darkness about a nanosecond before he turned on the light.

"Gah," I said and shielded my eyes from the glare. "Other than that I'm now blind, Bill's gone rogue. He's over at the town office messing up their filing system. Dolly came to warn me. She says he's muttering to himself, and she couldn't get him to respond. I need to go over there and do something about him."

I felt two long steps from alert as I fumbled for something to wear, but Drew looked like he'd been down for a solid eight. Clear-eyed and moving fast, he got dressed before I remembered underwear goes on the inside. If I didn't love him, I could almost hate him for that.

"I'll get the car out of the garage." And since we were up, Molly decided she had to pee. He took care of her while I finally managed to dress myself, and he waited in the car when I got outside. The night chill blew the rest of the cobwebs out of my head.

"You didn't have to come," I said, "but I'm glad you did." Dolly had gone back to keep an eye on Bill until we got there.

"Where else would I be in the middle of the night? What's the plan?"

That he thought I had the brainpower to put one together at that time of night said more about him than it did about me. "I don't have a key to get in, so I guess I'll stand around outside and call to him. Really, you should have stayed in bed. I can't see this going well."

As we made the turn ahead of our destination, Drew

proved why I needed him. He flicked off the headlights and picked a parking spot around the corner.

"We don't want to draw attention to ourselves, so keep your voice as low as possible. If someone calls the station, Ernie or whoever's on duty will come from the other direction. Should give us plenty of time to skedaddle."

Skedaddle. What a word.

"Okay, Bugsy. You can be the lookout, and if the fuzz shows up, we'll make a run for it." I wasn't mocking him for getting into the spirit of the thing because he had a valid point.

"Stick with me, Sweetheart. We'll take it on the lam."

I hoped not. With any luck, I'd get through to Bill with minimal fuss and be back home in bed before the sun came up. I should have known better.

The sound of filing cabinet drawers slamming in and out reached our ears before we even got close to the building. At least Bill hadn't bothered turning on the lights, but the noise would draw plenty of attention.

Dolly popped her head out the nearest wall and said, "He's getting worse."

"I can hear that for myself," I whispered back, then raised my voice and called out Bill's name. Total waste of time.

"He can't hear you," Dolly confirmed. "You need to put some oomph into it."

"Sure, because getting arrested for disturbing the peace is what I need right now."

Head and shoulder leading, Dolly stepped right through the wall. "I didn't mean with your voice, silly. Use your power."

"What power? The only power I have is seeing people like you whether I want to or not. You all find me, remember. It's not like I'm lighting candles or whipping out my crystal ball and holding séances in the hope some random ghost will pop up and restore my faith in the afterlife."

You have not experienced a withering stare until you've had one from Dolly. Hers somehow managed to indicate I was being wilfully stupid, and that she felt sorry for me. I didn't care for it. "You could have just said you didn't know how," she said.

"Fine. I don't know how."

Plopping her hands on her hips, she showed herself to Drew. I knew she'd made the effort because he sucked in a breath but also because her edges went sharper. After a moment, she let go of the effort and returned to her normal state.

"It's like that. Only instead of wanting to be seen, you want to be heard."

"Everything okay?" Drew said, his voice low.

"Fine and dandy, I guess. Give me a second here."

I looked in the window and saw Bill had moved from the filing cabinets to the drawers of the three desks on the opposite side of the room. I heard him mumbling something unintelligible. He turned once and looked right through me, his face wild with whatever emotion drove him. Martha would not be happy when she saw what he'd done, but that couldn't be helped. All I could do was get Bill to stop before he made things worse.

"Bill Cavanaugh," I focused on him with both my attention and my intention.

He paused and looked at me briefly, then returned to the task at hand.

Renewing my efforts, I tried again: "Bill Cavanaugh. Come to me." Okay, it sounded cheesy, even to me, but it worked—sort of, anyway. He pawed through the drawer he'd just opened and seized a folder, which he held aloft as if it were a first-prize trophy.

"Come," I repeated, putting everything I had into the command.

Bill came. Right through the wall, just like Dolly had. Papers still in hand. Was that even possible? Apparently so.

"What? Did you need something?"

Wearily, I rubbed my hand over my eyes, then let it drop. "Do you have any idea what you've done?" I may have spoken louder than I intended because someone's dog began to bark. "Never mind. Just come with me. We'll talk about this somewhere where I'm not two minutes away from going to jail."

We were hitting the final countdown to the wedding and still hadn't found Bill's killer. If Ernie was any closer than we were, he wasn't sharing that information with me. We'd ruled out Red and Brandon, but that still left us with a handful of suspects.

What I needed was the log book from the hardware store to see who else had a key since Bill said he didn't.

"Listen," I hissed low enough to keep the dog from barking again. "Put those papers back and do it fast. I've got a job for you."

Bill perked right up and did as he was told. If everything went according to my plan, I'd send him back to clean up the mess he had made, and with any luck, Martha would never know what he'd done. In a moment, he was back.

"What do you need me to do?"

"Be quiet and follow us back to the car now." It took longer than it should have because we detoured around the house with the dog in case it was still on the alert, but finally, we pulled back out onto the street.

"Where to?" Drew's voice sounded loud when he spoke in his regular tone. I winced.

"Drop Bill off at the hardware store and then pull in at the gym. No one will think it's weird if they see one of our vehicles parked there. Bill will go into the hardware store and find me that log book, which I suspect went missing because he was in there messing with Tim's filing system in the first place."

Turning sideways, I watched Bill's expression, which gave me my answer.

"You know where the log book is, don't you?"

"I guess so." He wouldn't look at me.

"That book might be the key to this whole thing if you'll pardon the pun."

"Technically," Drew said, slowing to a stop in front of the hardware store, "it's a play on words."

"It's the middle of the night," I retorted without much heat as Bill winked out. "You can't expect me to be witty on almost no sleep."

"I think your wits are fine any time of day." He gave me a cheeky look as he pulled back onto the road.

"Now, who's making a play on words? Keep your eyes off my wits before you get us in an accident."

We hadn't been parked long enough for the engine to

stop ticking when Bill reappeared in the back seat. "Here." He passed me a small, spiral-bound notebook that looked like it had been carried around in someone's back pocket for a hundred years. Drew clicked on the dome light so I could leaf through the pages and I realized Bill might have had a point about some business owners in town lacking organizational skills. Tim had listed the entries by date going back to the eighties when he'd put in the key cutter.

"There must be thirty pages here," I grumbled when I flipped through to nearly the middle before finding a blank sheet. Not wanting to sit in the car half the night, I opted to take photos of the pages with my phone. I could look at them at home. Besides, with all the energy Bill had expended, he wouldn't last much longer before he had to go recharge his ghostly batteries.

Even though I could shoot two pages at a time, the process took several minutes. When I finally handed the book back to him, Bill's edges were blurry.

"Don't forget to leave it where Tim can find it this time," I warned, hoping he had enough juice to get the book back into the building. All I needed was for Tim to show up and find his log embedded in a window or something. "And try to clean up your mess at the town office before Martha sees what you did."

Nodding, Bill picked up the log book and blinked out.

On the way home, I scanned the first two photos to see if I could figure out Tim's method for identifying the keys he'd duplicated. I'd probably have kept scanning, but Drew reached over and took my phone from me.

"Tomorrow's soon enough." He wouldn't give it back.

"I know," I sighed. Today was a long day, and tomorrow

will be even longer with the rehearsal dinner and everything else that's going on."

We'd already had to reschedule the rehearsal to make time for the emergency town meeting where Patrea hoped to be elected the town treasurer. Otherwise, the rehearsal would have been short a bridesmaid, and she'd have missed out on our votes. We'd go from the election to what I'd decreed would be the lowest key bachelorette party in the history of them. I had no intention of being hungover at my wedding, but Jacy insisted we had to do something since the guys were throwing a bash in Drew's man cave.

Bess might be disappointed in me, but Drew and I had both called a moratorium on strippers and getting trashed in a bar. Frankly, there's not much happening in our area on a Tuesday night, anyway. I didn't know what Jacy had planned, but she'd agreed to my stipulations, so I wasn't worried.

Just exhausted. Tomorrow would be soon enough to look at the photos I decided as, too close to sunrise, we finally climbed back into bed.

CHAPTER TWENTY-NINE

"Don't you worry about a thing," Mabel assured me when I visited the kitchen to make sure she had everything she needed. It was her rehearsal just as much as it was mine. "Patrea's done a bang-up job of whipping this place into shape. It's time you stopped trying to organize things and just enjoy yourself. I don't need you mucking around in here, so get out." She hugged me to take the sting out of the order, but I knew that didn't make it any less final.

The guys had worked overtime the day before setting up tables for the big day. We'd be eating in what Patrea called the atrium—a room with windows running nearly from the floor to the ceiling facing the back gardens. Three sets of French doors led out to a covered patio. Chris had hauled over a trailer load of potted shrubs which Patrea dotted with white fairy lights. She'd also gone behind my back to order several arrangements matching the ones on the tables but on a much larger scale.

After dinner, there'd be dancing on the patio. The place could have been built specifically for this kind of event.

"I will. I promise. If you need anything…" I trailed off when Mabel glared at me. "But you won't. Okay, I'm gone."

Jacy met me at the foot of the grand staircase. "It almost doesn't seem real, does it? I feel like I've stepped onto a movie set or something." She waved a hand at the chairs lined up to form an aisle down the middle, the fireplace filled with flowers at the end, and the small dais on which I would stand when I took my vows. More fairy lights twinkled in a pair of miniature topiaries flanking the fireplace, and electric candles flickered from every surface.

"It takes my breath away."

"You're getting married here," Jacy squealed, grabbed my hands, and spun us in a dancing circle. I joined in the squealing because, yes, I was getting married here, and it was perfect.

"Hey! No dancing for joy without us." Neena dragged Patrea into the circle.

That was what my mother saw when she and my father walked through the door, and then, when she glanced past us at the rest of the room, tears glittered.

"Oh!" her hand went to her heart. "Would you look at this, Lee? It's even better than I expected."

Dad looked pretty well overcome, too, but he didn't have time to say much because Drew arrived with his parents and older brother, who would stand as his best man. His sister's husband, his best friend from back home, and the two Army buddies who would round out his half of the wedding party came in behind them.

Jacy wasted no time trying to talk me into coming down the stairs for the processional. Unfortunately for me, my mother and Drew's took her side, which left me with no choice but to put on my heels and try it.

"The key to keeping your balance is not looking down at your feet the entire time," Drew's mother advised. "Put your hand on the rail, but keep your shoulders and arm relaxed.

Look ahead, nudge your heel against the back of the step, and take your time. This is your day, no need to rush."

"You make it sound easy."

"I've walked a few flights in heels. Remind me to tell you about that sometime." The twinkle in her eye promised a good story. Drew got his easygoing personality and sense of humor from his mother. He got his good looks and sense of duty from his father. They were night and day from my former in-laws, making becoming part of their family something to look forward to, not something to dread.

As it turned out, she was right. Navigating the stairs in heels wasn't as scary as I'd expected. Even when Jacy tied a tablecloth around my waist to form a train, I had no trouble. Once past the curve, I locked my eyes on Drew's and barely noticed the rest of the flight. Getting to him was all I needed to do.

"You win," I grinned at her. "I'll come down the stairs."

"And I'll be waiting at the foot," my father said. "You don't need me cluttering up your entrance."

"You're just afraid you'll be the one who trips."

"I can neither confirm nor deny that statement." His grin said otherwise.

The rest of the rehearsal went smoothly. We ran through the sequence several times to work out the timing and gave everyone who hadn't seen it already a tour of the mansion.

Once the ceremony ended, Patrea planned to cordon off the staircase to keep guests contained from wandering up to the dressing area. Doors to unfinished or unfurnished rooms on the main floor would be locked on the day. But that still left plenty of places for guests to spread out and enjoy a quiet moment.

In the main living room, Neena's work on the mural drew oohs and aahs, as it should. She'd done a spectacular job. Patrea had added several occasional tables, a pair of matching period-appropriate sofas, and three armchairs since I'd last been here. I recognized two of the chairs from Jacy and Neena's shop, and both console tables had come from my storage room.

"You almost expect to see Daisy Buchanan draped over that sofa with a glass of gin and a cigarette holder in her hand," said my future mother-in-law, drawing a laugh from everyone. Then, she turned to Drew and hinted, "This would be the perfect place to throw a thirty-fifth-anniversary party for your parents."

"Duly noted," he said, then turned to Patrea. "I'd better book the date before you're fully open, or I might not get the chance."

"Don't worry," she beamed. "I'll hold it for you. With the family and friends discount, of course."

The tour ended in the dining room, where Mabel would serve the rehearsal dinner.

Because she'd said I should, I'd left the menu up to Mabel. I was glad I did when she served a variety of dishes family-style, which made for a warm and intimate feel. Under her roller-derby queen exterior beat the heart of a saint. She even got Thea Lombardi to drop her usual scowl and be pleasant. Probably through intimidation or a bonus, but she made it happen.

"That woman is a genius in the kitchen," Drew's father said, toying with the last bite on his plate. "The last wedding we attended, we had a choice of fish or chicken. Both dry and over seasoned."

"The Blue Moon delivers to the inn," David reminded him. Not technically in the wedding party, he, along with Chris and Brian, would be helping behind the scenes, so we'd invited all three to the rehearsal.

Surrounded by family and friends, I couldn't help but contrast this night to my first wedding rehearsal, where I'd felt overwhelmed and out of place. I should have trusted my gut and walked away, but I'd put the impulse down to a case of cold feet. This time, everything felt right. It fit. We fit. And it wasn't just my feet that were warm. It was my heart, too. My father laughed at something Drew's brother said. My mother smiled at Drew, and if her eyes misted a little, it wasn't with worry but with welcome.

Sometimes, you need to be tested by the bad times to recognize when the right thing comes along. This was one of those times for me.

Soon enough, the place cleared out. Despite her vehement protest that they weren't doing it right, Brian and David loaded both dishwashers while Chris helped Mabel carry empty containers to her car. When she'd gone, taking Thea with her, the six of us collapsed on the living room sofas to rehash the evening.

"That went well," Patrea said. "Don't you think?"

"It was perfect." I hugged her. "I can't thank you enough for all you've done. That goes for the rest of you," I turned to address the group. "You've all gone above and beyond to make this the wedding of my dreams."

"That goes double for me," Drew added.

"Let's not gush, okay," Patrea waved away the praise. "You've been far too easy to please. Lousy test case, really. Not a single bridezilla moment. Not even from your mother."

"Sorry to disappoint. She's been caught up in helping me with Bill, so I guess that distraction worked in our favor."

"Any progress there?" Neena propped her feet on the mahogany coffee table, then put them back down when Patrea sent her an arched brow. "Or will he be going on your honeymoon?"

"I sincerely hope not," I shuddered. "Speaking of which, we got some new evidence last night, but I haven't had time to even look at it today. We overslept, so the day got away from us right at the start."

"What evidence?" David asked. "Can we help?"

"Bill snitched the key log from the hardware store," Drew said.

"We made him put it back," I added, "After I took photos of the pages. And I told him to leave it where Tim could find it this time, so Ernie probably has it by now."

"Send us the pics," Jacy perked up. "We'll split them up and go through them right now. Shouldn't take long between all of us."

She was right. In less than fifteen minutes, we had a list of ten names.

"We've already ruled out my father and Max Montayne," I said. "Delly's dead and crossed over, so he's off the list."

"My father has a pretty solid alibi," Chris said, since his folks had been in Kentucky at the time. "If he even has the key still after ten years."

"Same goes for mine," Jacy glanced down at the two names she'd found, "Plenty of witnesses put him at home the whole evening, and I sincerely doubt they let Able Gallow out of jail long enough to commit murder. Including the two your dad made, we've knocked seven off the duplicate list right there."

"Eight." David held up his phone. "Unless you think Ernie Polk had a grudge against Bill because the police department is listed as having a key for security purposes."

Drew shook his head. "Even if he was capable of murder, he isn't a good enough actor to fake his way through what happened when we found the body. If there's a key at the station house, I'd say Ernie doesn't know about it. Plus, since he's Harley's alibi, that makes Harley his."

"You're right," I said, "Which brings us right back to our two top suspects. Clive Thompson and Walter Prescott. It had to be one of them."

"Are they even members, though?" Jacy frowned. "I don't recall seeing either of them at any holiday gatherings."

"I'll check with my father, but Clive has an alibi, so I guess we're looking at Walter. Maybe there's something in the water at the bank that turns all their managers into murderers. Except—of the two, Walter is the one I suspect the least. Don't ask why because I'm not sure, but something about him just doesn't play for me."

"Even though he and Clive were in cahoots to get him elected treasurer?" Patrea, also running for the position, took a dim view of what she considered cheating. "I'm going to win, by the way. Clive can run his mouth all he wants."

"Remind me again, what was Clive's alibi?" Chris said.

"He was at the Gas N Go. Bill said Clive told him they were closing in a few minutes when he stopped there at about 7:30 for windshield wash on his way home, but Clive told me he didn't close until nine."

"And Bill was certain about the time?"

"That's the last thing he remembers clearly before he died? He has no idea why he stopped at the lodge?"

Brian and David tossed questions at me.

Drumming my fingertips on the arm of the sofa, I pulled the conversations with Bill from my memory. "According to him, he looked at the clock in his car when he pulled in at the gas station. We don't know why Bill stopped at the lodge, and we know he didn't have a key. Whoever killed him must have already been there. It couldn't have been Clive. The timing's too far off."

Neena decided she'd had enough. "It's time to be done with murder talk for tonight. I say you turn over everything you know to Ernie and let him figure it out."

"Or," Jacy contradicted, "we confront Walter at the town meeting tomorrow night and see what happens. For all we know, they were in on it together."

That was a possibility I hadn't considered but, given what Edie had overheard, should have.

CHAPTER THIRTY

I woke up to a misty rain and a full schedule the day before my wedding. The rental tuxes needed to be picked up and, along with the dresses, dropped off at the Wentworth. In the afternoon, we'd enjoy what passed for a spa day at Do or Dye—facials and mani-pedis for the bridal party and mothers of the bride and groom. Later, we'd attend the special town meeting to elect a new treasurer and, finally, my low-key bachelorette party, starting at Cappy's and ending with spending the night before my wedding at the mansion. Even if I hadn't wanted low-key, I doubted we'd have the energy left for a blowout bash after a day like that.

Despite what seemed like a possible breakthrough on the case, I wasn't any closer to finding Bill's killer than I'd been before. Everything rested on getting our two main suspects to reveal something during the town meeting. Unless Ernie beat us to it, which wouldn't hurt my feelings a bit, but I wasn't holding out hope.

The first surprise of the day came when I wandered into the kitchen to find Drew's mother making blueberry waffles. From scratch.

"Good morning," Marie beamed when she saw me. "Drew let me in. You don't mind, do you? I wanted some time with you, so I fed him and sent him off to walk the dog."

"Not at all." I kissed her on the cheek before pouring a cup of the coffee she'd already brewed. Tea just wouldn't cut it today. I needed the extra boost. "Those smell amazing."

"Sit right down," she said, plopping a loaded plate on the table and taking the chair opposite. "I want to warn you, I might cry a little, but you should know they'll be tears of joy. I couldn't have chosen better for Drew. You're his shining light, and I think he's yours."

She wasn't the only one who might cry. "He is. I didn't plan to get involved again. You probably know my first marriage ended badly. Most people do since it was all over the news."

"My heart broke for you," she said. "I remembered you from visiting the Dean family at camp."

I first met Drew at Jacy's parents' camp on the lake when we were kids. I didn't remember him as clearly as he remembered me, but he didn't hold that against me.

Gesturing for me to eat, she continued, "Today is not the day to bring up the past. It's a day to look to the future. I wanted you to know I'm glad you'll be part of ours. Welcome to the family."

"Thank you," I said, reaching across the table to take her hand in mine. "I want you to know that my family feels the same about Drew. My folks just love him."

"Good," she sniffed back her tears and squeezed my hand. "Eat your breakfast, dear. We have a busy day ahead. I'm looking forward to that facial."

"Me, too."

When David showed up twenty minutes later, she talked him into a waffle before he could tell me why he'd come.

"I volunteered to pick up the dresses and run them out to

the Wentworth while the guys sort out their tuxes." When I cocked an eyebrow at him, he assured me, "Don't worry, Dupree, I'll be careful with your gown."

"Good thing, Barrington. I wouldn't want to have to kill you on my big day."

"You don't scare me, but your mother does. Kitty would kill me harder."

Laughing, I agreed. "Thanks, though," I said, turning to my future mother-in-law, "David's my honorary brother. You could probably tell by the way he talks to me."

"Drew speaks highly of you." Marie smiled at David, and he got all embarrassed.

"Thanks for the waffle. It's the best I've had in a while," David said, rising to rinse his plate and put it in the dishwasher. "Point me toward the dress and the shoes and whatever else goes along with them. I already picked up Jacy's stuff, and I'm headed to Neena's next."

By the time he carried my dress out to his truck, my kitchen was spotless.

"It looks like we've got some extra time before we have to head to the salon, and Molly's out of food," I said, gesturing toward Drew's note on the refrigerator. "If you don't mind a quick stop at the grocery store, I can give you a tour of the town."

"Not at all."

We ran into Ernie coming out of the grocery store. "Any news?" I asked once he decided he couldn't avoid me and had been introduced to Marie.

"Nothing good. The forensic lab identified the saw marks on the rafter supports."

"That's something, right?"

Ernie huffed out a breath. "Sure. There can't be more than twenty or thirty Stihl chainsaws kicking around town. Narrows the suspect list right down." Annoyed—not with me but in general—he brushed past and headed for his car.

"Poor man. It must be hard to carry the weight of the law sometimes," Marie said as she followed me inside to pick up what I needed.

Moments later, I hefted a large bag of dog food onto the conveyor of the only open checkout. Robin's, naturally.

"You should just leave it in the cart," Marie said after watching me struggle with the heavy bag, "and let her scan it with the hand scanner. It's so much easier."

"In a perfect world, it would be." My answer probably sounded cryptic to her, but a checkout scanner could be a weapon of mass wallet destruction in Robin's hands.

"Hey, Everly," Robin said, running the bag over the scanner and surprising me that she remembered my name again.

"You could have used the hand scanner," Marie spoke up.

"You're right. Why do I always forget we have those?" Without even blinking, Robin grabbed the scanner and ran it over the barcode twice. "Aren't you getting married this weekend?"

Beside me, Marie sucked in a breath, and I had to hold back a giggle at Robin's expense.

"Tomorrow night, actually." The fact that her memory cylinders were firing led me to say, "Did you happen to hear any other noises from the lodge the night Bill was killed?"

"You mean the chainsaw? Sure."

Mentally, I slammed my palm against my forehead. "Why didn't you say anything about this before?"

"You only asked me about the roof and the gunshot." Her answer made me want to choke her, but I took a deep breath and tamped down the urge while I ran my debit card through the reader.

"What time did you hear the chainsaw running?"

Robin screwed up her face trying to think. "Oh, it was just before Da...I mean, around seven, I think."

That was before the power went out and before Bill stopped at the Gas N Go, which confirmed the theory his killer had already been in the building before he arrived.

"Thanks, Robin." I took my bag of dog food and headed for the door.

"Wait," Marie grabbed my arm gently. "She charged you three times for that. Shouldn't you say something?"

"Next time," I said. "I'll keep the receipt and get my money back later."

"They won't believe you if you don't show them you didn't get three bags." Marie looked shocked by my lack of concern.

"Oh, they will. This is not the first time she's done something like that. Trust me, I know the manager, and he won't even blink when he refunds my money."

"Why do they keep her on, then?"

"Because Kirby's a saint, and Robin needs the work. It could be worse. Before she got hired here, she applied at the bank."

That one had her shaking her head all the way to the salon.

Rather than spoiling the fun, I kept Robin's bombshell to myself and didn't have time to tell the others about it until just before we filed into the town office to discover the former cafeteria packed with people.

"Good turnout," I said. It was standing room only, so we found a spot along the wall on the left side of the room.

"Are you nervous?" Jacy rubbed a hand down Patrea's arm.

"Determined," Patrea replied as we waited for Miles to call the meeting to order.

The Board Chair, Miles Higgins, wasted no time getting to the point. "Our only order of business this evening is the election of a new treasurer," he said, raising his voice to be heard above the shuffling crowd.

I wasn't surprised at all when Dolly Tibbets walked through the wall and took an empty spot off to the right of the table where the board members sat. Nor was I shocked when Bill joined her.

"I nominate Patrea Evergreen," Martha Tipton wasted no time raising her hand.

"Second the motion," my mother beat Bess Tate to the punch.

"I nominate Walter Prescott," Dale Crawford jumped up and spoke before Miles could announce the first motion had carried. Beside Dale sat none other than Robin Thackery. Something about them being together triggered a thought that slipped away before I could grab onto it.

"Seconded," someone shouted, but I didn't see who.

After a short pause, Miles asked if there were any other nominations, and when no one spoke, they invited the nominees to come to the front and take one of several seats lined up in front of the table. As the two sat and faced the crowd, Miles asked anyone who wished to speak on the nominee's behalf to stand.

Bess shot out of her chair. Not waiting to be called on, she said, "Patrea Evergreen is the only logical choice. Not only is she a damned good attorney, but she also served as a financial advisor at her former firm."

Since the cussing was the only part of her speech that actually sounded like Bess, I assumed someone had coached her on what to say.

"I don't know about all that," Harley Stanfield stood and addressed the room. "But I do know Walter Prescott has worked at the bank for several years, and we all know him. I don't know this other person from a hole in the ground. I say it's best to go with someone you know."

Miles nodded to Harley but didn't respond to his statement. "Putting aside my official position on the board for the moment," he said, "I'd like to state that in all my dealings with her, Mrs. Evergreen has proved to be fair, above board, and knowledgeable. Reading her business plan revealed a keen mind for creating and handling revenue, which is exactly what we need right now. As a practicing attorney, she would not only be held accountable for the ethics required of a town official but also to the state bar, giving us an extra layer of assurance."

The discussion continued for quite some time. Patrea sat calmly and surveyed the crowd. Walter, on the other hand, glanced over his shoulder as if trying to get Clive's attention. Clive never even glanced in Walter's direction. Whatever deal they'd made seemed to have gone south. Maybe Clive realized Walter was a killer.

All I needed to do now was figure out what to say to draw a confession out of Walter.

"Why would you want someone else from the bank? Clive's been telling everyone who'd listen how Bill embezzled funds from the town," someone yelled.

Bill bristled and shouted back, "I never did." But, of course, no one heard him except Dolly, my mother, and me.

"Now, now." Clive held a hand flat out in front of him, motioning for everyone to calm down. "I think you misunderstood what I said. Bill only acted on the board's orders when he paid for the new handicap ramp."

"What about Duckie-Gate?" She didn't stand, so I couldn't see for sure, but I would have put money on Mara Tibbets being the one who shouted the question. Especially after her conversation with Edie at the salon.

Clive's face went red. "That was a misunderstanding—one that is long past and has no bearing on tonight's proceedings."

"Speaking of long past," Bess stood up again. "This meeting started an hour late, as it was, and I like to be in bed by eight. Can we move this along and just get to the voting?"

Confused silence lasted a full thirty seconds before Martha broke it. "What are you talking about? The meeting started at six, and it's barely 6:30 now."

"It's 7:30. See," Bess held out her arm to show Martha her watch.

"Oh, for heaven's sake, Bess. No wonder you haven't been on time for anything since the middle of March. You forgot to reset your watch for Daylight Savings Time."

Daylight Savings Time. The phrase reverberated through

my head, blocking out everything else while a whole new view of Bill's death fell into place.

"Brian," I said after switching places with Jacy almost by force. "Did you happen to look inside Bill's car when you saw it for sale at Bennie's?"

"No. Why?"

"What if Bill's car clock was off by an hour? That would mean he stopped at the Gas N Go right before Clive closed for the night, not an hour before."

"It changes the timeline some."

"It changes everything and puts Clive back in the game. I need to know if I'm right. Do you have Bennie's number? Or Brandon's? Maybe he'd remember."

"I don't. Brandon moved to Fairfield already, but Bennie's here." Brian nodded toward a spot across the room. "I don't see how we can get over there to ask him right now."

"What if I cause a distraction? Can you go ask him?"

"Sure."

Switching back with Jacy, I caught Dolly's eye and crooked my index finger. She took the hint well enough.

"What do you need?"

"A distraction. Can you..."

She cut me off. "On it." Before I could give her a suggestion, she'd taken matters into her own hands. Approaching the board table, she shot a grin back at me over one shoulder and flipped the ballot box onto the floor. When Clive leaned over to pick it up, his chair tipped up on two legs. Dolly helped it the rest of the way over, depositing Clive onto the floor. As Miles leaped up to see what had happened to his fallen colleague, Dolly shoved the stack of ballots off the front of the table. Bits of paper fluttered toward the front row of seats.

People in the first row rose to help. Others stood merely to get a better look at the ensuing chaos. Ginger Martin got up and pulled Clive's chair out of the way as he struggled to regain his feet. Practically dancing now, Dolly hip-checked Miles when he leaned down to help Clive up. Miles lost his grip, and Clive went down again.

Amid the chaos, Brian circled the room. No one paid him much attention as he made his way to Bennie. After a moment's conversation, Brian caught my eye, nodded, and slipped easily back the way he had come.

"You were right," he said. "The clock was off by an hour when Bennie took it in."

Given the choice between Walter and Clive, I'd been leaning toward Clive all along. I'd turned up too many bits of shade to fully trust him. This new evidence not only screwed up his alibi but proved he'd lied. My gut instinct said Clive was the bad guy, but he and Walter could both be in on it.

What to do?

"All good," Dolly showed up beside me. "Or do you need something else?"

"I need something else." That quickly, a plan formed, but it all hinged on Dolly. "Remember what Edie told Mara about Walter and Clive and the bribe?"

"Sure."

"Any way you could repeat that? Right now. In a loud voice. Without anyone seeing you?"

Dolly clapped her hands, and her face lit up like a Christmas tree. "You mean use my spectral voice?"

"Yeah."

"Hell, yes. Just watch me."

Before I could tell her to wait for my signal, she faded out and popped back up in the middle of the crowd.

"Is it also a misunderstanding that Walter Prescott bribed Clive Thompson to help him win this election?"

When Dolly's voice lifted with the accusation, every head swiveled to see who'd spoken. Well, most of them, anyway. Knowing full well I was behind what was happening, my mother and Patrea looked at me. Clive finally decided Walter could use his attention, but Walter wasn't having it.

"That's a bald-faced lie," he stood up and shouted. "I never bribed anyone."

"Did you, or did you not, offer Clive Thompson a thousand dollars after discussing how the town needed someone like you in charge of the money?"

Shock rounded Walter's eyes and mouth until they matched his round body and face—a complete contrast to Clive's furious expression.

"That money was not a bribe," Clive clenched his jaw but still managed to make himself heard. "It was a donation to the fire department."

"It had nothing to do with this election—nothing at all." Walter stood, a dull flush rising across his cheeks. I don't even care if I get elected. It was all Clive's idea to run, not mine."

"Is that because you backed his plan to bring in an outlet mall near the bypass?" Now that Dolly got the ball rolling, Martha decided to kick it through the goalposts.

"I...we...I never would have done anything that wasn't

right for the town," Clive stood and stared as she made a direct hit.

"Is that why you and Bill Cavanaugh were fighting in his office the week before his death?" Dolly popped up again and lobbed the ball back into play.

Martha ran with it again. "Because the deal was still on the table, right? And if you could get Bill to cooperate, you figured you could force the board to do things your way."

Between the two of them, they might get Clive to confess to murder without me having to say anything at all, but I couldn't let them have all the fun.

"I think it was," I stepped forward and faced Clive while Bill watched from his spot near the table. "And I think you asked him about it again on the night of the storm, and when Bill refused, you followed him to the lodge and killed him. Then, you tried to get Walter to run for treasurer because he'd fall in with your plans."

"You're all crazy. Ask Ernie," Clive scanned the crowd, looking for the man he expected to back him up. "Didn't I tell you Bill had stopped in for windshield wash at around quarter to eight? That was over an hour before I closed. How could I have followed him to the lodge if I didn't close up until nine?"

"You did." But Ernie wasn't looking at Clive. He was looking at me because I'd been the one who gave him wrong information. "Everly?" Ernie said.

Shoot. I hadn't thought this through. Oh well, nothing to do but get on with it.

"But that's not how it went, is it, Clive? You only repeated back to Ernie the time he'd mentioned to you to give yourself a better alibi. You didn't count on the fact that

Bill might have told someone where he was going and when. He'd forgotten to change the clock in his car for Daylight Savings Time, so when he said he'd stopped at the Gas N Go at 7:30, it was really 8:30. You didn't stay open as you said, but locked up and left right after he did."

While Clive sputtered, Bill's gaze traveled from Clive to me and back.

"The drive took some extra time, but you figured you'd catch up to Bill at home and try to change his mind. But when he came through town, I think Bill noticed something funny at the lodge and stopped to see what happened. Someone had been in there earlier and cut the roof supports with a chain saw, but we'll come back to that in a minute."

"That's ridiculous," Clive insisted. "It wasn't me. You need to talk to Dale Crawford. I gave him my key."

"The hell you did," Dale denied.

Max Montayne stood taller than most, his head and shoulders above those clustered around him. "How did you get a key? You weren't a member of the order."

"I told Tim we needed one for the town office."

Max thought that through for half a second, "Yes, I can see where that might have worked, but who gave you theirs to duplicate?"

"I plead the fifth," Clive clamped his mouth shut.

"This isn't a courtroom," Patrea rolled her eyes and shook her head, "you idiot." She surveyed the room, her gaze landing on each person present who had access to the keys.

"It was me." Walter's shoulders slumped.

As one, Dad and Max turned their attention in his direction.

"You weren't a member, either," my father said, anger

turning his face red and making his hair go poofy. "How did you get a key?"

Wearily, Walter lifted his hand and pressed his palm to his forehead as if it had begun to hurt. "From Martin Warner, who got it from Max three years ago when he was the town assessor and had to update values because of new state regulations. I was supposed to go in and take measurements on a Thursday afternoon, but I couldn't go, and Max needed the key back by the end of that, so I made a copy and went in early Friday morning to get it done."

That tallied with the dates Tim had listed in his log.

"And how did Clive get hold of it?"

Sucking in a breath, Walter went for broke and spilled his guts. "It was the rubber ducks."

I wasn't expecting that, and I don't think anyone else was, either.

"The ducks?" Max finally asked.

"He needed a place to keep some of the boxes for a couple of days and we knew you wouldn't have a meeting until the next week, so I gave him my key and let him hide the ducks in there. I didn't know he made a copy."

"Those ducks are the worst things that ever happened to this town," Martha Tipton declared loudly.

"Murder is worse," I said, trying to pull the conversation back to where it should be. "Why did you give Dale your key, Clive?"

Tugging at his bow tie as if it were getting too tight, Clive said, "He wanted payback for being blackballed, and I was annoyed with Max for coming down against the outlet mall. When he said he wanted to trash the place, I thought he meant to paint stuff on the walls, not sabotage the roof. Bill must have caught him, and Dale killed him to cover his tracks."

Hearing the wheels of the bus he'd just been thrown under getting close to his head, Dale knocked Robin over as he tried to bolt but only made it halfway to the door before Harley Stanfield knocked him flat with a single punch.

"Harley," Ernie shook his head wearily. "You know better."

"He earned it." Harley went willingly when Ernie signaled for a deputy to take him into custody.

"I didn't do anything," Dale mumbled when the second deputy hauled him to his feet.

"What do you want me to do with this one, boss?"

"Take them both to the station and put them in separate cells for now."

"See," Clive said. "There's your murderer, right there. Dale did it."

"No, he didn't." I hadn't finished my story. "Because when Dale got done sawing the supports, he went to Robin Thackery's place. Based on what she told me...or tried not to tell me, he'd been there for over an hour before the murder."

"He practically admitted it, didn't he?" Clive insisted. "I'm telling you, Dale killed Bill."

"No, he didn't." It wasn't just me who heard him this time. Bill made the effort and appeared before the entire town. "I remember now. It happened almost exactly like she said. You pitched for the outlet mall again and wanted me to cut a check for a couple of nights at the inn so the company rep could review the property. I refused and said I intended to tell Miles what you planned to do, and then I left. The rest of the drive was awful. I could hardly see where I was going, but there was a lull just as I got to the lodge, and I could see the door was open."

No one moved the entire time Bill spoke. I don't know if they were too scared or too interested.

"I pulled in, got out of my car, and went inside. I thought maybe someone had come to check on the place and didn't get the door latched. When I got inside, I saw sawdust everywhere. I was just getting my phone out to call Lee when you came in."

"I didn't. It wasn't me. I don't even own a gun."

"Sure you do." The guy who owned the bait shop spoke up. It took me a few seconds to remember Joe Parnell was his name. "A .22 Ruger. I sold it to you."

"It looked bigger when he was pointing at me." Bill's form began to waver as the memory returned, and then, he poofed. Unless I could get Dolly to do it for me, I'd still have to help him go into the light, but it would have to wait until he had enough juice to show himself to me again.

Chaos erupted as people spilled into the aisles and headed for the doors. Trying to get to Clive, Ernie fought the crowd like a fish swimming upstream. Realizing he was busted, Clive shot out of his seat and looked for another way out. With too many people between him and the main doors, the only option left was to go through the kitchen-turned-storage room and try for the emergency exit on the other side.

"Get him," Ernie ordered.

Since we were closer, Drew took off at a sprint with the rest of our group right behind him. Clive was two steps from the emergency exit when Dolly appeared out of thin air in front of him.

"Boo," she said, stopping the man in his tracks. Stunned, he spun to try another ploy, but Drew had already closed the distance.

"Get out of my way," Clive grabbed a box of file folders—the first thing he put his hand on—and swung them at Drew's head. When Drew ducked, Clive got past him and tried to run by me, but I jumped on his back and rode him to the floor.

"I've got him now." Only a little late to the party, Ernie helped me up and placed Clive under arrest for suspicion of murder. I hadn't noticed we had an audience until applause broke out behind us. I turned to see my parents among the small group who had followed.

"See, Dad. Catching killers isn't always dangerous."

Before he hauled Clive out, Ernie turned and said, "Anyone want to tell me how you managed the special effects?"

CHAPTER THIRTY-ONE

While we dealt with Clive, Miles, and Ginger had enough presence of mind to go out and reassure the townspeople it was okay to come back inside. They, like Ernie, had jumped to the conclusion Bill's appearance had been an elaborate ruse intended to force a murderer out into the open. Other than Dolly, the rest of us were happy to let them think whatever they wanted. Best of all, she agreed to escort Bill to the edge of the next plane of existence and toss him into the light if he balked.

As soon as everyone sat back down, Walter renounced his candidacy, and the town elected Patrea by a simple show of hands. In a surprising turn of events, Miles also put Clive's seat on the board up for nominations. Harley Stanfield nominated my father, who won by a landslide.

With Bill's murder solved, Patrea's triumph, and my father's surprise election, our mood when we walked into Cappy's Tavern for my bachelorette party couldn't have been higher.

For once, David had followed through in a timely manner and persuaded Miranda to take the management position at the inn before Patrea snapped her up.

"Since this is my last night here and several special occasions rolled into one, your first round is on me," she said when she came to our usual table—not to collect drink orders but to deliver a bottle of house white to the table. She hadn't attended the town meeting, but news travels fast in Mooselick River.

"To Everly," Jacy raised her wine glass. "On this last fling before the ring, may her life be full of love, and her love be full of life."

"Cheers," rang out the chorus as we all took a drink.

What with the town meeting keeping folks occupied, the nearly-empty bar seemed like a ghost of its usual self—even for Karaoke Tuesday. But Jacy was determined we had to do at least one number as a group for this to qualify as a bachelorette party, so we humored her and took the stage while she chose a song.

Even Patrea had to laugh when the first notes of Like a Virgin blasted out of the speakers. Before we hit the second chorus, we were dancing around the stage and having fun with it while Miranda cheered us on.

"One more," Jacy said when the song ended and programmed in Girls Just Wanna Have Fun. "Then we can go to the Wentworth and jump on the beds."

"I think the management will take a dim view of such activity," Patrea warned.

"Party Pooper," Jacy proclaimed as the music started up again, and we picked up our microphones. Hamming it up with my friends, I didn't notice Jerry Kaminski walk into the bar, but he certainly noticed me.

"Sing it, baby," he hollered from in front of the stage, thrusting his hips to the music and never taking his eyes off me. His performance sapped all the fun out of the evening.

"Come on, Jerry," Miranda approached him. "That's enough now. You know Milo will kick you out for good if there's another complaint about you." She took his arm, but he shook her off.

"Sing another one and shake it for me. Come on, just one more." If you couldn't tell he was drunk from the slurring, the smell of alcohol coming out of his pores was enough to peel paint.

"Do you want me to call Drew?" Miranda raised her voice, mainly for Jerry's benefit.

"No. We'll just leave," I told her.

"Come on," Neena said, casting Jerry a look of pure disgust. "I think we're done here."

I wholeheartedly agreed and followed her off the stage with Patrea not far behind us. When Jerry made the mistake of grabbing my ass on the way by, I didn't even stop to think before letting Drew's self-defense training take over. I put Jerry on the floor before I even realized I meant to do it. Not that it took any incredible feat, mind you. He wasn't steady on his feet, to begin with, and I didn't hurt him other than a bruise to his ego. Given the state of him, he probably wouldn't have the sense to notice or care, anyway.

Led by Miranda, a half-hearted cheer erupted from the few patrons who'd wandered in after the town meeting. I wasn't sure I deserved it since I hadn't intended to resort to physical violence. Still, the man needed to keep his hands to himself. Eyes, too, for that matter.

"Don't touch me again, Jerry." I leaned down to make sure he heard me. "Not ever."

"I'll get someone to take him home." Miranda shook her head. "And thanks for making my final shift one to remember."

And that was the end of it. We left the bar, drove to the

Wentworth house, and spent the rest of the night enjoying the ambiance. Patrea did not let us jump on the beds, but she did attach her phone to a nifty little speaker, and we danced on the patio. Later, we retired to what she now called the pink bedroom to talk and laugh long into the night.

CHAPTER THIRTY-TWO

As predicted, the sun beamed from a perfect sky the following morning. I couldn't have asked for a more beautiful day to get married or for better people to share the day with. Patrea surprised us with breakfast pastries and ordered me to let her handle all the last-minute details—not that we'd left many of those. Just after noon, she went downstairs to oversee the flower delivery and again a bit later to let Mabel into the kitchen.

"Are you nervous?" Mom said when she arrived a short time later.

"Not a bit. I just want to get on with it, but at the same time, I wish this day could last forever."

"Forever is what it's all about," she said, pulling me into a hug.

It wasn't long before Mara and her crew arrived. While they got everything set up, we heard male voices in the hall. Jacy looked out. "The men are here. And the photographer."

Controlled chaos is the best way to describe the next two hours, which went by in a blur. Finally, though, it was time for Jacy and my mother to help me slip into my dress and for Mara to finish my hair and makeup.

"What about now?" Mom asked while she knelt to adjust the strap of my shoe. "Any nerves?"

"I'm excited, but no. No nerves. It just feels right."

"Good." She hugged me and kissed my cheek.

Just as we'd rehearsed it, I laid my hand on the railing and took my first step down the stairs. This moment would mark the rest of my life with Drew, and I couldn't be more ready.

My mother had cried when she'd zipped up my dress and had to have her makeup repaired. I had my somethings—old, new, borrowed and blue. At Jacy's insistence, she'd spritzed me with perfume from her grandmother's Sweet Honesty stash while the photographer immortalized the moment.

"Be happy," Mom whispered as she left me to take her place downstairs.

"See you down there," Jacy grinned, the last one out the door.

Alone, I counted off the time it would take everyone to find their places, took mine, and listened for the music that was my cue. Calm drifted over me like silk, settling into all my contours.

I didn't think about tripping. All I could see was Drew and the life we'd make together.

Halfway down the stairs, I paused while my attendants made their way down the aisle, then continued until, at the bottom, I tucked my hand firmly in the crook of my father's arm.

"I'm not giving you away. I'm only loaning you," he whispered, handing me off to Drew. "Take good care of her, son."

"I will, sir." Warm and safe, his hand closed over mine. "You ready for this?"

"More than. You?"

"Best day of my life so far."

Standing in front of friends and family, I promised to love him through whatever life would throw at us—the words not just coming from my lips but from my soul.

His promise to do the same felt as real as the ring he slipped on my finger. I swear I heard Grammie Dupree's happy laughter as we kissed. Or maybe it was mine.

The rest of the night went off without a hitch. We ate, laughed, and cried at the toasts, cut the cake, and danced until our feet hurt.

Neena acted like it was my fault she caught the bouquet, but I didn't hold it against her.

At first, I wasn't surprised to see Ernie Polk walk into the atrium. He'd been invited to the wedding, after all. It was his expression that gave me my first pang of worry. He didn't look like he'd come to offer us his best wishes. Instead, he had his cop face on.

What now? I thought as he spotted me standing beside Drew and saying goodnight to one of the guests.

Ernie wasted no time crossing the room. Dread built in me with every step he took.

"Drew Parker," he said without sparing a glance in my direction. "I'm placing you under arrest for the murder of Jerry Kaminski."

So much for the honeymoon.

We hope you enjoyed the twists and turns leading up to Everly and Drew's big day. But the journey doesn't end here.

In Ghost of Honor, Everly faces a new challenge when Drew is arrested for a murder he didn't commit, and she must clear his name.

~Also Available in Audiobook & Paperback Versions~

Quick Author's Note

Writing Wedding Presence was our version of throwing a haunted party—and you were all invited! We loved giving Everly and Drew their moment in the spotlight (complete with the usual supernatural interruptions), and honestly, it felt like such a fun reward after everything we've put them through.

But we also knew the peace wouldn't last long.
This book marked a turning point in the series: the stakes are getting higher, the ghosts are getting bolder, and Everly's abilities are still evolving. Let's just say the honeymoon phase isn't going to be all sunshine and sangria.

Anyway, if you've come this far with us and not decided we're complete and total whackadoodles...and especially if you have, we're offering a chance to sign up for our newsletters— the best place to get new release updates, sales notifications, and other fun content.

You can sign up for ReGina's newsletter and/or Erin's newsletter and as a thank-you gift for hanging out with us, you'll also get a FREE novella that isn't available anywhere else. And of course, we promise not to SPAM your inbox!

Love, hugs, and happy reading,
ReGina & Erin

P. S. If you enjoyed this book, it would be great if you could leave a review or recommendation on Amazon, GoodReads, or BookBub.

Your reviews help indie authors sell more books!

BOOK 13 OF THE HAUNTED
EVERLY AFTER MYSTERIES

At first, I wasn't surprised to see Ernie Polk walk into the atrium. He'd been invited to the wedding, after all. It was his expression that gave me my first pang of worry. He didn't look like he'd come to offer us his best wishes. Instead, he had his cop face on.

What now? I thought as he spotted me standing beside Drew, saying goodnight to one of the guests.

Ernie wasted no time crossing the room. Dread built in me with every step he took.

"Drew Parker," he said without glancing in my direction. "I'm placing you under arrest for the murder of Jerry Kaminski."

Over Ernie's shoulder, the ghost of Dolly Tibbets winked out—presumably to find and welcome the town's newest ghost to the post-living community. I had no illusions whatsoever that Jerry would have gone into the light, and neither, it seemed, did she.

"Jerry's dead?" And for once, I hadn't found the body. Should I feel bad for feeling good about that? Probably. The relief lasted about a nanosecond before the enormity of the situation hit me again. "What happened?"

"I'm not at liberty to give details about an ongoing investigation." Ernie began to read Drew his rights. "You have the right to remain silent."

"And that's just what you'll do." Patrea had appeared at my side. "Let him take you into custody." Not that Drew had put up a struggle. "And don't say a word until I get there."

"Until we get there," I insisted. "I'm coming with you."

I didn't care that I was still wearing my wedding dress. I didn't care if all of these people were my responsibility. I only cared that something was happening to someone I loved, and I needed to do whatever I could to make it better. That's who I am—who I have always been—the kind of person whose mind immediately goes into problem-solving mode whenever there is a crisis. It's not just a skill but a personality trait.

But Patrea touched my arm while Ernie finished his spiel and pulled me aside. "Not this time, Everly. This is what I do, and you need to trust me. I've got him, okay?" I wasn't the only problem solver in my immediate group of friends.

"Stay and deal with things here," Drew finally said. "I'll be fine. I haven't killed anyone."

"I know that." I glared at Ernie, who should have known better. He didn't even flinch, which didn't bode well. Thanks to him, my bright and shining, perfect day was now a tarnished mess.

By now, guests were filtering in from other areas of the house to see what the fuss was about.

"What's going on here?" Junior Pease's booming voice cut through the murmurs like a chainsaw through balsa wood.

I didn't remember inviting him, but since they were both

active in the VFW, Drew could have, or Junior could have been someone's plus one. Either way, he planted himself squarely in front of Ernie and Drew, his face reddening to match the color of the lobster puff appetizers we'd had earlier. His question was rhetorical since it didn't take a giant leap to see what was going on here.

"You can't be arresting a veteran on his wedding day in front of God and everyone. I won't have it. Do you hear me, Ernie Polk?" Junior's voice cracked with indignation, his hands clenching. "You oughta be ashamed, slapping cuffs on this good man like he's nothing but a common criminal! Explain yourself."

The room seemed to hold its breath, guests exchanging wide-eyed glances. Even the music went quiet. I could practically feel their collective disbelief morphing into a thick fog of speculation that would surely blanket the entire town with gossip by morning.

Ernie declined to elaborate. "I'm doing my job. That's all you need to know."

"Junior, please." Drew's words tried to cut through the older man's fog of anger, but they went ignored, lost in the sudden swell of conflict.

"Shame on you, Ernie!" Junior continued, jabbing a finger towards the officer whose jaw twitched beneath his stern facade. "This isn't how we do things here. We look after our own, and we certainly don't drag them away on what should be the happiest day of their lives. Your mother would be mortified."

"Enough, Junior," Ernie finally growled, his patience wearing thin as river ice in spring. "Step aside."

But Junior was a force unto himself, a gale that wouldn't be stilled. His outburst echoed off the walls, stirring up a storm within the once-serene reception. And just like that, my wedding had turned into a scene straight out of one of those thrilling crime novels – minus the thrills and double the drama.

Worse, now that more of the guests had been drawn to the source of the conflict, a commotion swelled like a cresting wave, crashing down to wash away all remnants of wedding cheer. Not that Ernie hadn't done that already.

My father stepped forward, his presence like a lighthouse amid the brewing storm. He placed a firm hand on Junior's shoulder, leaning in with the quiet authority he always carried.

"Junior," he said, voice steady and clear, "lets you and I have a word outside, hmm?"

There was something about the way Dad squared his shoulders, the imperceptible nod, that settled even the most obstinate folks down. Maybe his years of standing in front of high school students gave him the presence needed to deflate Junior's bluster. The older man's eyes flickered toward my father with a hint of respect.

"Fine," Junior huffed, allowing Dad to steer him away from the crowd, albeit with one last glowering look at Ernie, who paused as he took Drew's arm.

"I didn't kill Jerry Kaminski." Infused with certainty, Drew's voice echoed across the room.

A murmur of agreement spread throughout the guests, but I knew their support could be fickle. By morning, the roots of doubt would be set in the fertile soil around the local grapevine. Phone lines would burn with talk about attending a wedding where the groom had been arrested. Some would decide he'd done something to earn it.

Ghost of Honor is available now or, if you want to save money, you can get the box set of the next three books 13-15 at a discount. Keep reading for a preview of the free novella you'll get for joining our newsletters.

Excerpt from A Snowball's Chance in Spell

~

Lightning flirted in shadows of the dark clouds hovering over my house when I came home from work the afternoon before my twenty-second

Christmas Eve. Nothing unusual there. With three elemental faeries living in the house, weird weather happened all the time. Or rather, every time my temperamental godmothers mounted some sort of snit.

The godmothers idled at snit.

Going back to work wasn't an option. I'd cleared the last match of the year—a lovely couple with a shared affection for online gaming—and I was no coward. When it came to diffusing faerie fights, I consider myself an expert, and this one didn't look like it rated more than a two on the volcano scale.

Yes, you heard right. I measure faerie fights on the scale of whether or not a volcano might erupt in my backyard. Living with faeries is never boring. Occasionally dangerous —especially because I have yet to come into the magic that is my birthright, but never boring.

A quick check proved they'd contained the madness to the inside and/or the backyard. The two feet of snow on the front lawn was still there and still white—you try explaining black snow to your neighbors sometime. I didn't see any winged denizens—fae or otherwise—dotting the roof ridge, or hear any ominous sounds. If not for the fact that lightning is rare in Maine during the winter, and rarer still when confined to a single area, I'd have thought it was a quiet day in the household.

In my head, I downgraded the threat to a level one, and went inside.

For the most part, my place looks like an ordinary, New England style home. Built by my great grandparents, it's the oldest house in a neighborhood that grew up around it when the suburbs expanded into what was once a rural area.

Because, I think, the faeries wanted to give me a normal upbringing, they left the house in mostly the same condition it was in when they came to take care of me and only added on a wing for their own use.

I stepped into the front hall expecting...well, just about anything. Did I mention the faeries love holidays? Maybe they don't have them in the faelands, or maybe they do and go overboard there, too. I can't say since I've never been, but I could tell at a glance there were more decorations than there had been when I left.

"Terra!" I yelled, but got no answer. Terra, faerie of earth, held sway over all the flora and fauna found on dry land. She would be the one responsible for the pine boughs twining over anything that held still long enough. Fire faerie, Soleil, contributed by setting sparks of faerie light to twinkle inside the delicate ice bubbles crafted by her sister, Evian, mistress of water. The effect was lovely, but not as lovely as the three women could be when their faces weren't twisted, as they were now, with rage.

I came upon them in their favorite fighting grounds: the kitchen. It looked like I'd caught this one early since there was relatively little damage done so far. Steam rose from a puddle of water at Soleil's feet which I assumed had come from Evian. Vines snaked from between the kitchen tiles to twine around Evian's ankles, and there were a few smoking embers dotting Terra's hair. Nothing more than a minor spat.

Keeping it casual, I asked, "What's going on?" There's no rhyme or reason to what will settle a fight or send one into the red zone.

Terra turned one granite pink eye in my direction. "This

doesn't concern you." The fingers of her left hand twitched and the vines slithered from Evian's ankles to her knees.

Retaliating, Evian conjured a gush of water from thin air, and doused the smoking embers. The scent of pine boughs couldn't compete with the stench of burnt hair, or the pungent funk erupting from the flowers that burst into bloom near her feet.

"Now look," I pointed out to Terra before she conjured something worse. "Evian is trying to help."

"Was not." Evian snapped her fingers and turned Terra's wet hair white with frost, except because the vines were now questing higher, she overshot the mark and doused a few of Soleil's decorative sparkles.

That was the moment I lost control.

Oh, who am I kidding? I never had control.

Soleil let out a screech and lobbed a fireball at Evian, who encased it in a ball of water and batted it toward Terra. I felt scoured clean when Terra called all the dirt and dust in the house to form a layer over the bobbing ball of doom which now resembled a small planet whizzing back toward Soleil.

It might have ended better if I'd have kept my mouth shut, but I didn't.

"You're going to put an eye out with that thing."

The ire of three faeries is a potent thing, but not as potent as a flaming mudball. I ducked, rolled, and hit the latch on the patio door in what I'd like to think was a graceful move. Probably looked like a seal rolling off a rock.

The flaming fireball arced over my head, its warm breeze tossing my hair, and rocketed off into the sky.

Crisis averted. Except, it wasn't. I should have known.

A Snowball's Chance in Spell is only available by signing up for one of our newsletters here:
https://reginawelling.com
https://erinlynnwrites.com

If you'd like to meet more people who live rent-free in our heads, here's a list of other series we've written. Our books are all set in fictional towns in Maine, and some characters like to flit back and forth between series. The cast of Psychic Seasons hangs out with Everly and also with Lexi Balefire from the Fate Weaver series. Mag and Clara Balefire are Lexi's grandmother and aunt!

Psychic Seasons
Four women, four love stories, and a whole lot of supernatural surprises. In the quaint town of Oakville, Maine, psychic visions, ghostly whispers, and fate itself conspire to change lives—and hearts—forever

Haunted Everly After
Everly Dupree came home for a fresh start—not a full-time gig solving ghostly murders. But when the dearly departed start demanding justice, what's a reluctant medium to do?

Ponderosa Pines Mysteries
Nothing bad ever happens in the weird little town of Ponderosa Pines...until someone dies. Now it's up to best

friends Chloe and EV to solve the mystery—before the town's secrets bury them too.

Fate Weaver
Lexi Balefire—matchmaker, witch, and accidental fate-weaver—must balance love, magic, and a family legacy of chaos before destiny decides for her!

Mag and Clara Balefire Mysteries
Sister witches Mag and Clara Balefire move to a sleepy Maine town for a fresh start—only to find themselves conjuring up trouble, solving murders, and keeping their magic under wraps in this charmingly witchy cozy mystery series

Laurel Haven Witches
Four witches, destined by blood and magic, must embrace their power, battle a dark legacy, and surrender to the love that could break the curse—or bind them to it forever.

Nell Page: Accidental Investigator
Nell Page owns a bookstore, drinks too much coffee, and has a habit of noticing things she probably shouldn't. With warmth, wit, and an accidental talent for investigating, Nell tackles mysteries that don't always involve murder—but always matter.